In Secret Sin

Rose Doyle graduated in English from Trinity College, Dublin, and went on to become a successful journalist. She is the author of three bestselling children's books, written following the broadcast of her first radio play. Her first adult novel, *Images*, was published in Ireland in 1993, followed by the UK publication of *Kimbay*, *Alva*, *Perfectly Natural* and, most recently, *The Shadow Player*. Rose lives in Dublin with her two sons.

D0508975

Also by Rose Doyle

The Shadow Player
Perfectly Natural
Alva
Kimbay

ROSE DOYLE

In Secret Sin

PAN BOOKS

First published 2000 by Pan Books
an imprint of Macmillan Publishers Ltd
Pan Macmillan, 20 New Wharf Road, London N1 9RR
Basingstoke and Oxford
Associated companies throughout the world
www.panmacmillan.com

ISBN 978-330-45535-0

1 3 5 7 9 8 6 4 2

A CIP catalogue record for this book is available from
the British Library.

Typeset by SetSystems Ltd, Saffron Walden, Essex
Printed and bound in Great Britain by
Mackays of Chatham plc, Chatham, Kent

Visit www.panmacmillan.com to read more about all our books and to buy
them. You will also find features, author interviews and news of any author
events, and you can sign up for e-newsletters so that you're always first to hear
about our new releases.

**To Clodagh and Eamonn –
there for two pages a day**

Acknowledgements

In Seattle I was given the guided tour, and a sense of life in that wonderful city, by Ellen and Gerry Coyle and by Eileen West and Adrian. Many, many thanks to all of you.

'Keep up appearances; there lies the test;
The world will give thee credit for the rest.
Outward be fair, however foul within;
Sin if thou wilt, but then in secret sin.'

from 'Night' by Charles Churchill

Chapter One

Victor Francis Baldacci died on a morning in June while listening to a patient whose marriage was on the rocks.

It was 10.37 a.m., he was fifty-eight years of age and Constance Brady was his third patient of the day. Victor Baldacci had worked hard and his psychotherapy practice was large and successful.

Because his consulting rooms were in the family home his wife, Bridget, was close at hand when the fatal cardiac arrest occurred. Even so, her husband was well and truly dead by the time she got to his side.

'It wasn't my fault.' Constance Brady was beside herself, more ashen-faced and stricken than the peaceful-looking corpse. 'I was just telling him the usual things ... there was nothing new ... nothing for him to go and die about ...'

Bridget Baldacci, standing over her dead husband, thought that never, in their thirty years of marriage, had she seen so serene an expression on Victor's face. He had not been a tranquil man and, though he hadn't been an angry one either, he'd been someone with a lot of unspoken disquiet about him. While Constance Brady clutched at her and wept, Bridget stretched out a hand and touched Victor's long lashes and gently closed the lids over his beautiful brown eyes.

She felt shock and she felt disbelief. Victor hadn't been the sort of person to do anything without warning, least of all die.

'Of course it wasn't your fault.' She helped Constance Brady into an armchair opposite Victor and looked again at his peacefully folded dead face. 'It must have been his heart . . .' though his lips weren't blue and he didn't appear to have had pain, '. . . he smoked such a lot . . .' sixty a day at least, never even trying to give them up, 'but he never complained, never said there was something wrong . . .'

Victor keeled over slightly in the armchair as, very gently, she rested a pillow under his head and put a rug about him. He was still warm.

'Sweet mother of God, why did you do this to me?' Constance Brady threw herself from the armchair to her dead therapist's feet. 'He was the only man who ever listened to what I had to say and you took him from me . . .'

'Listening was his job,' Bridget observed.

She felt detached and calm. In shock, she supposed. Victor would have approved of her demeanour. Raw emotions unnerved him, though he had indeed been an excellent listener. He'd been less good at talking, a reticence ideal in a therapist. He had appeared, and often had been, wise and consoling and unnaturally patient. He'd been so handsome too. Her lovely Victor.

'You've had a shock. I'll make you some hot, sweet tea,' she tucked the rug gently around Victor's knees as she spoke to Constance Brady. 'But first I must ring for an ambulance.'

'An ambulance! What's the good of an ambulance? He's dead! The man's dead!' Constance Brady embedded her hands in her hair and seemed about to tear it out by its blonde roots.

Bridget slapped her hard, twice, once on each cheek.

'It's the thing to do,' she said.

Constance Brady sobbed quietly, her face buried in her hands, as Bridget first dialled an ambulance and then Victor's doctor from the phone on his desk. Constance, in the meantime, seemed to shrink in the armchair.

'I'll make the tea.' Bridget, sighing, gave her a reassuring pat on the head as she slipped past and into Victor's kitchenette.

The consulting rooms were well equipped; Victor had sometimes spent days at a time alone in their quiet, cream-painted spaces. Bridget chose camomile from among the herb teas.

Bridget Baldacci, née Durcan, was a woman who trusted her feelings and instincts and was not much impressed by psychotherapy. Victor's knowledge and training hadn't, after all, helped him release his demons. 'My gut,' Bridget often half joked, 'is the most accurate barometer of tides and events round here.' Her stomach, depending on the circumstances, turned, sank or felt queasy. It never let her down.

Much later, when the events of that morning were memories and Victor had been long cremated and she'd put a great deal of distance between herself and his consulting rooms, she would blame shock for the fact that she'd had absolutely no premonition of the terrible consequences his death would bring.

But on that bright, sad June morning, as she filled a couple of mugs with the tea and laced them with whiskey, she was glad not to have whispers of foreboding, to be without knowledge of any kind about the sickening truths and other deaths Victor's passing would lead to. All she felt was mildly bereft as she sat with Constance and Victor and quietly sipped the tea until the doctor and ambulance arrived. That was when she discovered that Victor had died instantly from a huge coronary thrombosis.

'It simply interfered with the pacemaker function of the heart,' said the doctor. 'He didn't feel any distress.'

Bridget could have told him that herself.

In the weeks which followed she dealt with the business of death efficiently: with the funeral, the acknowledgements, the closing down of Victor's practice. She was a rock for their two grown children, listening and consoling her beloved Anna and Fintan as they talked their way through grief.

She contacted Victor's family in Seattle, his mother and his sister who he hadn't seen, or wanted to see, for thirty years. They sent flowers. She had Victor cremated because of a confused feeling that his homeland should have something of him and ashes were a movable feast.

And through it all she kept thinking that when it was over and she was alone she would collapse and weep and slowly die a bit herself.

Grief didn't come quite like that. She missed things about Victor: his hard, questioning mind, his body turning to hers in bed at night. The problem, as she saw it, was that her entire adult life had been lived within the framework of her marriage. Now that it, along with Victor, had been so brutally taken from her she had nothing against which to measure or identify herself.

Memories of their first meeting, on a summer afternoon in the west Canadian city of Vancouver thirty-one years before, had replayed themselves in her head. She went with them, reliving that time and understanding, all over again, how she had come to give her all to a handsome American nearly nine years older than she'd been and about whom she'd known nothing at all. But their meeting was all she could remember.

When she tried to call up other memories they wouldn't come to her so she stopped trying, understanding that it was her mind's way of protecting her from too unbearable a pain. At times she couldn't even remember his face and had to keep checking photographs to see how exactly he'd looked.

She still felt no aching pain or loss, existing in a fog in which only certain realities had substance and in which all thoughts were a blur. When she met friends she found she had nothing to say to them. Watching television she was bemused and puzzled by the lives of the people she saw there. Everything except her beloved garden appeared to her shapelessly indifferent and beyond her understanding.

The garden saved her because there she was needed. Its paths and bowers and rampant plant life were her creation, she knew every corner and stone. She had been the one to coax life from the barren, stony field which had passed for a garden when she and Victor bought what became their first, and last, home twenty-five years before. It had to be got ready for winter, couldn't be ignored, and so became the place where she spent her days, and a lot of her nights too, in the months after Victor died. She wasn't unhappy.

What she felt most of all was suspended, caught in the calm before a storm.

But by the end of October the fog had lifted and she knew what she had to do.

It was at the end of October when her daughter and first born, Anna, said she felt Bridget was suffering from Post Traumatic Shock Syndrome and should talk to someone, a therapist of some kind. A decent psychologist might do the trick Anna said or, better still, a psychiatrist.

She came to her mother in the garden, in a navy-blue suit and full of sharp, city energy. Bridget, who by then had started to form a plan of her own about what she was going to do, was not encouraging.

'Don't be ridiculous,' she said, though gently, 'there's nothing wrong with me.' She knew far more about PTSS than Anna, who was twenty-eight years old and a steadily achieving lawyer with a good firm. Constance Brady was indulging in a rash of treatment for PTSS on account of Victor dying in front of her eyes.

'All I'm suggesting is that some counselling might help,' Anna said.

'Of course it wouldn't,' said Bridget. 'It didn't help your father, did it? With all that he knew he couldn't heal himself.'

Anna and her brother Fintan, who was twenty-five years old and a sculptor in west Cork, knew their father had gone to the grave with the secrets of his early life intact. Acceptance of his silence about his family and his youth in Seattle had been a family thing.

'You're in shock.' Anna backed away from any probing about her father. 'You need to acknowledge your grief so you can move on . . .'

'You'd be surprised how much movement I'm a part of just by being out here.' Bridget, on her knees planting tulip bulbs and anemones, looked thoughtfully about the garden. The day was shining and warm, one of many that autumn fine enough for Bridget to need a straw hat. The decision about what she would have to do to make sense of her life and marriage had germinated and taken root and grown, over days such as this in the garden. She wasn't ready to tell Anna yet, mainly because she didn't want to deal with her objections. These would be loud, when they came.

'This isn't enough.' Anna, pacing the flag-stoned path, dismissed the garden with a sigh. 'You need to do something *focused*, something you can rebuild your life around, structure a future – '

'These are for the early spring' – Bridget shoved another bulb into the warm earth – 'or is that too near a future?'

'Oh, for God's sake!'

Anna, pacing on her thin, elegant shoes, stopped and killed an instinct to tap her foot. She stood instead with her ankles crossed, studying her mother and thinking how interesting she looked, in spite of everything, with her red hair straggling loose from under the straw hat (the red, she knew, was helped along these days, though her mother would never admit to such a thing), her small bones and wistful, sheepdog eyes seeming not much different than they'd always been. 'Your mother's eyes,' her father had once said to Anna when she was young, 'are the colour of the Atlantic ocean in March. She's a bit like the Atlantic herself. Unpredictable.'

The unpredictable bit worried Anna. Interesting-looking, age uncertain, unpredictable, that was her mother.

Interesting was, of course, far more useful than beautiful now she was getting older. She was hardly going to be looking for lovers, at her age, which was at least fifty.

But that's where the unpredictable came in. Because maybe she would take lovers, might even be planning to. Bridget Baldacci might do a lot of things – but Anna hated surprises and wanted to know what, exactly, her mother might do.

'I'm talking about *you* getting a life' – she snorted at the general selection of growing things – 'not the frigging plants. You're still young . . .' she hesitated, 'youngish, anyway. You've got a life to live. What're you going to do with it? You can't go on like this for ever. I'm worried about you. So is Fintan . . .'

'There's no need.' Bridget, separating the bulbs into groups, didn't for one minute believe her son was worried about her. Fintan rarely thought about anyone but himself. Anna didn't mean to be insensitive either. It was just that she had no interest in gardening and no facility much for understanding others. Bridget looked up with a sigh and saw with surprise that storm clouds had gathered in the clear sky.

'You both know I'm more than able to look after myself. I'm biding time, is all.' She smiled at her beautiful daughter, so very like her father to look at. 'To every thing there is a season.'

Anna gave an impatient toss of her head and a clump of

7

black hair, Victor's hair, fell loose onto her collar. She wound it sleekly back into its coiled topknot. Tumbling locks were not the thing in court and Anna, who specialized in family law, spent a lot of time in the courts. The fact of her being here, in the garden, in the middle of a working day, said a lot about how sincerely worried she was about her mother.

'You need more than a seasonal change,' she said, 'you're too alone here. Have you thought about going back to work?'

'I've resigned, you know that.'

Anna knew but preferred to think that Bridget's resignation from her job as a school secretary had been an aberration. It had been no such thing. To Bridget, in her new circumstances, it had made complete and logical sense.

Victor, no surprise to Bridget, hadn't made a will. He'd been so obsessively private that the idea of detailing his affairs for another to see would have brought on an even earlier coronary. Victor, when all was said and done, had trusted no one. Not even her. But he'd been clever about investments and Bridget had given up her job once she had realized she wouldn't have to struggle financially, at least. The job had become routine, in any event.

'You need to retrain for something,' Anna caught herself tapping her foot and stopped.

It was hard to know exactly what her mother should retrain for. She'd never been easy to categorize and as children Anna and Fintan had been mortified by her difference from other mothers. Bridget had always been too something – exuberant, colourful, opinionated. She'd never been the sort of obligingly background figure their father had been.

'You must have some idea what you want to do.' Hating the limp, ineffectual sound of her own voice she finally gave in to the urge to tap her foot.

'So much for the bulbs,' her mother, ignoring her, stood up, 'now for the montbretia. It's lost the run of itself altogether.'

Trailing Bridget to the end of the garden and the montbretia Anna dallied with the notion that perhaps her mother was glad to be a widow, was relieved to be free of her husband, glad to be on her own.

The intensity of her own grief had been a surprise, given her father's reserved temperament and the fact that he'd been difficult to get close to as an adult. She knew she was like him in many ways, and when he died she'd become swamped in memories of the loving care he'd surrounded her with as a child. Until they'd grown old enough to question him he'd been besotted with herself and Fintan. He'd lived for them during their childhood years, only growing cautious when adolescence and defiant questioning began.

He'd always lived for their mother.

By the fiery blaze of the rampaging montbretia Anna hunkered down beside Bridget. Not easy, in her straight skirt, but it didn't look as if her mother was going to stop what she was doing. Bridget was catching the flowers low, pulling the bulbed roots briskly out of the ground.

'Have you thought about selling the house? It's far too big for you.' Anna turned a calculating look on the grey stone pile she'd grown up in. 'You'd make a killing. You've never really liked it anyway.'

'No, I haven't thought about selling my home.'

Sitting back on her heels Bridget also turned toward the house. It was true that she'd never liked it. She'd felt herself devoured by its Victorian pedigree and too many rooms. Victor had liked it though, a lot.

'And I'm not going to think about it, yet.'

She wished wearily that Anna would make some concessions to the shining day. An open-necked shirt would have been a start. 'Might as well give those roses the chop while I'm here.' She got off her knees and marched to a clump of rose bushes. 'There's a time to pluck that which is planted' – the secateurs advanced and stems fell – 'and my time isn't right yet, Anna, for a lot of things . . .' she handed her daughter a vermilion rosebud, 'one of the last of the summer.'

'You're being evasive and sentimental and you know it,' Anna took the flower and turned it irritably between her fingers.

'Give it back.' Bridget took the rosebud and slipped it into her daughter's coiled topknot. Anna became Carmen in a suit. 'You look lovely.' Bridget touched the young woman's face, in a wistful gesture. Love had long resigned Bridget to an impatience she sometimes felt with her first born. Because Anna was so darkly beautiful it was easy to assume she was passionate about life. People usually did. She was, in fact and by nature, a pragmatist. 'I'll get you a bite to eat,' said Bridget, 'I don't suppose you've had anything all day.'

The clouds grew suddenly heavier as she led the way briskly back to the house. When a low tree snagged the straw hat from her head she left it where it fell and shook her hair loose. Anna, walking behind her, picked it up.

'I don't want anything to eat.' Anna hung the hat on a hook in the sun room. She didn't want to be in the sun room either. It was where her mother insisted on keeping the casket with her father's ashes and she couldn't quite reconcile herself to sharing space with them.

'You need nourishment.' Bridget, angling the casket more firmly into its niche in the brickwork, resisted what had become a regular urge to flush the contents down the lavatory. One quick, businesslike gush and they would be gone, dispersed for ever into the city's sewers, all decisions and maybe even Victor's pain gone with them. The urge was irrational, she knew, as well as wrong-headed, futile and horribly appealing.

'Any word from Seattle about the ashes?' Anna, calling from the kitchen, broke her train of thought.

Going into the kitchen and closing the windows against the approach of evening, Bridget didn't immediately answer her daughter's question. When she went on evading it, pulling back her hair to catch it in a rubber band, Anna tried again.

'Well? What about Seattle?'

Bridget, hair secured, began to wash her hands at the sink. 'I got a reply to my letter last week.' She removed and studied her wedding ring before, with infinite care, placing it on the window sill.

'You could have told me before now.'

'I suppose I could.' Bridget's mildly apologetic tone, as she dried her hands, didn't do much to mollify her daughter.

'I have a right to know.' Anna, abruptly and stiff backed, left the kitchen.

The sun room was no less inviting than before but if she'd stayed in the kitchen she'd have rowed with her mother. She touched the casket. Just because she couldn't bear to be around the damn thing didn't mean she didn't care about her father's ashes. How could her mother not know their fate mattered to her? She hated the way Bridget took things on herself and to herself, and didn't share. It had always been a problem between them.

'I'm sorry,' Bridget, standing in the doorway, spoke quietly, 'the letter wasn't what you'd call encouraging, exactly . . .' She paused. 'They don't want his ashes, in part or in whole, for scattering or otherwise—'

She stopped, choking back a sudden urge to howl at the cold, malign cruelty of it, as the same sense of impotent rage which had swept through her when first she'd read the letter, engulfed her again. She'd given in to the urge then, in Victor's rooms, systematically ripping every book on psychotherapy he'd owned from the shelves, kicking at them where they fell, cracking the spines of some of them. The rage had moved on, taking her detachment with it, and she'd been thinking ever since, memory piling upon memory, as her plan had started to form.

For a long time after they met, Bridget had wanted to meet Victor's mother. His evasiveness, then his obdurate refusal to arrange a meeting, had forced her to face the reality of his flawed and secretive nature. But by then she'd been hopelessly in love and couldn't imagine a life without him. They married when she was twenty and Victor twenty-eight and his secrecy about his family had continued relentlessly.

When Anna had been born, and then Fintan, Bridget had sent cards to Seattle. She'd got back printed, unsigned acknowledgements. The cold indifference had angered her and made it easier to accept Victor's rejection of his family. In time she'd even stopped wondering why.

Until now. Until his mother had written to say the family didn't want anything to do with his ashes.

'You don't look great, mother, are you all right?'

Anna's voice came to her as if down the shaft of a tunnel. 'I'm fine,' Bridget turned a sigh into a rueful smile, 'and I *am* sorry I didn't tell you about the letter.'

She was certainly sorry she'd told her today. In time she would have shown Anna the letter just as, in time, she would have discussed her future with her. The way this visit was developing she was going to have to tell Anna what she planned any minute. 'I really am OK' – of its own accord, and as she tried for damage limitation, Bridget's smile became even more rueful – 'and the letter, in its own way, wasn't so bad. Reasonable, really. She simply said that she saw no need to divide the ashes into two parts . . .'

'Who saw no need? Who wrote to you?'

'Victor's mother . . . your grandmother, Veronica Baldacci.' Bridget hesitated. 'It was in one sense quite a civil letter—'

'Can I see it?'

'Of course,' Bridget said. Reading it wasn't going to do Anna one bit of good. 'Make yourself a sandwich while I go and get it.'

In the bedroom she'd shared with Victor, Bridget re-read the letter. Its condescension and its discouraging tone struck her again. It began with a 'Dear Bridget' but that was about as familiar as it got.

> Your letter, together with its suggestion that a portion of my son's cremation ashes might find a resting place in Seattle, came as a surprise. Victor made certain, early, decisions about his life. This family did not feature in those decisions. He chose to live in Ireland and I think it more fitting that his ashes remain, intact, with the life and family he created there.

Her signature, black and very bold, took up most of the rest of the page. Clearly, Veronica Baldacci was not a woman to be cast aside, by anyone and for any reason. But then Bridget had sussed as much when she'd telephoned Seattle to tell the woman her son was dead.

'He died at home?' The elderly voice had been coolly disinterested.

'Yes, in a manner of speaking . . .' Bridget explained about the consulting rooms.

'I see,' said Victor's mother. 'Had he been ill?'

'No.' Bridget hesitated. 'He'd been having some discomfort is all. He'd talked to his doctor about it . . .' But not to her. More secrecy. Dr Russell had had to explain to her that Victor had been to see him about chest pains.

'His father had a stroke when quite a young man,' Veronica Baldacci sounded businesslike. 'He died as a result.'

'I see,' said Bridget. Veronica, in Seattle, did not volunteer any further information. Bridget told her about the funeral arrangements. 'Victor will be cremated. The ceremony can be delayed a few days if you or any of the family would like to—'

'That won't be necessary. I myself do not travel and Victor's sister would be unable to go to Ireland. Please convey our sympathies to . . .' When she stopped Bridget decided against reminding her of her grandchildren's names. Veronica, with an audibly impatient sigh, carried on, 'Our sympathies to the young people. Our thoughts will be with you.'

When a grotesquely large wreath arrived on the day of the funeral Bridget went to the end of the garden and carefully took it apart. She buried the flowers, lilies and white roses for the most part, and foliage. As compost it had an honest function.

But it wasn't good enough. Dealing with Victor's family had left a large, unresolved pain in her gut. For peace of mind alone she would have to do something about it.

Downstairs, in the sun room where Anna was eating a sandwich, Bridget gave her the letter from her grandmother. She sat and watched while the younger woman read it, anticipating the words, wishing she could change them. Anna read it twice before, without looking at her mother,

14

tearing it into careful pieces which she scattered across the glossy, cherrywood table.

'She doesn't want his ashes. We don't want her letter.' With a stabbing forefinger she manoeuvred the scraps into a neat pile. 'You don't need her either. But she's quite right, about one thing at least. *We* were Dad's life. He *should* stay here.' She took a deep, shaky breath and faced her mother. 'Bitch,' she said, 'rotten, lousy old bitch.' Tears ran in a flood down her face.

Bridget went to her and held her, silently and hard, until the wave of tears and neediness had passed. Anna's long, thin body felt no less fragile to her than it had when she'd been a child, and no more secure in the world. She patted her daughter's face dry before letting her go.

'I should correct myself,' Anna picked up and began to nibble again at the sandwich, '*you* were Dad's life, not us.'

'No.' Bridget shook her head as she gathered the scraps of letter and let them fall again, like confetti, on to the polished wood. 'I was his retreat from life.'

Victor had used his love for her to create his own, private world. That was one of the things which had become clear to her since his death. She'd been his cover, the children his insurance, this house his personal island. Even what he did – all the probing and the listening – had been on his terms. People came to him, into his lair, and there he took them apart and rebuilt their lives. As a defence it had been perfect, and impregnable.

'Well, it's over now,' Anna's voice was harsh. 'He's gone and his mother's rejected him, even in death.' Hearing the courtroom drama of her phraseology she allowed herself a half smile. 'So it's time to get on with the rest of our lives. Yours in particular, mother.'

'You're right,' Bridget said and Anna, surprised, sat forward.

'I'm right?' She leaned her elbows on the table.

'I've decided on something.' Bridget stopped to listen as rain began falling gently on the glass roof. She'd always liked rain, its power to soothe, wash clean, absolve. She was sure its beginning to fall now was a good omen. 'This is probably as good a time as any to tell you—'

'Don't do me any favours, mother,' Anna said dryly. 'I've only been trying to get sense out of you all afternoon.' Her eyes flickered involuntarily towards the wall clock as she stood up. 'You need a drink. So do I. Don't go away.'

Her heels made precision clicks on the Valentia slate of the sun room's floor before the door to the kitchen swung closed behind her. Bridget hadn't missed the glance at the clock, nor the inference that the time Anna had allocated to this visit was running out. Not a bad thing. If they dealt with the subject quickly then Anna's lawyerly mind would have less chance to cross-examine.

'Drink.' Anna handed her mother a liberal measure of whiskey. Her own glass held white wine with ice. 'Now talk to me,' she poked at the ice with a finger and watched Bridget carefully.

She's worried, Bridget thought, that's why she got us the drinks. She's afraid she's going to lose a mother as well as a father. And she is in a way.

'I've decided to go to Seattle,' Bridget said.

'You've decided to go to . . . Seattle.'

'Yes. I'm going to visit the Baldaccis, get to know a little about them. I plan to go after Christmas, very early in the new year.'

'You're going to Seattle in the new year.'

'It's time I met your father's family.' Bridget's tone was reasonable.

'I would have thought the time for that long past and gone.' Anna carefully extracted a piece of ice from her drink and began to suck it. 'Doesn't sound to me like a spectacular way to move on' – she shrugged – 'more like a step backwards, into the past.'

'Perhaps,' said Bridget, 'but then perhaps I need to do that too.'

'I don't see why . . .' Anna stopped.

She looked from her mother's quietly smiling face to the darkening garden. She'd wanted her mother to open up but now that she had Anna realized that she'd been afraid, all along, that Bridget would do something like this. Going to Seattle wasn't the answer to her grief. It would just prolong the holding on to her father. She had to be talked out of it.

Her father's family wouldn't want to see her anyway, any more than they'd wanted his ashes.

The rain, she saw, was falling heavily now, the sun room becoming cold as the heat of the day escaped fast through the glass.

Anna had never shared her mother's love of growing things. As a child garden shadows had held unnamed terrors for her, though she'd never said anything about such fears to Bridget, who would have laughed. Anna had talked about it to her father though. He'd stroked her hair, gently and for a long time, and assured her over and over that there was nothing in the garden which would ever hurt her. She'd believed him. She wished he was here now.

'As a family lawyer,' Anna took a deep breath, 'I feel I should point out that Dad may have been married before. It's fairly common you know, in situations like this.'

'Situations like this . . . Like what, exactly?' Bridget asked.

'Situations where there's been a lot of secrecy about the past. I've seen—'

'If he was married before then I want to know about it,' Bridget cut her short. 'I want to know everything there is to know.'

She meant it. She was fifty years of age and for thirty of those years had lived with a man about whose background she'd known hardly anything because he had decided it was his secret and none of her business. But now he was dead and she wanted to know everything. He'd been her sounding board and her ballast and she'd loved him for the way he'd brought her to life and given her an awareness of herself that first, golden afternoon in Vancouver, BC. She'd loved him for loving her from that beginning, when she had thought herself so very unlovable.

And it was because he'd been all of those things that now she needed to know who the real Victor had been.

'Why?' demanded Anna. 'You've lived without knowing all these years. What difference does it make now?'

'The difference is that your father is dead . . .' Bridget paused, 'and I'm alive.'

'And that's a reason for going to Seattle? For prostrating yourself in front of people who don't want to know you? Who never did?'

'Yes, that's a reason. And I'm not just going to Seattle. I intend to visit Vancouver too. A sort of pilgrimage, you might say.'

Anna ignored this and tried another tack. 'You respected his decision to put the Baldacci part of his life behind him when he was alive. I really think you should afford him the same courtesy in death.'

'No, you don't.' Bridget was resignedly dismissive. 'You don't believe that at all. But you think *I* believe it and that you can work on my guilt.' Ignoring Anna's protest she got up and walked to where Victor's ashes sat in their bright casket. 'The thing is, Anna, my love, I don't feel guilty. Not one bit. The dead have no right to judge and dictate to the living.' She stood over the casket, looking at it, but not touching it. 'I *would* feel guilty, however, if I didn't go to Seattle.' She turned to her daughter. 'On the positive side it'll mean you'll finally get to know about your paternal relations.'

'You know I don't give a fuck about them.'

'I would have preferred your good wishes.' Bridget smiled at the familiar, Victor-like intensity in her daughter's dark eyes. 'I'll take half the ashes with me.'

'They don't want them. They said so . . .'

'I'm going to give them a chance to change their minds.'

'Has it occurred to you that they may not even want to meet *you*?'

'Oh, yes. But they're not going to have a choice about that. I want to meet *them*,' Bridget's smile became rueful, 'for better or for worse.'

Chapter Two

It was raining in Seattle. The one thing everyone had said about Seattle was that it would be raining. It's a watery city, they said, in the way that Dublin is, with mountains and sea and lots of rain.

Bridget found the grey, misty views of the city reassuring.

Vancouver, where she'd spent three days, had been full of bright sunshine and sharp, wintery air. But it had refused to surrender anything of the girl who'd fallen for and given her all to an American lover there, thirty-one years before. She'd found nothing much of Victor in Vancouver either. Memories had come faintly and been so inert they might have belonged to someone else. Since the city hadn't changed, was as ordered and naturally stunning as ever, she was forced to acknowledge that it was she herself who had changed.

There were times when, even more than at home, she couldn't recall how Victor had looked, could see only the peaceful, unsurprised face he'd worn the morning of the cardiac arrest. She missed not having Victor to think about; he'd made up so many of her thoughts for so long.

By the time she climbed aboard a Greyhound bus for Seattle she'd been impatient to be gone.

First impressions matter and Bridget's of Seattle were mixed. Afterwards, whenever she tried to capture her uncertainties, the things which came to mind were the way the air smelled of cinnamon and coffee, the hordes of stylishly cool downtown winter people, the shining spires of skyscrapers against ever-changing skies – all of it juggling with a darker, unsaid something she couldn't pin down.

It was as if there was a blemish, an unacknowledged evil or wrong of some kind, hovering about the life of the city.

At the time Bridget put such confusions down to her nervously dire expectations of Victor's family. But it was not long before, her expectations proving right, the city came to have an even more aberrant edge for her.

The Greyhound bus cruised into Victor's home town just after one o'clock. By the time the passengers had been unloaded at 1150 Station Street the low-lying cloud had turned the city as dark as early evening.

'Enjoy your stay,' the bus driver, who had fought in Iwo Jima, handed Bridget her bags, 'and enjoy the weather.'

He said the same thing to everyone. On the bus he'd told Bridget that people were people, wherever you went, if you gave them half a chance. Even the Japanese were people. Bridget had agreed that people were people and hoped it was true.

The bus station was full of people. She hadn't expected to be met but now that she'd arrived, and was tired, she found herself searching faces, and hoping. She had no idea who, or even what, she was looking for. She'd written to Victor's mother about her visit and had got back a letter which wondered about 'the wisdom of such a trip' and reluctantly encouraged her to 'get in touch when and if' she arrived in Seattle.

There had been no invitation to stay, no welcoming encouragement.

The taxi which stopped for her was driven by a pale, infinitely miserable-looking Pole. As it drove on the look of the city improved, the streets becoming wider and the buildings higher and more elegant. Bridget, hoping the taxi driver knew where he was going, wondered why people so often felt compelled to tell her their life story. Maybe the reason she'd fallen in love with Victor was because he'd never told her anything.

The driver was talking about his girlfriend.

'She has my children too,' he said. 'Fine children. I never will see my children in Poland again. Now I don't see my American children. My girlfriend will not allow it . . .'

'Is the hotel much further?' Bridget was losing her patience.

She was wet and cold and 9,000 miles from home. She did not want to listen to a Polish taxi driver with a dandruff problem and offspring on two continents mangle the English language. She should never have got into his car. This came of being out of travelling practice. God knows where he was taking her. She'd read a lot, in her research on Seattle over Christmas, about the city's serial killers. There were several of them currently on the loose, notably the Green River Killer. It was said too that one in four citizens of the area was classified as a sociopath, that the low-lying cloud, stormy nights, dark days, mist and fog gave cover to, and attracted, any amount of evil doers . . .

'Not far now,' said the Polish driver, 'only a cupla blocks.'

'I'm in a hurry,' said Bridget.

'The world is always in a hurry. Me, too. I hurry so much I never have time to learn American, never.' The driver's eyes on her in the mirror were like wet cement and full of tears. 'I just work and work for a few dollars. Sometimes, life is such a bitch to me that I drink a little bit . . .' A tear fell and he sniffed and blinked.

'Everyone needs to relax now and again,' said Bridget.

Relax. She was sitting in a car driven by a depressed drinker who might very well be the Green River Killer, forty-nine victims so far and presumably on the lookout for more since he hadn't yet been caught.

The rain had slowed to a drizzle.

'I'll get out here.' She leaned forward and tapped the driver's shoulder. His jacket felt cold and sticky. 'Please stop the car and get me my bags.' She was polite and she was firm.

'You're a nice lady. I take you to de door.'

He didn't turn around. In the mirror she could see his eyes fixed on the road ahead. He seemed to be perspiring and the taxi seemed to be for ever going downhill, passing high, glass emporiums and coffee houses. The bottom of the street came in sight, and an expanse of water. Seattle's waterfront, the Puget Sound. Bridget felt ridiculously relieved.

'I'd like to walk the rest of the way.' She didn't touch his shoulder this time.

'Bags too heavy for you.' He was firm. They stopped at a red light and he lit a cigarette. He didn't speak.

'There are people waiting for me at the hotel,' Bridget lied.

'We get there soon.' Ash fell from the cigarette as the car moved forward again.

'Tell me about an area called Madison Park,' Bridget said. 'Truly upscale' and 'extravagantly wealthy' were the words used to describe it in the guidebooks. 'Do you know it?'

'I don't go up that neighbourhood much,' his short laugh was like a stone hitting a grating, 'and the kind live up there don't much pick up cabs in the street.'

They drew up in front of a small hotel. It looked reassuring as it had in the brochure from which Bridget had made the booking.

'Thank you,' Bridget said. 'How much do I owe you?'

'Seven dollars.'

Far too much. Only a fool would have paid without a quibble. Bridget told him to keep the change from a ten-dollar bill and clambered out. The wet air felt cold and invigorating.

'My bags . . .'

He jerked his head and she saw that he'd opened the boot from inside the car. She retrieved the bags. The car was lost in the traffic before she got to the door of the hotel.

The Hotel Pacific Nights, which had advertised itself as 'European in style', was chintzy and brocaded with a log fire burning in the lobby. But this was Seattle, after all, and there was also a bank of coffee-dispensing thermos flasks and newspapers stacked beside reading lamps.

'And how are you today?' The Filipino woman at reception flashed a gold front tooth. Her eyes didn't quite meet Bridget's. 'You'll be with us for two weeks, is that right?'

'I hope so. It depends on—'

'We've put you on the fourth floor. You'll like it up there.' The tooth, flashing again as she studied her computer screen, looked like an accessory to the hotel's gold-braided uniform jacket. 'Hold it,' she said, 'seems we've got a special delivery correspondence here for you. Arrived yesterday. Also your keys, of course, and our very helpful guide to the hotel and city.' She made a hand signal and an elderly porter appeared. 'Mrs Baldacci will be going to the fourth floor.' She didn't smile at him.

'The elevator's this way, ma'am.' The man picked up Bridget's bags and headed briskly across the lobby. His silver hair was crew cut.

'Enjoy your stay with us.' The receptionist turned away.

'My letter,' Bridget reminded her. 'You did say you'd some correspondence for me?'

'One letter.' Without looking at her the woman put a manila-coloured envelope on the desk in front of Bridget.

'Thank you,' Bridget said.

She decided against opening it straight away. She was too tired, and far too wound up, to absorb whatever Veronica Baldacci had to say with any sort of equanimity.

If it was rude she would lose her temper, if it was kindly she would be embarrassingly grateful.

After the porter had departed with her dollar tip and a laconic nod, she leaned against the door and allowed herself a quick study of the envelope. Oblong, in decent quality paper, it had her name, Mrs Bridget Baldacci, printed in blue-inked, block capitals. Her fingers itched.

'Now now, Bridget,' she told herself, 'first you pour a drink, then you unpack. After that you will top up your drink and sit with it and slowly absorb your special delivery. It may need all your concentration.'

Her room was filled with dark furniture: desk, armchair, chiffonier and high-backed bed. The wallpaper was embossed, the bed covering tasselled and the roller blind had a lace trim. It was a sombre room, overshadowed and made gloomy by the taller building opposite. Bridget turned on all of the lights and, deciding against Scotch – the only whiskey in the mini-bar – poured herself a gin and tonic and topped up the glass with ice. Unpacking took twenty minutes; boots, rain gear and woollies had been the general advice of friends and family and, with a few exceptions, these were the sort of clothes she'd packed. It had helped eliminate decisions about what to bring.

She put the casket in which she'd carried half of Victor's ashes on the desk. It was small and plain, a gun-metal grey colour, and immediately became the only thing she could see in the room. She shoved it into the desk drawer and felt at once both guilty and relieved.

The envelope, when she opened it, held a single folded sheet of cream-coloured paper. Its message was written in block capitals and was not from Veronica Baldacci. The style was not right, the wording all wrong. There was no indication who it was from, no signature of any kind.

Dear Mrs Bridget Baldacci,

It is unlikely, since you have come this far, that you will leave Seattle without meeting your dead husband's family. It was unwise of you to come here and I would advise you to turn about and go back to Ireland immediately. Victor Baldacci's family do not want the past disturbed and therefore do not care to meet you. There is nothing unnatural in this; mistakes are best left in the past where they can cause less pain.

Meeting his family will not bring the dead man back. Neither will you be helped to find peace or understanding. I cannot be of assistance if you decide to stay; no one can. The best help I can give you is my advice to you to go home as soon as you read this letter.

Bridget put the sheet of paper down, flattened it on the desk and sat looking at it while she finished the gin and tonic. She picked out phrases over the rim of the glass.

'It was unwise of me to come, was it now? You'd advise me to turn about and go home, would you? I won't be helped to find peace and understanding? Well, in that case, you anonymous shit . . .' she picked up and tore the letter in two, then tore it in two again, 'I'll have to settle for trouble and strife.' She dropped the pieces into the bin. 'Because you're dead right, my friend. I didn't come all this way for nothing.'

She stood looking at the scraps of paper for a moment, willing them to tell her something, give a hint even of why so many people wanted what had happened in the past in Victor's family forgotten. She hadn't expected a red-carpet welcome but the basic civilities would have been nice. The letter could, of course, be the work of a crank, either a family member or a jealous friend. One way or another, she wasn't going to give it too much credence. Not unless something else happened.

She rang Anna, then Fintan. Given that day was just breaking in Ireland they were quick calls to say she'd arrived. She joked about her minor hysteria in the taxi, said nothing at all about the special delivery letter.

'When do you plan to see Dad's people?' Anna was a morning person.

Bridget hadn't planned. She did now.

'I'm going to give your father's mother a few hours to make contact. If I haven't heard by then I'll take a taxi out to the house. Five o'clock seems to me a respectable time to go calling, anywhere in the world.' She looked at herself in the mirror. Her wet hair resembled seaweed and her face looked pale and tired. 'She can hardly close the door in my face.'

'Why not?' Anna asked.

Why not indeed? Bridget said goodbye but felt better, reassured by her daughter's cynical expectations of her grandmother. She had a hot bath and washed her hair. On the very large television she got a weather report delivered by a glossy, blond man in a brown suit. 'Looks like it could be the coldest night in the region,' he said cheerfully. 'There's snow across the Cascades and southern Washington Cascades.' When he was replaced on the screen by a snow-laden palm tree she switched channels and found herself face to face with a coquettish Fergie, Duchess of York, lisping about weight control through a wide, soft-focus smile. Everywhere else the news was of Sonny Bono's death on a ski slope at the Heavenly Valley Ski Resort on the Nevada–California state line. He'd skied into a tree.

'Looks like it got you, babe.' Bridget touched the widely grinning screen face of the dead politician-entertainer.

Sonny and Cher had been riding the charts with 'I Got You, Babe' when she'd first met Victor in Vancouver in 1966. They'd danced to it, sung along with the words, laughed at the way it fitted them.

Bridget decided the death wasn't an omen. The TV said Sonny Bono had been skiing at the resort for more than twenty years. He was a victim, she told herself, of the law of averages. She just wished his average hadn't come up that day.

She was suddenly impatient with the room, with Veronica Baldacci's rudeness and lack of contact. From the window she saw a lightening of the sky, and clouds scudding above the tall building opposite. It was looking as if there was going to be a hiatus before the snow, rain, ice and cold promised for later on; if she was to see anything of the city she'd better do it before a blizzard arrived.

She might even come across the ghost of the youthful Victor out there.

She pulled on boots and a jumper and lifted the phone. Nice, healthy buzz. No technical problems then. Just no one trying to get through to her.

In the street she walked quickly, not clear where she was going but keeping a sniping wind to her back. The freshly rained on footpaths were vitreous and the shining skyscrapers like cliff faces after a storm. At an intersection she ignored the 'Don't Walk' sign and continued with fellow pedestrians across the empty road. The small, anarchic act made her feel better, as if she'd bonded with the city. Dubliners, too, notoriously ignored pedestrian lights.

She stopped to take stock. She was standing on 4th Avenue, elegant and wide. To her right a street plunged recklessly down to the waterfront. If she were to keep on going, veering uphill she would come to the International District, home to the city's Asian community. The prospect seemed a cosier one than exposure to the Puget Sound.

This proved to be a mistake. The International District was bleak, full of wide, windswept streets and small, cluttered shops. Not since he'd died had she felt so totally without Victor. She began retracing her steps to the hotel.

'Hey, most beautiful woman in the entire world.' A black man, small and wizened and with shining, perfect teeth, touched her on the arm. Bridget stepped away from him and he looked at her, full of admiring disbelief as he held out a begging hand.

Confused, Bridget shook her head and turned away.

'You're not the world's most beautiful woman?' his voice followed her, sadly. When she turned, relenting, he'd gone.

She wasn't beautiful but she had been, sort of, once. Beautiful enough for a good man to love her for his lifetime – and to use the words said by the black man the first time he met her. 'There isn't a woman as beautiful as you in the entire world,' was in fact what Victor had said, only half joking. She heard him say it again now, the words setting up a lonely echo in her head.

Then the memories she'd been looking for in Canada came crowding in.

Victor hadn't lived for her since the morning he'd died but he did so now, coming alive to her so intensely she cried out and closed her eyes. For a while she leaned against a hoarding, glad to be remembering at last, careless of the cold. 'Where were you until now, Victor?' She wrapped her arms about herself and watched the clouds break and regroup. 'You went from me so completely I had to come to this place to find you. Don't leave me again ... I'm not used to being without you ... you were always there, before ...' The street was so quiet the urge to call aloud to him was huge.

She faced into the wind and it drew tears from her eyes as she walked on, slowly.

The first time ever she'd seen Victor Baldacci he'd been

leaning against a tree on the campus of the University of British Columbia in Vancouver. She'd been lying on the grass and had looked up lazily to catch him watching her. He hadn't looked away. He hadn't smiled either. He had simply stood, immobile and languid against an old maple, and held her gaze. She'd been the first to look away, turning her head to laugh with a companion on the grass. She knew he would come to her.

'Walk with me, please.' His hand touched her shoulder lightly. With the sun behind him she couldn't see his face but knew it anyway from the way the dappled light had picked out its planes and shadows under the tree.

'Where would you like to walk?' she asked and he held out a hand.

'You'll see,' he said and linked her fingers with his and pulled her from the grass to his side.

He was older than she'd thought, taller too and broader. She didn't quite reach his shoulder. He held her hand tightly and led her quickly back toward the wooded area.

'What's the hurry?' she asked but knew, because she wanted it too, that the rush was to get away from her companions, to be on their own. She never once looked back, even when voices called to her. When they were in the middle of the trees he let her hand go and smiled at her and said, 'There isn't a woman as beautiful as you in the entire world.' It didn't seem extravagant at all the way he said it, just a statement of what was for him a fact.

Bridget spent the rest of the day with him, and a lot of the night too. She was a virgin and she didn't sleep with him, just listened while he talked to her about the life he'd lived in Alaska, where he'd gone to university, and about the Indian peoples he'd lived with and studied. He talked, as the night went on, about things they could do together while she was in Vancouver.

Bridget knew that one of the things she was going to do was sleep with him.

'I'm supposed to study while I'm here,' she said. She was doing a summer course in Canadian literature.

'Of course.' Victor grinned.

She didn't study. She went to classes and opened books and wrote down words and the only thoughts in her head were of Victor. Waking and sleeping her thoughts were of him. She lived the week in a state of expectation. Expectation was what she felt when she walked with him or when they sat in a cinema or listened to music.

They made love, within a week of meeting, on the narrow bed in the rooms the university had given him to live in while he delivered a summer seminar on the Aleut and Indian peoples of Alaska.

They had been to an open-air concert that day, a fund-raising event with a mixed bag of rock musicians. Bridget had loved it, the spirit as much as the event. Victor had been amused and gently mocking of her enthusiasm.

'Bunch of ego trippers and bad musicians,' he said.

'Not what you'd call brilliant.' Bridget sniffed. 'But they tried and it was fun.' She felt flattened and all at once a lot younger than him.

'I enjoyed it.' He held her against him and spoke into her hair. 'I enjoy everything I do with you.'

They were crossing the campus to his room and she lifted her face to his, smiling, and saw what she had not previously realized: he cared about her happiness more than he cared about his own. She touched the small frown between his eyes, liking the way it made him appear vulnerable.

'That's good,' she said, afraid and too cool to tell him she felt the same.

'Will you stay with me tonight?' he said.

'Why not?' Bridget said and held on tight when he kissed her.

He'd done some decorating in his rooms, hanging Eskimo paintings on the walls and covering the floor with rush matting. His rooms told her everything she needed to know about him, that summer. As soon as he had closed the door behind them she turned into his arms.

'You'll have to show me.' Her heart was thumping.

'You're sure this is all right?' He held her away from him.

'Very sure.' She lifted her arms and slipped her T-shirt off over her head. Her white lace bra made the most of a tan built up over days swimming and lying in the sun but she was all at once self-conscious, wanting to bury herself against him.

'Maybe we should wait.' He didn't touch her. 'You have to be sure about this . . .'

'I'm sure,' she said again. 'I've been thinking about it all week. I want the first time to be with you.'

'And what about the second and third and all the other times after?' His voice was hoarse and uncertain.

He didn't want to lose her. She was not too young to understand that, or to know that she was not something casual and summertime to him. But even then, weightless with desire and abandon, she worried that his love might be too intense, too needy.

'All of those times too,' she said to him and put her mouth against his.

Lying on the bed, naked on top of the Eskimo cover because it was too hot to lie under it, she traced the shapes and parts of his body with her fingers. She'd never seen a man like him, could never have imagined the beauty of a mellow gold skin sprinkled with black hairs.

'I meant what I said,' he spoke against her neck, 'there

is no woman, anywhere that I've ever been, so beautiful as you are.'

'And where have you been then?'

'Enough places to know.'

He held her tightly against him and she could feel his heart beat as his hands moved to show her about loving and the ways they could give each other pleasure. Beneath him she felt like silk, all fluid movement as she moved with him, lost to the ecstasy of the feelings he brought to life in her. She cried out and laughed softly at the idea that the sounds of her pleasure might be heard through the open window and identified for what they were across the campus. Victor laughed with her and a little later he came and so did she.

Afterwards they wound their hot, sweaty limbs together and lay and talked until a cool, night breeze came through the window and Victor got up to close it lest she get cold.

They spent every minute together after that, most of it lying on his bed, holding each other and making love as if the world was about to end and this was all the time they had.

'Don't go back to Dublin,' he said one night when it began to rain.

'I have to.' She felt like crying. Her life would end if she left him.

'Marry me,' he said, 'stay here and marry me.'

'Just like that?' she said. 'Life is not so simple, you know.'

'We can make it simple,' he said.

And he did. They didn't marry in Vancouver, but by Christmas he had come to Ireland and they had been married in Dublin.

Their love-making had always been good, for all the years they'd been together. If Victor were to come to her today, ask her to make love with him on a narrow bed anywhere, she would go with him.

33

The night before the morning he'd died they'd made love. She was glad of that.

The Filipino woman on the reception desk at the Hotel Pacific Nights didn't remember her.

'Baldacci, I'm on the fourth floor,' Bridget said and the woman gave her the key with a wide, unknowing smile. I could be anyone, Bridget thought, and didn't bother asking if there were any messages.

She'd turned off the lights before going out so that almost the only thing she saw when she opened the bedroom door was the flashing red light on the telephone.

'Well, Victor,' she murmured, 'it looks like we've got lift off.'

She felt quite calm as she picked up the receiver and pressed the button to hear her mother-in-law's dry, unfriendly voice.

'I am told by the hotel that you have arrived. I have arranged for some of the family to meet you this evening. We dine at seven. My grandson will collect you from the hotel at five thirty.' There was a pause, during which Veronica Baldacci sighed before going on, 'I will presume, unless I hear otherwise, that this arrangement suits you.'

The digital clock beside the bed showed 4.30 p.m.

Bridget changed into a skirt and light-weight green woollen sweater. The Baldaccis were probably expecting an avenging, warrior widow so she wore the long, jade earrings Victor had given her the Christmas before he died and tied her hair back to show them off to best effect.

At two minutes to 5.30 p.m. reception rang to say a Mr Jack Carter had arrived and was waiting for her in the lobby.

Chapter Three

She saw him as she stepped out of the lift. He was tall, with sun-bleached hair and dark eyes. It was the eyes, and a pair of wide shoulders, which helped Bridget identify him as a Baldacci. Victor had had both. Similarities appeared to end there.

The man standing in the middle of the lobby in a long, stone-coloured raincoat looked bored. Victor had been acutely, awkwardly and often painfully alive to everything and everyone. He'd never been bored.

The man in the lobby was young, about thirty, and he was checking his watch as Bridget approached. Women turned to look at him as they passed. Women had noticed Victor too.

'I'm Bridget Baldacci.' Bridget stood in front of him. He was taller than Victor had been. 'I hope I haven't kept you waiting.'

He smiled and gave her an openly assessing look. 'Hi, Aunt Bridget,' he said and held out a hand. 'I'm John-Francis Baldacci-Carter. My mother is your late husband's sister.' His handshake was firm, and brief. He kept his eyes on her face as Bridget stepped back.

'It's good to meet someone from Victor's family at last.' She smiled too, but carefully. John-Francis Baldacci-Carter's stare had begun to verge on the rude.

'You're not like I thought you would be,' he voice had lowered and softened and Bridget realized with astonishment that he was flirting with her.

'It's hard to be right about someone you've never met and know little about.' She was brisk. 'For my own part I'd no idea you existed.' She paused. 'You're about the age of my children, who aren't children any longer, of course, and are your cousins.'

'So I hear.' His teeth were white in the pale-gold tan of his face. 'You've got a boy and a girl. Same set-up as my own family. There's just me and my sister, Lindsay, in the Baldacci-Carter end of things too. Looks like we've got that much in common anyway.'

'Victor didn't know he had a niece and nephew,' Bridget said, 'so let's hope my coming here is a case of better late than never.'

'Let's hope – ' he took her elbow – 'and let's go now too. I'm pulled in around the corner.'

Pulled in meant just that. The black Porsche he helped her into had two wheels on the pavement and lights flashing on four sides.

'Traffic's a bastard in this town.' Victor's nephew nosed the Porsche assertively into a fast-moving lane. 'It's survival of the fittest.'

'I know the feeling,' said Bridget, who did. Dublin grid-locks were constant and paralysing. Not unlike the Seattle traffic, stalled on every side and with a horn belligerently blowing in the near distance. 'Makes me feel quite at home,' Bridget said, which wasn't true. Her stomach had started a nervous tumbling and she was feeling an awfully long way from anything she was familiar with. 'Tell me about your mother,' she said, 'is she older or younger than Victor?'

'He really never talked about us? Didn't ever fill you in on things?'

'Never.' Bridget paused, studying his profile for a min-ute. It was a good profile, jawline, nose and forehead all well defined. It gave away nothing of the thoughts of the young man behind it. 'I always thought,' she looked ahead, into the traffic as it moved off again, 'that we would grow old together and that Victor would one day tell me about Seattle and growing up here—'

'My mother is the eldest,' he said cutting her short, 'by two years. That makes her sixty years old, though she stopped counting a long time ago. Her name's Magdalena' – he pressed a button and the sound of a jazz combo rippled into the conditioned air – 'and that's what she's always been called. She's not a Mags or a Lena.' He shifted lanes again and they got a clear, fast run for 500 yards or so. Coming close to a bridge they got bogged down again. 'I don't recall her talking much about her brother,' John-Francis Baldacci-Carter said, 'not what you'd call a talkative pair.'

'Maybe your mother will make an exception in my case and open up,' Bridget said.

'Yeah, maybe.'

They turned onto and crossed the bridge, the city ahead and behind them like fields of spangles in the dark. The stretch of water beneath them was a chilling swell of inky blue.

They'd reached the other side, and a more suburban scenario, before John-Francis Baldacci-Carter spoke again.

'Why'd you come here? Why put yourself through this shit now he's dead?'

Bridget didn't answer immediately. When she did she gave him the reply she'd given Anna to the same question months before.

'I'm here because Victor's dead,' she said, 'and because I'm alive and curious.'

'Don't you know what curiosity did to the cat?' He was smiling.

'I've heard.'

They were silent again as he swung the car into a narrow, tree-lined road and began to climb.

'One of the things I'm curious about, John-Francis—' Bridget began.

'Call me Jack. Jack Carter is what my friends call me, though not the family . . .' He stopped, grinning. 'You strike me as the friendly type.'

'Jack it is, then. My question has to do with why you think my coming here is such a bad idea. Is it just that you've got a negative view of your family? Or is there something I wouldn't want to know about why Victor wrote his family out of his life?' She turned to look at him. The excellent profile had become fractionally more chiselled. 'Because that's what he did.'

'Sounds to me like you've answered the question yourself, Aunt Bridget,' his smile didn't waver, 'whatever happened was before my time and no one wants to talk about it anymore. Seems to me that for a man to write his family out of his life he'd need to be pretty fed up with some situation or other. I just dunno why you'd want to rake over all of those dead ashes, that's all.'

He understood all right, Bridget thought, he just didn't want to be involved. Briefly, she wondered if Jack Carter had written the letter which had been waiting for her at the hotel. He didn't seem the type, but you never could tell.

'I get the feeling, Jack, that I'm a not altogether welcome visitor to Seattle,' she said.

'I don't know, Aunt Bridget, why you get that feeling. It's a free world and we're a hospitable lot around here. As far as I'm concerned you're entirely welcome to Seattle.'

'Thank you. And please call me Bid. My friends and family all do.'

The road became more steeply inclined, more heavily lined by a virtual wall of evergreens on either side. Here and there, as they passed, distant lights indicated the presence of secluded houses. The car climbed steadily, smooth and silent.

'Have you always lived in Seattle?' Bridget hated silences.

'Born, bred and now livin' the good life here.'

'I'm told half the city works for Microsoft. Do you?'

'Do I look the nerdy type?' he said irritably. 'Microsoft's a sweatshop for nerds and high-tech workaholics. I don't fit either category.'

'What *do* you work at?'

'I'm part of the family set-up. My father's the vice president and CEO. Grandmother's the president.'

The road straightened and he drove faster, turning too quickly and with a squeal of brakes into a short avenue leading to a pair of high, grey gates. The headlights shone on large, gently falling snowflakes as he pressed a remote control and the gates began to slowly open.

The inner part of the avenue was lined with an erratic growth of old trees, the bald and wintry mingling with heavy evergreens. They rounded a sweeping bend and a large, colonial-style house came into view. The snow, swirling and denser now, made it hard to see clearly.

'Before you, Bid, is the ancestral home,' said Jack Carter, 'the house your husband grew up in. The house my mother grew up in. Their mother, my grandmother Veronica, lives there now. Alone for the most part.' He shrugged. 'I stay with her from time to time, or sometimes my mother does. But basically she's the independent type and prefers to be alone. She has Hugo, of course, her faithful Hugo—'

'Hugo?'

'You'll meet him.' He spun the car in a wide arc on the gravel in front of the house. There were lights on in several rooms. 'My grandmother's father built this place.'

'So she moved back home with her husband, your grandfather, when she married?'

'That's what she did.'

He brought the car to a halt and turned off the engine. Bridget stared at the long, white clapboard building which had been Victor's childhood home. There was no apparent movement behind the lighted windows and the front door remained closed. An elegant portico ran the length of the front, and the black-painted door was framed by two smaller pillars. The palatial effect was spoiled by two rows of giant evergreens. Leaning smotheringly close on either side they gave the place the look of a mausoleum. They were already sprinkled with a covering of snow.

'How old is it?' Bridget asked.

'Turn of the century, colonial revival. I'm told the portico was inspired by Mount Vernon.'

'George Washington's house?'

'Right.' He got out of the car and came round to open Bridget's door. 'My grand-grandfather, John Langan, was Irish and one of the big social climbers of his day. Don't hold that against the house though.'

Victor had never even hinted at Irish blood or ancestry. Bridget climbed out and tilted her face so that snowflakes fell on her closed lids. It was two winters since there had been snow in Dublin.

'Do you know where in Ireland your great-grandfather came from?'

'Nope. Grandmother will fill you in though.'

The front-door bell was shaped in the nose of a bronze lion. Jack Carter had pressed it a couple of times before they heard slow, even footsteps cross the hall on the other side.

'Come on in.' The small man who opened the door had dust-white hair and narrow, foxy features. The hair was caught into a skinny ponytail. 'It's a bad night to be standing outside.'

He ignored Bridget, and spoke directly to Jack Carter. He was wearing a black suit, red waistcoat and black, red-spotted bow tie and his accent was distinctly Irish. Cork unless Bridget was badly mistaken. She stepped into the house ahead of Jack Carter and smiled at the small man.

'They're waiting for you in the sitting room,' he spoke again to Jack Carter and took his raincoat. Underneath the younger man was wearing a dark wool suit, very designer.

'This, Hugo, is Bridget Baldacci.' Jack Carter looked at his watch and ran his fingers through his hair in a quick, continuous movement. 'She's—'

'I know who she is.' The old man turned close-set eyes on Bridget. His expression was one of lively bad humour. 'I'm Hugo Sweeney.'

'You're Irish.' Bridget extended a hand.

'I am.' He ignored the gesture. 'I'll take your outer garments from you.'

Bridget gave him her coat and scarf and with Jack Carter followed him across the high, wood-panelled hallway. Austere and gloomy, it was relieved by a wide, artfully curved staircase which looked to have been designed for grand entrances.

'Nice staircase,' said Bridget.

Hugo Sweeney opened a door and stepped aside while Bridget and Jack Carter went into the biggest sitting room Bridget had ever seen. It ran from the front to the back of the house and was grotesquely overstuffed with furniture. Everywhere Bridget looked there were gilded chairs and chaises, fat, embroidered sofas, fragile tea tables and lacquered card tables, velvet-covered stools, a pink ottoman. Oil paintings of sombre and bewigged colonials hung in clusters on the walls.

Directly opposite the door, round a marble fireplace with a burning, fake log fire, a group of people sat watching Bridget and Jack Carter.

There were four of them, two women and two men. Bridget took a couple of steps further into the room. Her stomach lurched uncomfortably.

'Hello,' she said, 'I'm Bridget—'

'We were pleased you were able to visit at such short

41

notice.' A tall woman, older than Bridget but not old enough to be Veronica Baldacci, unwound herself from a gilded armchair. 'And on such an unpleasant night too, though I'm afraid it's fairly typical of this time of year in Seattle. You would have found the spring a more pleasant time for your visit.' Her voice was low and modulated, the words only slightly slurred. She extended the hand not holding a drink to Bridget. 'I'm Magdalena Baldacci-Carter. I hope my son watched his manners on the ride here.'

Bridget, crossing the expanse of room to take the proffered hand, could see nothing of Victor in his sister's handsome blonde looks, except that she was tall. She was elegant too, a single string of pearls breaking the severe lines of a sheath-like black dress.

'I didn't come to Seattle for sunshine.'

Standing in front of Magdalena Baldacci-Carter, Bridget saw how bone thin she was. That close too it was impossible to ignore the faint alcoholic fumes from her breath. Her hand in Bridget's was limp and warm.

'It's good to meet you at last.' Bridget smiled.

'Likewise,' said Magdalena Baldacci-Carter. 'You'll doubtless want to meet the rest of the family. My mother is busy right now but will be with us momentarily. Allow me to introduce you . . .' She sipped her drink and gestured vaguely towards the others in the room.

Any one of the three people who stood to greet Bridget could have sent the warning note to her hotel. They were all tall, seeming to tower over her. Her mouth dried and they became a blurry triad as she tried to focus. She wished she had a drink in her hand, wished too that she'd never got the damned note.

But she had and it was more than likely that one of these people had sent it – and extremely likely that none of them wanted her here. She managed not to flinch when a slightly stooped man, sixtyish and with a neat white beard, put a hand on her arm and gave a small, nervous cough.

'Hello there, Bridget. I'm Thomas Carter,' he said. 'I married into the family as well. Married Magdalena too many years ago now to keep counting.' He smiled at his wife. 'We're a small enough bunch, as families go, so why don't we get the introductions over with quickly so we can put a good, stiff drink into your hand.' He adjusted a pair of gold-framed glasses and cleared his throat again. 'My wife Magdalena and my son John-Francis you've already met. But not my lovely and intelligent daughter' – a fragile blonde gave Bridget a nod – 'Lindsay—'

'Enough, Dad,' the blonde woman's smile was impatient. 'Good to have you here, Bridget,' she said. Her voice was neutral to cool as she indicated the fourth person in the group. 'This is my husband, Russell Segal.'

Russell Segal was dark-haired, sun-tanned, fit-looking and film-star handsome. There was an unnerving perfection about the sculpted bones of his face.

'Glad to make your acquaintance, ma'am.' He had even, shining teeth.

'Nice to meet an aunt at last.' Lindsay lit a cigarette with a gush of flame from a silver lighter. 'I've been a bit short on them until now. What would you like me to call you?' She watched the smoke as it circled. 'Aunt Bridget? Bridget? Or would it be more to the point to call you Mrs Baldacci?'

'Bid will do fine,' said Bridget, 'it's what most people call me.'

'Cute name.' Russell Segal rested a long arm across Bridget's shoulders. 'Suits you too.'

'I think it a rather sad diminution.' Magdalena, back in her gilded armchair, crossed a pair of very good legs. The honey blonde colour of her shoulder-length hair had probably been natural ten years before. She swung an ankle outward and looked at it critically. 'Shortening names always seems to me rather childish, not something to be carried into adulthood.' She yawned. 'I'll call you Bridget.'

Boredom, Bridget decided, was probably the reason she drank so much.

'We all know why you feel like that, mother.' Jack Carter sauntered to the fireplace and rested an elegant arm on the mantel. 'Magdalena is not a name to mess around with.' He threw a brief, conspiratorial look Bridget's way. 'Too many lousy possibilities. Mags? Lena? Not your style at all.'

'I do like it when you see things my way.' Magdalena Baldacci-Carter's expression, as she looked at her son, became quite animated.

'Don't I always?' said Jack. Magdalena gave a laugh and shrugged.

Bridget's need for a drink was becoming desperate. She wished someone would invite her to sit: the multitude of chairs and sofas was confusing, most of them looked too old and too precious to risk sitting on.

Thomas Carter came to her rescue.

'Dinner could be a while yet, so let's sit back down. John-Francis will get you a drink.' He indicated a spindle-legged chair next to him and Bridget sat. 'Veronica is overseeing the meal. She likes to be involved, doesn't like to keep a lot of help in the house. What would you like to drink?'

'When in Rome,' Bridget said. 'I'll try a Martini Dry. Three olives.' Victor had liked a Martini Dry with three olives.

'One Martini Dry on the way.' Jack Carter disappeared to a long table with drinks at the other side of the room.

'You have two children?' Magdalena stared into the evenly dancing blue-gold flames.

'Two, yes. Though they haven't been children for a long time,' Bridget said. 'They're in their twenties, late twenties.' The room was unbearably warm.

'They had no interest in coming to Seattle?'

'None. They live very full lives . . .' Not like me, Bridget thought, unable to live any kind of life since Victor had died. Magdalena raised an eyebrow and waited for her to go on. 'But they're as curious as I am about their father's family,' Bridget said.

'That's nice,' said Magdalena.

'One Martini Dry.' Jack Carter stood between Bridget and his mother. He handed her a white napkin with her drink and raised his own glass. 'Welcome to Seattle,' he said.

'A drink seems like a good idea,' Magdalena spoke loudly, rattling the ice in her empty glass. Her eyes were still half closed. 'See if you can pour me a decent gin Martini, John-Francis.'

'Oh, God, here we go again,' Lindsay groaned, stubbed out her cigarette and fiddled with one of her small, silver earrings. 'If you people will excuse me, there's something I have to do.' She lifted a small shoulder bag from the lacquered card table nearest her. 'I won't be staying to eat.'

Her mother's eyes opened fully and her ankle stopped swinging. 'You have not been given permission to leave,' her voice had become harsh as well as loud, 'and so you will stay. We are going to make the best of this situation. We are all, as a family, going to share a meal with our guest.'

'I've already eaten,' said Lindsay. 'I wasn't told about this . . . dinner until today. There are a couple of work issues I should be—'

'You will stay here, Lindsay,' Magdalena said. 'You are not in the boardroom now. The business will wait. Your obsession with it has, at any rate, become unhealthy.'

'Unhealthy! You have to be joking, Mother!' Lindsay's laugh was genuinely amused. She lit another cigarette.

Magdelena stood a little unsteadily and Bridget saw her knuckles whiten when she gripped the back of the chair. Thomas Carter moved unobtrusively closer to his wife.

'You, Russell,' Magdalena fixed an imperious glare on her son-in-law, 'get your posturing ass into gear and deal with your wife. I want everyone here to sit down to dinner tonight with Bridget . . .' she paused, 'and I am holding you responsible for Lindsay's presence at the table.'

'I'm not my wife's jailer,' Russell replied laconically, 'I can't even stop her smoking so I don't know as I can exactly put her in chains, Magdalena.'

'Californians! You're all the same. Lazy, dumb, useless, retarded . . .' Magdalena took a long, hissing breath. 'Just tie her down, Russell, do whatever it takes. You're a man, aren't you?' Her eyes narrowed. 'Or are you . . .?'

'Why don't we all calm down.' Jack Carter moved closer to his mother and put an arm round her shoulder. 'Seems to me things are getting a bit out of hand around here. Mother, I'll get you that drink now. Lindsay, why don't you take Bridget outside onto the back patio for a couple of minutes, show her the tree? I'll bet it looks good with the snow falling on it.'

'Jack the peacemaker.' Lindsay gave a short laugh and blew a small spiral of smoke into her brother's face. 'I'll bet you haven't looked at that tree once this Christmas. Come to that, I'll bet you didn't know it was there until Grandmother decided not to take it down—'

'Do I have to get my drink myself?' Magdalena, sitting back into the chair, interrupted sharply. Thomas stood behind her massaging her shoulders.

'Want to come with me see Grandmother's Christmas tree?' Lindsay's face, when she turned to Bridget, was smiling and smooth and lovely. 'Having it out there in the yard's been a yearly event since for ever.' She gave a short laugh. 'You're in luck. As you probably picked up just now, Grandmother has decided to let it stand for longer than usual this year.'

'I'll get Hugo to bring your coats—' Thomas began.

'We won't need them.' Lindsay took Bridget's arm and started with her towards the rear of the room. 'We're not going to climb the tree.'

Circumnavigating the furniture they made their way towards a set of closed double curtains. The room behind them was silent, the rattle of ice as Jack Carter mixed his mother's drink the only sound.

'Peace and goodwill to men.' Lindsay opened a set of French windows the other side of the curtains and stepped out onto a patio. 'What you see before you, Bid, is Grandmother's yearly tribute to the season just past. The Baldacci Christmas just wouldn't be complete without it.'

Bridget stood beside her on the patio, sheltered from the falling snow by a porch, and stared at a colossal fir, lit up and shining in the murky dark of the garden. It was all of thirty feet high, uniquely and dazzlingly impressive as it stood with the snow falling softly about its blue and white lights and settling gently on the bright-green pines. A reindeer, at the very top, had a radiant red nose. Tree and reindeer together made for an eerily peaceful, perfect triangle of light in the dark emptiness of the garden.

The arrival of the snow had taken the cold sting from the air and Bridget took in calming gulps as she went down a set of steps and into the garden proper. A light covering of snow lay on the grass.

'It's a wonderful tree,' she said, 'how long does your grandmother intend leaving it there?' It was now the seventh of January.

'Until she decides Christmas is over.' Lindsay came and stood beside her. 'She's decided it should go on longer this year. She's waiting for a friend to call . . .' She let out a long breath. 'She's more than eighty years old, did you know that?'

'Victor was fifty-eight when he died. I knew his mother had to be about that age.' Bridget studied the tree. Now that she was closer it seemed to her that there was something slightly off about it. She couldn't quite decide what, exactly. 'Are you telling me Victor's mother is senile?'

'God no.' Lindsay shook her head. 'Just that she's an old woman, and that old women do strange things, break the rules a little. They're allowed.'

'Rules are for all women to break,' said Bridget, 'only they don't do it half enough.'

'Are you a rule breaker?' Lindsay looked at her thoughtfully.

'Not often enough.' Bridget smiled.

'Women are, by and large, the law-abiding element in the human race,' said Lindsay. 'By and large. Snow's stopping . . .'

Slowly, as the snowfall tailed away, the Christmas tree came into sharp relief against the pitch black of the garden behind it. Only the occasional flickering of a tree light broke the unearthly silence.

And into this Veronica Baldacci walked.

Bridget had imagined Victor's mother as a woman of height and bearing with an imperious air. It was an image built on a combination of Victor's silence and her own telephone conversations.

The woman walking toward them was all of those things. What Bridget hadn't expected was someone who must have once been very beautiful. Even allowing for the dancing lights and distance she was the possessor of a pair of remarkably high cheek bones and wide-spaced eyes. She wore a long, silver fox-fur coat and was using a black, silver-topped walking cane.

'You're about to meet your mother-in-law,' said Lindsay, 'and God knows when we're going to get some food if she's been wandering about out here.'

Veronica Baldacci, walking slowly and seemingly unaware that she had company in the garden, reached the tree and began to adjust a light bulb. When Bridget made a move toward her Lindsay put a staying hand.

'Wait,' she said.

'Why don't you introduce me?' said Bridget.

'She knows we're here. Better to wait until she comes to you.'

'Is that a rule?' Bridget raised an eyebrow.

'Sort of . . .'

'I haven't broken enough rules in my life . . .' Bridget watched as Veronica Baldacci moved back and stood looking up at the tree. '. . . maybe I'll break one now.'

Veronica Baldacci couldn't have failed to hear Bridget crunching across the snow. But she didn't turn, leaning on the cane and staring at the tree even when Bridget stopped a couple of feet behind her.

'Hello,' she said, 'I'm Bridget, Victor's wife.'

'I was aware you'd arrived,' the voice sounded more tremulous than it had on the phone. 'Dinner will be served in a little while. We will talk then.' Veronica Baldacci turned. She was wearing too much make-up and her expression was stern. 'I would have preferred us to meet formally, indoors.'

'I've waited a long time to meet you.' Bridget smiled. Her first and distant impression of Veronica Baldacci had been an accurate one: Victor's mother had been a stunner, once. She'd known it too. The make-up covering her thin, tight skin and outlining her features was a defiant scream at beauty's passing.

'It would have been better manners to wait for me to come to you,' Veronica Baldacci said.

'It would have been mannerly to receive me when I arrived,' said Bridget.

'Touché,' said Victor's mother and smiled. 'Though I'm inclined to think it would have been better by far had we never met.'

'For you, perhaps,' said Bridget.

'For both of us, I think. Why have you come here?' The older woman sighed. 'Why could you not have left things as they were?'

Bridget studied Veronica's face for a moment before answering: it told her nothing. 'I lived for thirty years with your son,' she said at last, 'why wouldn't I want to meet his mother? His family? Don't you think it natural that I would want to see the place where he grew up?'

'Why bother? He's dead.'

'It seems even more important now he's dead.'

'Death comes to us all.' Victor's mother turned back to the tree and Bridget, closer to it now and following her gaze, saw what it was that had struck her as odd. The giant fir was artificial, every branch and pine needle a tribute to the art of plastic imitation.

'Sometimes,' Bridget said, 'death comes too soon.'

'That's a point of view, certainly,' said Veronica Baldacci.

Snow slipped from a plastic branch with a low plop as Bridget waited for the older woman to add something regretful, kind, even enquiring, about her son. Her feet were becoming cold and wet from standing in the snow. Veronica Baldacci remained silent.

'Forgive me if I'm wrong but you don't appear to feel grief at your son's death,' Bridget spoke quietly, 'your falling out must have been very terrible . . .' she paused. 'It could be, of course, that I am altogether wrong.'

'I ceased to grieve for Victor many years ago,' the older woman didn't turn around, 'long before you met him. He was not a grateful son. I reared him, as any mother would, happy to have the son my husband and I had wanted so much. My husband put everything into his boy, believing in him. By the time Victor left, in 1962 when he was just twenty-three years old, his father was dead, and sadly disillusioned.'

'Are you telling me that Victor was responsible for his father's death?'

'Not in any physical sense, no. But it is not too fanciful to say that he broke his father's heart.'

Bridget stomped her feet, testing that her toes still had life in them. 'None of this sounds like the man I knew. He was intensely loyal to me and our children.'

Veronica Baldacci turned then. But her focus was clearly inward and it was doubtful that she saw Bridget.

'He left himself no other choice,' she said, 'he had cast aside everyone else in his life by the time he met you.'

'But why?' Bridget stared, hating the ambiguity, resisting an entirely irrational urge to shake direct answers from the other woman. 'Why did he leave here? What happened that was so terrible it kept him away?' Rubbing her hands together, the better to keep them away from Veronica Baldacci, she didn't hear Lindsay's approach until she stood shivering beside her grandmother.

'I want to get back indoors even if you two don't.' She hugged herself, her blue silk blouse spotted with snow. 'The temperature's dropping again. Let's go get some food.'

'You have a point, my dear, as always.' Veronica gathered the fur around herself. 'I left the inept woman I pay to cook for me to finish preparing the meal. She should have it ready by now.' She tested the ground with the cane and began walking toward the house. 'She brought her daughter in as help with tonight's occasion but she would have been better off leaving her at home. We will have to hope that Hugo has salvaged things.'

As they climbed the steps onto the patio, Victor's mother turned for a final look at the tree.

'I will leave it stand for a further week. Another seven days is as much as I am prepared to wait. Any longer would be ridiculous.'

51

'Right.' Lindsay sighed. 'Ridiculous is just what all of this is.'

Shivering violently now she went ahead of them to open the French windows. Bridget walked slowly beside Victor's mother.

'I do hope your journey hasn't exhausted you,' the older woman spoke as if they'd just met.

'Not at all,' said Bridget. 'It's given me an appetite though.'

'I don't like to have my plans hijacked,' Veronica Baldacci said, 'and I had planned to make your acquaintance and speak with you before dinner. So we will talk, briefly, in the library before eating.'

'If you like.'

'I do.'

In the sitting room Lindsay eyed Bridget's sodden boots and said, 'Your feet look about as wet as mine are. I'll get Hugo to bring you a pair of slippers.'

'He can bring them along to the library.' Veronica didn't stop. 'We'll be spending a short time there together.'

Chapter Four

The library was small, too warm, and as overstuffed with furniture as the sitting room had been. Bridget sat in one of three wing-backed chairs and within minutes saw steam begin to rise from her wet boots. Veronica Baldacci shed her waterproof boots and her fur coat and rang a bell. A dress in beige cashmere hung loosely on a body as bonily thin as her daughter's.

'I will come to the point straight away.' She sat down so that she was facing Bridget directly. 'It will prevent us wasting one another's time.' She secured a hairpin and patted her hair into place. 'I did not encourage you to come here because I would have preferred the past to lie at rest. My son, your husband, was the cause of great hurt to this family. You will no doubt say that I should forgive, that I am his mother and should also forget. But I cannot and will not do either of those things, ever.'

'I think that very sad, for all concerned.'

'You may think so, but then you are speaking from ignorance. It is my prerogative and privilege to hold onto my anger and to my hurt.' Victor's mother fixed her gaze on the marriage ring on Bridget's left hand. 'Neither you, nor your children, have any right to sit in judgement, to expect anything else from me. I knew my son. I knew him for what he was and knew what he could not change in himself. It is useless for you to come here expecting reconciliation, or an understanding of some kind.'

'Reconciliation?' Bridget was curt. 'There is nothing for me to be reconciled to – I was never part of this family. Nor do I want to be. That's not why I've come here.'

She left the armchair and walked to the window, the heat and sense of claustophobia in the small room was getting to her. Outside a wind had come up, lifting the powdery white cover from the ground and sending it, circling, into the air. The Christmas tree was still beautiful, the garden still a dark abyss behind it. She leaned her hands against the cool of the glass and told herself that the sane thing would be to leave now. She'd met Victor's family.

The really sane thing, of course, would have been not to have come in the first place.

But why shouldn't she be helped to understand? What right had Veronica Baldacci to deny her knowledge?

She turned back to the room, her hands behind her back, palms still against the soothing cool of the window.

'Reconciliation's a different thing to understanding,' she said. 'It's important to me that I understand why my husband denied his mother. Why he denied his entire family. I came here because I want to know what it was that he could never tell me.'

'He said nothing of his life here?' Veronica Baldacci's hands moved from her lap to clutch at the chair's arm.

'Nothing. Ever.'

Was there relief in the pale eyes? Or was it shock which made them freeze and glaze over?

'Yes. That would have been his way. He didn't change then.' The older woman shrugged. 'I should have known . . .' For several seconds she massaged her forehead with her fingers, a cluster of rings on her fingers making the action cumbersome. 'He bore grudges, always silently, as a child. Obviously it wasn't in him to change, any more than it was in his . . .' She made an irritable gesture with her hand. 'Please sit down. Since you're here we will talk. Some.

54

We will also have drinks – if that manservant of mine can be got to answer the bell.'

She reached forward and pressed a bell in the wall, long and hard. It could be head, loudly echoing, through the bowels of the house.

'I hope, in spite of what you've told me,' said Veronica Baldacci, 'that you have not come here looking for money. Victor was not entitled to anything from this family.'

Bridget didn't move from the window. She held her breath for a while and counted to five before she said, 'I have not come looking for money.'

'We will not discuss the subject of greed then,' Veronica said. 'Though I must tell you that there are some in the family who cannot conceive of you being here for any other reason.'

'That's understandable, I suppose. But they're wrong.'

'I hope so.' Victor's mother drummed her fingers on the arm of the chair.

Bridget watched her for a minute, wondering if she'd always been so cold, so controlled. She'd half expected that Victor's family, and this woman, would think she'd come for money.

What she hadn't bargained on was the complete absence of regret, of a mourning of any kind for Victor.

'You may not grieve for your son's death,' she left the window and began to circle the room, 'but do you grieve for his life?'

She turned quickly, and caught a flickering disturbance on the older woman's still, made-up face. It could have been pain, a grief denied, it could also have been anger, or simple irritation.

'Victor was too young to die. Of course I regret his death.' Veronica Baldacci shrugged again. 'Victor choosing to live the greater part of his life at a distance naturally affects the nature of my grief. He created another life for

55

himself and I applaud his independence.' She paused. 'However, I deplore his cruelty.'

'Victor wasn't cruel. He simply didn't know—'

'I don't care to know about his emotional problems. I'm an old woman, not a state I enjoy. I have decided to concentrate on certain priorities for the time left me to live. Victor, and the past, are not priorities.'

This time, when Veronica leaned forward impatiently to press the bell again, Bridget took a minute to study the room.

Excess, when it came to furnishing and decor, was definitely the Baldacci way. The room looked to be a perfect cube. Three of its walls were filled, floor to ceiling, with books; beautifully bound, matching leathers many of them, classics and history titles predominating. Green, in different shades, was the main colour. The lighting came from a collection of ornate reading lamps. Touching one of a pair of bronze noblemen on a table beside her Bridget thought how nicely Victor's casket would sit between the two of them.

'Please be careful.' Veronica Baldacci gave an impatient tsk. 'This room has been put together with great care.'

'I can see that,' Bridget said. The reading lamp behind the older woman gave her face the look of a skull with a blonde halo. Bridget decided against mentioning Victor's ashes, yet.

The door opened without warning and Hugo Sweeney, arms laden, stepped into the room.

'I brought you these.' He put a pair of leather moccasins on the floor in front of Veronica. 'By rights you should be in your room resting before dinner.'

'I can't wear those.' Veronica lifted the walking stick from beside her chair and poked at the moccasins. 'Bring me my cream pumps. And why are you talking about a rest before dinner? Is the meal not ready to be served?'

'Just about,' Hugo said in a mollifying tone, 'another twenty minutes or so. I'll take you to your room.'

'I'm entertaining, as you can see.' Veronica glared at him. 'And I would like you to bring us drinks.' She pointed at the moccasins. 'You may give those to our guest. Mrs Baldacci insisted on an uninvited viewing of our tree. She was not dressed for the occasion.'

Hugo, silently and without once lifting his eyes, placed the moccasins close to where Bridget was sitting.

'You can bring us the drinks straight away, Hugo.' Veronica Baldacci lifted the walking stick from beside the armchair and tapped impatiently on the floor. 'I will have my usual bourbon, a double measure. Mrs Baldacci will have . . .?'

'A cup of tea. No sugar, no milk.'

Hugo Sweeney's face took on a stubbornly resentful look and Veronica tapped more sharply with the stick.

'Get her the tea, Hugo. And while you're in the kitchen check with that wretched Amy about dinner.'

Hugo picked up the fox fur. 'I'll be setting an extra place at the table.'

'I did not ask you to do so,' Veronica's voice dropped and became almost inaudible with fury. 'We will be six, no more.'

'You can't ignore her. She arrived back twenty minutes ago. She'll come to the table and make a scene. You'd be better off accommodating her. It'll cause less trouble.' Hugo Sweeney's tone was deferential, wheedling. Its cajoling rhythm seemed to soothe Veronica.

'You'd better make sure then that she doesn't place herself anywhere near me at the table. Go now, and bring me my pumps and the drinks.' She closed her eyes and leaned back into the chair, balancing the stick in front of her across the arms. 'And be quick about it.'

Hugo Sweeney closed the door quietly and gently after him.

57

'He runs the house for me. He's useful.' Veronica tapped her fingers on the stick, her rings catching the light from the lamp. She kept her eyes closed. 'He's loyal. You have to be my age to appreciate loyalty truly.'

'How long has he worked for you?'

'Long enough. He's seventy-two years old. He was thirty-one when a priest in the parish asked me to give him a job which would keep him out of jail long enough to stop him being deported. I took him on because he was Catholic.' Her eyes snapped open. 'You are Catholic too, I presume? Victor didn't marry a non-Catholic, did he?'

Bridget didn't answer immediately. First she worked out something about Hugo Sweeney. He'd been forty years ministering to Veronica; he would have known Victor. She might, if she worked on him, get an objective view of what had happened.

'I was a Catholic when Victor married me,' she said eventually, and slowly. The faith she'd been reared in hadn't been of much interest to Victor. It was of much less interest to Bridget now than it had been.

'I'm glad to hear it.' Veronica leaned toward Bridget. 'We must hold hard to the faith of our fathers. The old country has always stood by the church.'

'Your grandson Jack mentioned that your father was Irish,' Bridget said.

Veronica straightened. 'My grandson is known as John-Francis within the family.' She began tapping the stick again with her fingers. 'So. You didn't even know that your husband's ancestry was part Irish?'

'No. All of this is news to me. I presumed, because of his looks and his name, that Victor was Italian-American.'

'His father, my husband Frank Baldacci, was of Italian extraction. Catholic too, of course. Victor greatly resembled Frank, in looks.'

'Your father was Irish . . .' Bridget prompted Veronica when she fell silent.

'I am not deaf and I am not senile,' Veronica snapped, 'so do not prompt answers from me. It is simply that the subject does not interest me half as much as it does you. Yes, my father was Irish. He came here in the eighteen fifties. He'd got word of the gold rush when he was in New York, to where he'd made his escape from the potato famine in Ireland. My family name is Langan.' She spoke quickly, offhandedly, as if the story she was telling had nothing to do with her. 'It may be that Victor chose you because of your nationality—'

She stopped as the door opened and Hugo Sweeney reappeared. He placed a small table between the two women and a tray with a single cup of tea, a glass of bourbon and two napkins. Close to Veronica's feet he placed a pair of almost flat-heeled cream pumps.

'Dinner will be served in ten minutes,' he said.

Veronica took a long drink. 'I want you to attend in the kitchen, Hugo, and to make sure that six, good portions of food are delivered to the table. The seventh, uninvited, guest will have to be satisfied with what she gets. Do I make myself clear?'

'As glass,' said Hugo Sweeney.

'We were discussing the likelihood of Victor having chosen an Irish wife because of my family links with the old country.' Veronica watched Hugo Sweeney carefully as she spoke.

'Not likely at all.' Hugo stood stiffly inside the door. 'I never knew him to have any interest in those as went before him.'

'That sounds like Victor,' Bridget agreed and smiled.

Hugo looked at his watch. 'Time's marching on. Eight minutes now and the food will be ready.'

'I'd like you to tell me something before you go.' Bridget stood and took a few steps towards Hugo, who immediately opened the door. 'Please,' Bridget said. 'All I want to know is what sort of young man my husband was. You knew him . . .'

'He was a serious person,' Hugo Sweeney stepped into the doorway, 'not easy, hard enough to get to know.' With a curt nod he turned and pulled the door firmly behind him.

'Not an easy man to get to know himself.' Veronica slipped her feet into the pumps.

Bridget, sipping the lukewarm tea, was willing to bet Veronica Baldacci knew everything there was to know about Hugo Sweeney. It would have been one of the reasons for his loyalty.

'Hugo spoke of time marching on.' Veronica sighed. 'I find it more true to say time flies, as one gets older. It is equally true, of course, that death urges, knells call, heaven invites, hell threatens . . .' Her milky blue eyes stared at Bridget. 'You are a woman who has put thirty years of her time into my son. My advice to you is not to waste any more of it on this family. You won't listen, of course. You are obviously stubborn.' She paused. 'Thirty years . . . and then to come here. If it is true that you do not want money then you must be mad. We will talk again. I am not inclined to reveal family intimacies to a perfect stranger. I know nothing about you.' Veronica Baldacci stood and leaned on the stick. 'I had hoped that our small talk in this room would satisfy you but you are clearly not a woman who is easily . . . satisfied.' She hesitated. 'How long do you intend staying in Seattle?'

'A couple of weeks, at least.'

'We will talk again but right now we will eat.'

She stood tapping the stick impatiently while Bridget removed her boots and slipped her feet into the moccasins. They were much too big, slapping on the wooden floor of the hallway as she followed her mother-in-law from the library and across to where the dining-room door stood open. It was a long room with a long table.

'There's a place laid for you at the far end,' said Hugo Sweeney.

'Thank you.' Bridget took the chair nearest her. 'I'll be fine here.'

Better to be close to the door, she would not feel so hemmed in by Baldaccis that way.

Chapter Five

'Good to have you back,' said Thomas Carter with a smile and a nod.

Bridget looked at him and decided the remark was as innocent as it seemed. She would have to guard against paranoia.

'Sorry if I kept you waiting,' she said.

'Most of us had the wisdom to eat earlier.' Thomas leaned across the table, an attempt at confidentiality made difficult by the table's width. 'Entertaining is not one of Veronica's fortes.'

Bridget, faced with a basket of bread rolls, was suddenly aware of a rumbling hollow in her stomach. 'I haven't eaten all day myself,' she admitted.

'Oh dear, oh dear,' Magdalena, to her right, murmured reprovingly, 'how very optimistic you were. I would advise you to start on the bread rolls. They may be the best thing on the menu.'

Bridget took one. It felt soft and warm.

The dining-room decor reflected the by now familiar taste for sombre Victoriana. It was, if anything, more suffocating than either the library or the sitting room with bigger and darker furniture, numbers of landscape oils and heavy, burgundy-coloured curtains on all the windows but one.

Bridget found herself sitting opposite an empty place setting. Magdalena sat next to her, Thomas sat across from his wife and Lindsay and her husband bickered a little further down. At the far end Jack Carter sat close to where his grandmother had taken her seat at the head of the table. The table, of polished oak, was big enough to have seated eighteen people and swallowed up the six who now sat there. The place settings had been laid widely apart, presumably by Hugo Sweeney, so the occasion was not going to be an intimate one.

'We will begin, Hugo.' Veronica Baldacci tapped the floor with her stick. 'You and Amy may start serving.'

Hugo Sweeney, after a brief glance at the empty chair, all but clicked his heels before disappearing through a door.

'Is there someone I haven't met?' Bridget broke the bread roll and looked up as she reached for, and failed to find, the butter. No one seemed about to answer her question. She rephrased it. 'Hugo says there will be a seventh person joining us . . .'

'Veronica has a house guest,' Thomas said. 'She has just returned from a trip downtown and may join us . . .'

'There isn't a chance in hell of her *not* joining us,' Magdalena said. 'This is the occasion she's been waiting for. A captive audience, a God-sent opportunity to let loose with that crazy ego of hers.' She pushed her wine glass across the table to her husband. 'Just thinking about it makes me thirsty. Pour me a glass of the Chablis, Thomas, and fill it up.' She watched while her husband poured the wine, speaking out of the side of her mouth to Bridget. 'She's been waiting to meet you. It's your fault she's here in the first place.'

'Don't pre-empt things, sweetheart.' Thomas carefully eased his wife's drink back across the table. 'Let's try to keep this thing amicable.'

'Amicable! Amicable doesn't make people go away. Amicable doesn't change anything.' Magdalena gulped at the wine, shrugged and sat silently fiddling with an earring. She looked tired.

Bridget helped herself to a glass of the Chablis. It would help the butterless bread roll down and it didn't look as if anyone was going to pour it for her.

Hugo Sweeney arrived through the side door with a serving trolley and a large, square woman. At a finger-clicking command from him the woman began ladling the contents of a soup tureen into bowls which Hugo Sweeney then delivered to the table.

'Fish chowder,' John-Francis announced after a spoonful.

'That's right.' The square woman beamed. 'I knew you'd like it, John-Francis. That's why I made it.'

'God, is there *any* woman you don't turn it on for?' Lindsay looked disgustedly at her brother.

'That is not the question.' Magdalena smiled at her son. 'The real question is – where's the woman can resist him?'

'You're the only one for me, Mom, you know that,' John-Francis grinned.

'We will say grace,' Veronica said loudly and stood. 'Bless us, O Lord,' she began to intone without waiting against the sound of chairs scraping back from the table, 'and these Thy gifts which, of Thy bounty, we are about to receive. Give us patience too, Lord, and return absent friends safely.' Into a small silence she delivered a sharp 'Amen' and sat.

Veronica was facing the door from the hallway, her back to the one window without a curtain. This overlooked a floodlit, formal garden with two rows of classical statuary, a long, columned pergola and high, evergreen hedging. It had expense and self-conscious style written all over it. It was also, Bridget thought, another possible resting place for Victor's casket.

'Thought I'd take a few days skiing next week,' Russell Segal, speaking for the first time, aimed his remark at no one in particular.

'Might come with you,' said John-Francis. 'Where're you headed?'

64

'Thought I'd try the backcountry—'

'Forget it' – Lindsay abandoned her soup – 'I'm not financing any more of your vacations, Russell. And you can forget it too, John-Francis. You're expected to be around for the reinvestment deal with—'

'Take it easy, Lindsay, I'll deal with the business end of this later,' Thomas was cool. 'In any event, I don't think skiing's going to be an option for a while to come. The weather service is talking avalanche hazards.'

'Sonny Bono won't be taking any more skiing trips.' Russell Segal laughed. 'Pity he had to go like that though, he was one of the good guys. Cher wouldn't have gotten anywhere without him—'

'He wasn't a good guy,' Lindsay snapped. 'He was a vulgar little man who did a good job of self-promotion.'

'He'd become a useful Congressman.' Russell sounded petulant. 'He was a Republican. I voted for him.'

'I rest my case,' said Lindsay.

'Your wife is quite right, Russell, about Congressman Bono,' Veronica Baldacci said impatiently. 'He was nothing but a showman. Married three times.' She paused. 'Marriage is until death.'

'It is in this family at any rate.' Magdalena, fingers in a frenzy, was reducing a bread roll to crumbs on her plate. 'Our guest will agree with that, won't you, Bridget?'

'It was in my case,' Bridget said.

'Your experience is quite typical, believe me,' said Magdalena.

'Sonny Bono voted against same sex marriages,' Thomas spoke quickly, 'very unCalifornian—'

'Was your marriage to my brother a happy one?' Magdalena, cutting him short, gave Bridget a direct look.

'Yes. Very.'

'You surprise me.' Magdalena, ignoring the soup, made a pyramid of the crumbed bread roll. 'He was such a moody youngster. Strange that he should be the one to have an apparently happy marriage.'

'People change. They grow up.'

Veronica tapped the floor with her stick and Magdalena, through tightened lips, muttered, 'I wish she wouldn't do that.' Bridget found herself wishing the same thing.

'We will have the next course,' Veronica Baldacci called.

Hugo Sweeney, who'd been standing just inside the door, moved silently on the soup bowls. He was deft and quick and full of a resentful energy as he wheeled the laden trolley from the room. He took with him the bowl laid for the seventh diner.

'I brought some of Victor's ashes with me,' Bridget said as the door closed behind him. 'I thought you might like to scatter them in the garden.' She gave a half-smile and shrug. 'Or maybe keep the casket somewhere ... the library perhaps ...'

Thomas coughed. Someone else sighed. Through the window, in the spotlit garden, Bridget thought she could see the beginnings of another snowfall. She watched and waited, silently, until Victor's sister at last broke the silence.

'I'm sure you meant well,' Magdalena said, 'and maybe things are done differently in Ireland. But since my mother hadn't seen her son for thirty-five years or more, I doubt she would care to have his ashes as a daily reminder of his desertion.'

'Do you feel the same?' Bridget asked.

'Yes,' Magdalena said, 'I feel the same.'

'No one in this family wishes to be reminded of the unhappy past,' Victor's mother's voice was harsh. 'You should not have presumed to bring my son's ashes here.'

'Maybe you could scatter them in the Bay?' Thomas, after an anxious look at his wife, spoke gently to Bridget. 'There are regular, daily boat trips and you might – '

'Thank you. I may just do that.' Bridget gave him a wry smile.

The man was well meaning. He might just be her letter writer. She broadened her smile. Thomas, looking uncomfortable, straightened in his chair.

'Ah, the trolley's back.' John-Francis gave a low whistle and rubbed his hands together. 'What further delights have you got for us tonight, Amy?'

'Chicken.' Amy dimpled and Hugo Sweeney snapped at her, sharklike, across the trolley. She began lifting dishes from the warming plate and giving them to Hugo.

Bridget's mother, herself a bad cook, had habitually told her offspring that hunger was good sauce. Bridget had never before appreciated the wisdom of the old saying. Amy's chicken was sawdust dry and broke apart like a piece of rotted timber at the touch of a fork. The sauce appeared to be a mixture of salt and cream. Bridget, alone at the table, ate with something like relish.

'I'll have to forego the pleasure of your chicken, Amy,' John-Francis, studying the food on his plate, sounded regretful. 'I have to leave.' He stood. 'My apologies, everyone. Night and the city calls.'

'Thank you for your time, John-Francis.' His grandmother was icy as he bent to kiss the top of her head, lightly.

'You get an early night now, Grandma.' His grandmother didn't return his grin. 'Great food,' he called to the watching Amy as he made his way to the door. To Bridget, as he passed, he said, 'Sorry I can't give you a ride back to your hotel. But maybe we'll do the city tour together before you leave.' He gave a small salute. 'You won't get a better guide.'

'You shouldn't have come here, Bridget.' Magdalena flattened the pyramid of bread crumbs as the dining-room door closed behind him. She was crying, fat tears making tracks through her make-up. She sipped her drink, dabbing at the tears with a finger. 'It's like a cage was opened when Victor died . . . you've come out of it to rake up the past, take what's ours—'

'You're tired, sweetheart,' Thomas interrupted her, 'maybe you should lie down.'

'I'm drunk,' Magdalena snarled, 'how else do you expect me to get through an occasion like this? Doesn't mean I'm not right though. You know I am. You all know I'm right.' She shrugged. 'We are looking at the beginning of the end.' She reached for her drink, missed it and knocked the glass over, emptying the contents into her dinner plate. 'Accidents will happen . . .' She shrugged.

'Get her a black coffee, Thomas,' Veronica Baldacci spoke with cold distaste, 'it might put an end to this maudlin nonsense.' Hugo Sweeney, with Amy in attendance, cleared away the dinner plates. Through the window behind her mother-in-law Bridget saw that snow had, indeed, begun to fall again, feathery flakes of it dancing in the lights and the wind. It looked very lovely, another world altogether from this one.

'Tell me something about this part of Seattle.' She looked down the table at Lindsay.

'Well, where to begin . . .' Lindsay raised her remarkable, almond-shaped eyes to the ceiling and thought for a minute before going on. 'We're pretty good on our history in Seattle.' She smiled. 'We're sort of separatists, I suppose, considered hick until we became fashionable and environmentally PC a few years ago. As for this neighbourhood . . . well, it wasn't always the upmarket area you drove through tonight. In its early days Madison Park was known as White Beach, something to do with the huge numbers of hookers populating the place. We're told it was as close as Seattle ever came to having its own Coney Island. There were amusement parks and horse racing and even, at one time, a ferris wheel.' She became thoughtful again. 'I think I would have liked it then.'

'More than you like today's Madison Park?' Bridget asked.

'Who can say? I'd have had a different history, been a different person, if I'd lived then.' She smiled again and shrugged. 'We'd all have been different.'

'True,' said Bridget. 'And is that life gone from here altogether? Have the hookers all gone out of business?'

'Who's to say?' Lindsay gave a short laugh. 'Things aren't always what they seem. You must know that.'

'I know that,' said Bridget.

Dessert had been served, an elaborate concoction of cream, ice-cream and fruit, and the mood in the room had become almost relaxed when the door from the hallway opened.

Bridget stared. The young woman coming through was tall, dark and, differences in style apart, could have been Anna's twin. Not an identical twin, there were too many subtle differences for that, but her double nevertheless in all sorts of ways. Her hair was the same burnt-almond brown, her eyebrows arched as Anna's did and her wide-spaced eyes were the same inky black. There were differences about her nose, which was longer, and her lips, which were painted a shade of mauve Anna would never have used and were thinner. Bridget had never seen Anna wear anything like the black sequinned top and second-skin black jeans this young woman was wearing either.

Her eyes searched the table and stopped at Bridget.

'You have to be the daughter-in-law,' she said. 'I've been waiting to meet you . . .'

'You need not have waited so long,' Lindsay indicated the table setting, 'you were expected to eat with us.'

'How kind. Someone should have told me. Well, I'm

here now.' She dropped into the empty chair. 'And how thoughtful! You've put me right opposite Bridget.' She reached a hand across the table. 'I'm Eleanor Munro. Has anyone explained who I am? Why I'm here?'

'You're obviously family,' Bridget, stretching over the table, found her fingers gripped tightly, 'since you're remarkably like my daughter Anna.'

Eleanor Munro sat back, shook her head, and began to laugh. No one joined in. Hugo, at a nod from Thomas, put a plate of dessert in front of her. Removing her unused cutlery he dropped it with a loud clatter to the floor.

'Sorry,' he said.

Eleanor Munro's hilarity came to a stop. 'Irony is always worth a laugh. Do you find irony funny, Bridget?'

'It depends. Why don't you try me?'

'The irony of this situation, Bridget, is that I come from what could be called bastard stock while your daughter is the progeny of the son who got away, and yet we're the only grandchildren who remotely resemble our grandaddy. Is that an irony or isn't it?

'It seems to fit the criteria,' said Bridget, 'but fill me in a bit more, please.'

Chapter Six

'Can't say I'm surprised nobody told you about me.' Eleanor Munro looked around the table. 'Everyone here's been wanting me to go since I got here, hoping I'd just disappear. Disappearing's a sort of way of life in this family.'

'We thought we'd let you speak for yourself.' Thomas nodded at the plate in front of Eleanor Munro. 'Dessert's good. Best part of the meal, in fact. Try it.'

'Thanks, but no thanks.' She pushed the plate aside impatiently, 'I'd prefer to talk. You got any cigarettes, Lindsay? I left mine in my room.'

'The room you are sleeping in does not belong to you,' Veronica Baldacci said icily, 'and I do not permit cigarette-smoking at the dinner table.'

'You'll have noticed, Bridget, that one of the more lovable things about this family is the hospitality factor.' Eleanor Munro poured herself a glass of wine. 'You might also have spotted a certain honesty about the past, a desire amongst the people gathered here to set the record straight. Lindsay, have you got a cigarette or not?'

'I need a cigarette too, Grandmother, so just try ignoring us.' Lindsay, shaking a couple of cigarettes from a packet, efficiently ignored her grandmother herself. Veronica Baldacci, face expressionless, signalled Hugo, who immediately placed ashtrays in front of the two younger women. He didn't quite bow as, a miniature sentinel, he took a standing position behind Veronica's chair.

'I don't know why you do it, you two, you know how much damage—' Russell Segal's plaintive plea was efficiently cut short by Lindsay.

'Oh, shut up, Russell,' her voice was low and furious. 'You don't understand anything about anything so just keep out of this.'

'Right. I'll do that.' Russell pushed his chair back from the table. No one tried to stop him as he left.

'Well, Thomas, you're the only guy left – you going to leave too?' Eleanor Munro's voice was mocking. 'Letting the women get on with things is the Baldacci way, after all.'

'Think I'll stay and hear what you've got to say.' Thomas was polite. 'I take it you've joined us for a purpose?'

'Too damn right I've joined you for a purpose.' Eleanor Munro grinned. 'I'm here to tell Bridget a few things she needs to be straighened out on. In public. I don't believe in secrets, as you know. A little straight talking's what's wanted around here.' She sighed and stretched her arms above her head. 'I think this little session could be very therapeutic for all of us.'

'An act of compassion on your part.' Magdalena held up and studied the contents of her glass. 'You're here to tear this family apart and for no other reason. You will cause terrible harm before you leave here. I know it.'

'A terrible harm has already been done, Magdalena, so it's a bit late for agonized histrionics. That's why you drink. You know too well what went on in this family—'

'I drink because I like it.' This time, Magdalena reached for the bottle and refilled her glass herself.

'What is it you want to tell me?' Bridget said. She felt lightheaded, expectant.

'Where to begin . . .' Anna's double smiled through a cloud of blue smoke. She seemed to be enjoying herself. 'Let me introduce myself, properly. I am the grandaughter Grandma Veronica didn't want to know about, the cousin my cousins didn't want to know, the niece whose existence Aunt Mags has been able to deny, along with everything else, with the help of her drug of choice. Of course, I'm not the only issue was ignored. Your son and daughter weren't exactly taken to the family bosom either, were they?' She stopped, slowly and deliberately filled her water glass.

'Anna and Fintan weren't ignored exactly.' Bridget smiled encouragingly. 'But I'd really like to hear your story.'

'You're right, of course, since there was a choice involved in their situation.' Eleanor Munro looked around the table and back at Bridget. 'Their father choose to put this family behind him, to keep his children away . . .' She took a drink of the water. Nobody spoke. 'My mother, on the other hand, needed help and support and looked for it all down the years and got none. She's dead now, just like Victor's dead, and I'm here to put a few things right, just like you are.'

'You've come here to destroy what has been a content and functioning family.' Veronica Baldacci, breaking the family's silence, was coldly formal.

'Content! Functioning!' Eleanor Munro shook her head, laughing. 'What we've got here is hardcore dysfunction.'

'I'm leaving. I really don't care to listen to another of this woman's paranoid performances.' Magdalena got awkwardly to her feet. 'She's trouble and you all know it. Someone should shut her up. Bridget doesn't need to hear this.'

She staggered once as she left the room. Her exit, Bridget thought, would have done justice to an ageing movie star.

'And then there were five,' Eleanor Munro said as the door closed. 'Anyone else want to leave before Bridget and me have our heart to heart?' She turned her dark eyes on each of the table's occupants in turn. 'Everyone else is willing to deal with a dismantling of the world of make-believe you've created around yourselves?'

73

'You're the one in this room who knows most about make-believe.' Lindsay snorted. 'You're the novelist, the one who makes things up for a living. Trouble with you, Eleanor, is that you don't know the difference between make-believe and reality. Sure, things happened in this family. That's the way it goes. Families are made up of people and people do things to one another.' She shrugged. 'Good and bad things.'

'My granddaughter is right but I would add to what she's said,' Veronica Baldacci's voice was low and Bridget had to strain to hear her. 'You've never been a part of a family, Eleanor, you have no awareness of the concept of give and take. Like your mother you prefer to plunder and tear apart.'

'Quite an impressive two-hander you and Lindsay have got going there.' Eleanor examined her nails, long and tapering and painted the same mauve as her lips. 'But a good performance does not a truthful one make.'

Thomas gave his small, throat-clearing cough. 'This is highly inappropriate,' he said.

'Everything about this family's inappropriate.' Eleanor Munro faced Bridget. 'The only way to give it to you is straight, Mrs Victor Baldacci. You'll have to forgive my blunt, New York manners.' She took a deep breath. 'I'm Frank Baldacci's granddaughter. Difference is, I don't, fortunately, have Veronica for a grandmother. Good old Veronica was Grandaddy Frank's wife but she was *not* his first love. Nor was she his last.' She hesitated. 'In some ways, she's to be pitied. She was twenty-two when she married Frank. He was eight years older and it was all arranged for them, a bringing together in the late nineteen thirties of two ambitious Catholic families, one Italian, the other Irish. Veronica may have been virginal, I don't know,' she gave Veronica a languid look which the old woman ignored, 'but Frank Baldacci certainly wasn't. Fact is, Frank was about to become a father when they married though he didn't, of course, tell his bride-to-be about this. Honesty has never been a prime virtue in this family.'

'The baby was your mother?' Bridget asked.

'Right. The mother-to-be was Grace Munro, my grand-mother. She was sixteen years old and she'd already been Frank Baldacci's plaything for two years.'

When Eleanor stopped again Bridget waited for denials. They didn't come. Eleanor waited too, quietly turning her water glass round and round. She looked fragile and unreliable. She sipped at the water before going on.

'Grace was dirt poor, practically illiterate and besotted with Frank Baldacci. Frank was a man who was used to getting what he wanted and he got what he wanted then too. He wanted Grace and he wanted Veronica and he got them both.' She leaned back, unnervingly balancing the chair on its hind legs. 'He was a man who liked to make the most of opportunities and he used the fact that an hysterical Grace was threatening to make their affair public to strike a deal with his new bride.' The chair legs hit the ground with a thud as she sat forward. 'Veronica agreed to Frank's continuing to have my grandmother as his mistress and to an allowance for the child, my mother, Shelley Munro – she never did get her father's name. In return Grace stayed silent and Frank stayed out of jail—'

'Not what you'd call an ideal beginning to a marriage,' Bridget, feeling compelled to say something, interrupted. She needed the reassurance of her own voice, a few seconds to absorb what was being said. She felt sorry for Veronica but didn't dare look at her. Her feelings about Eleanor Munro was more confused.

'On the face of it, no. But Veronica wanted the marriage and she wanted Frank Baldacci and possession, after all, is nine tenths of the law. She probably reckoned that her charms, and the production of a son and heir, would firmly ensnare Frank and see his illiterate mistress off the scene.'

Hugo Sweeney, from his guardian position behind her chair, leaned over and spoke loudly to Veronica.

'Can I get you something?' He touched her arm and she shook him off impatiently. 'A nightcap?' He was persistent.

'Get me a bourbon,' Veronica said.

There was silence while he poured and brought her the drink.

'It's quite touching, the devotion Veronica gets from some men,' said Eleanor Munro. 'She never did get it from her husband, even if she did have him to herself at the end when no one else wanted him. But you didn't want him yourself then, did you Veronica?'

Veronica Baldacci gave no indication that she'd heard the question. She was looking quietly detached, eyes half closed, as she sipped her drink.

Thomas cleared his throat. 'You're talking about things which happened more than forty years ago, Eleanor. You weren't there. You're coming from the standpoint of your mother's hurt and a lot of second-hand information.' He glanced quickly at his mother-in-law. 'The fair thing would be to allow Veronica to take over now. Bridget's come a long way—'

'Bridget wouldn't be hearing a thing if it wasn't for me so don't give me shit about Veronica telling the family story.' Eleanor's face was contorted and paper white. She stopped then, lowering her voice, continued, 'And I wouldn't be here if it wasn't for Ted Morgan, would I, Veronica? Ted Morgan's the only reason I got through the front door.'

'You're quite right,' Veronica said calmly. 'I would never have allowed you into my home if you hadn't arrived with Ted. He's a good man but gullible. He made a terrible mistake bringing you here. He knows it too and that is why he is not with us tonight.'

'Oh, for God's sake, why can't you ever face the truth,' Eleanor Munro was close to shouting. 'Ted's not here because he doesn't want to be!'

'You are an evil and misguided young woman,' Veronica suddenly and violently banged her cane on the floor, 'just as your mother was evil and misguided. You are the inevitable consequence of her delusions. I should never have listened to Ted. I should never have made you welcome in my home.' She took a deep breath and sat back in her chair, hands tightly clenching the top of her stick.

'You didn't make me welcome,' Eleanor spoke softly. 'I insisted and Ted facilitated. Everything that is now happening was inevitable. What goes around comes around. Once your son died and the past came knocking on your door you were going to have to open it, sooner or later.'

'I would like you tell me' – Bridget took a deep breath – 'what Victor's death has to do with all of this – with your being here – '

'Your husband, in dying, created chaos,' Eleanor Munro spread her hands in a hopeless gesture, 'but that comes at the end of my story. What you need to know first is that my grandmother Grace disappeared when my mother was only fourteen years old. A police investigation failed to find her but it did turn up the fact that Frank Baldacci was the father of her child. There were rumours that Veronica had had a hand in her disappearance.'

Thomas tapped the side of his glass with a spoon. The sudden sound was sharp and as effective as a rifle shot. 'You are causing terrible hurt to an old woman.' He was curt. 'If you feel you must do this then stick to the facts.'

'The facts are more than enough.' Eleanor agreed. 'And they show that nothing was proven against Veronica. But, and this *is* a fact, she and Frank managed a pretty good damage limitation job by giving my mother a home in this house, bringing in an older sister for Magdalena and Victor. Kindness itself.' She stubbed out her cigarette. 'Here's another fact; my mother was taken in to live here but never given the Baldacci name. And another: one year after my mother came to live in this house Frank Baldacci raped her. His abuse of her went on for six years until, one day when she was twenty-one years old, she too disappeared.'

Bridget was feeling slightly sick. So, it seemed, was Veronica, swaying slightly in her chair and shaking her head.

'It is NOT a fact that my husband raped her.'

Hugo Sweeney put a steadying hand on her shoulder as she went on.

'Frank was too kind to your mother, to Shelley Munro. She was a manipulative young woman. Just as you are.'

Eleanor Munro, shrugged dismissively.

'There are a few more facts, Veronica, and you know it. You know too that they bear out my version of events. One of them is that Frank Baldacci hired a private detective who found my mother. She was living in New York and in a terrible state. Frank then turned up and tried to persuade her to come back to Seattle. She didn't go with him. She told me herself once, when she was in a bad way, that she was afraid of him, that she'd always been afraid of him and that her fear had made everything that had happened possible.' There was a long pause while Eleanor Munro appeared to gather her thoughts. 'Frank left. He didn't give her as much as a cent out of the Baldacci fortune. She was twenty-one years old, she was his daughter and had been used by him for sex and he left her there, friendless and without money.'

'He was not a well man,' Veronica spoke in a dull, flat voice. 'He had a stroke soon after getting home. He remained paralysed until he died.'

'And you had the debauched, incestuous bastard all to

78

yourself at last,' Eleanor Munro said harshly. 'Only he wasn't much good to you then, was he? But you got round that, Veronica, didn't you?'

She stabbed the air with an accusing finger, two spots of colour flaming high on her cheeks. 'You came into your own then, didn't you? Didn't you?'

Her voice cracked and she dropped her head into her hands. She sat there, her fingers agitatedly crawling at her hairline while she took deep, gasping breaths. Bridget wanted to go to her but couldn't. It was all she could do to sit, mouth dry and limbs leaden, as she tried to take in what she'd heard. She couldn't bring herself to look at any of the others at the table either.

Their silence was shocking, and it was frightening.

Even if only some of this young woman's claims were true then Victor would have known. This awful story was part, or maybe all, of what he'd grown up with. And, appalling as it was, she had to hear it all.

When Eleanor Munro at last lifted her head she spoke directly to Bridget. She was dry eyed and haggard-looking. 'When her husband became paralysed Veronica took over the business. She could have stepped back and let the board run things but she didn't choose to do that. She moved into the boardroom and took over. Nothing wrong with that – except that she took over the lives of everyone in the family too. She's been running them ever since.'

Bridget, afraid suddenly that she might not learn what she needed to know, found her voice.

'Did my husband know about . . . all of this when he was growing up?' She looked from Eleanor Munro to Veronica Baldacci to Thomas Carter. 'Did Magdalena?'

'You have been given a distorted version of how things were.' Veronica Baldacci was cold and in control of herself again. 'My son, as a child and a young man, was part of a caring family. As was Magdalena.'

'Bullshit,' said Eleanor Munro. 'They knew, both of them, that they were part of a diseased family. Look at Magdalena, for God's sake – a life devoted to obliterating everything with drink. Victor took his own way out and left it all behind, for good. We're all adults round this table, Veronica. Spare us the fairy tales.'

'You have done what you joined us to do.' Veronica Baldacci rose slowly from her chair. 'You have presented the past to my dead son's wife in a manner which is entirely destructive. I will not dignify it with denials, or explanations. She can believe, or disbelieve, as she sees fit.'

It was clear she expected everyone else to stand too. Thomas did so but Lindsay, her eyes on Eleanor, stayed sitting. Bridget didn't move either.

'If that's the lot, then I'll start clearing away.' Hugo Sweeney moved to the table.

Eleanor Munro spoke through her teeth. 'Why don't you clear yourself out of here and let us finish what is family business, and none of yours?'

'Hugo knows this family in a way you never could,' Veronica Baldacci's voice was low and harsh.

'I'll bet he does.' Eleanor gave a sharp laugh. 'I'll bet old Hugo understands exactly what's good for him. So do I and I'm here to get what my mother didn't get from this family. She asked you people for help, but you ignored her letters, Veronica, you didn't even reply to her. She was blood of this family, half-sister to Magdalena and Victor, and you just didn't want to know.'

'My children had to make their own way in life,' said Veronica, 'they didn't get handouts. They went into the company and earned what they got. Why should she have been any different?'

Eleanor stared. 'You knew she couldn't come back here. You people destroyed her—' She stopped, shaking her head

80

as if clearing it. 'Ted was right. He said the Baldacci's operated on a moral terrain that was all their own.'

'Don't bring Ted Morgan into this,' Veronica's voice had a shrill edge, but her face was as coldly formal as ever. 'What Ted has to say he will say to me himself, when he gets back.'

'He's not coming back, Veronica. Ted's gone. He couldn't take it any more. He didn't want to come in the first place. I made him come, but the fact is I should never have brought him here.'

'You're a liar. Ted Morgan came back to Seattle, and to this house, because he wanted to.' Veronica took a breath. 'He had unfinished business to attend to.'

'Where is he now then? Where is Ted tonight?'

'He is his own man. He will be back when he is ready. He has things to think about.'

'Jesus Christ, Veronica, did you always fool yourself like this? Ted's gone. I wish he wasn't,' Eleanor shrugged, the black sequinned top catching the light across her shoulders, 'but that's how it is.'

For a moment she seemed to Bridget to be frighteningly vulnerable, bereft looking. Then the expression was gone.

Veronica turned her back on the room and walked to the uncurtained window. The snow was falling still in light, gentle swirls. 'We were never in any doubt, Miss Munro, but that money was what you came here for.' She paused. 'An arrangement will be made.'

'You're damn right an arrangement will be made. But not without discussing it with me.'

'An arrangement will be made,' Veronica repeated.

'There are two of us now. Bridget wants to see right done too. We're not afraid of you people. We're together on this—'

'Stop it.' Bridget stood up.

Her heart was uncomfortably close to her mouth but

she'd come here on her own account and wasn't going to be a part of someone else's fight. 'I don't know what you think we're together on, Eleanor. All I want is to know why Victor left home,' she spoke to her mother-in-law's rigid back, 'and why he never came back.'

Eleanor Munro looked disbelieving. 'You want a hell of a lot more than that. You want what's due to Victor Baldacci's children. These people know that's why you're here. We just have to stick together and you'll—'

'You're wrong,' Bridget managed to keep her voice even. 'We're here for different reasons.'

She began counting, slowly, backwards from ten. It was an old trick, used when she felt panic rising. It usually worked. By the time she got to five she was breathing more evenly.

'But I'm here because you're here.' Eleanor Munro, rubbing her eyes, smudged her mascara. 'When I heard you were coming to Seattle it seemed so right to me, as if the day of reckoning had come and the wronged were to be avenged . . .'

'I'm sorry you thought that.' Bridget meant it. 'But our experiences are different. I don't feel aggrieved in the way you do.'

'This is all wrong.' Eleanor Munro was shaking, the streaked mascara ghoulish against the deathly white of her face. 'We were meant to work together on this thing, you and I. I know it. I feel it. When Ted went, I thought I would have you. I can't be alone. There's safety in numbers . . .' She was gabbling, pouring herself another glass of water, spilling it as she poured and again as she lifted it to her mouth.

'You're pathetic.' Lindsay disdainfully folded her napkin. 'I suggest you go to bed, sleep off whatever it is you're on.'

'And you're so fucking superior. Why don't you try living in the real world?' Eleanor Munro's voice rose. 'You live in this nest of vipers, sheltered by them, fed by them, doing their dirty work for them—' She gave a loud, gulping sob and all at once she was weeping, her head in her hands, her thin frame convulsing as she cried great, hacking tears.

'And this is the creature we have been giving credence to.' Veronica left the window and walked slowly down the room, past the weeping Eleanor to the door. 'She is completely unreliable, just as her mother was. Goodnight, Bridget. We will meet again.' She patted her perfect hair, fingers like a set of bleached bones scattered with rings. 'Thomas, Lindsay – I am leaving the foolish Miss Munro in your hands. See that Bridget gets safely back to her hotel too.'

Hugo Sweeney opened the door, then slipped through it after her.

The sobbing went on, Eleanor's head still buried in her hands, black hair veiling her face. Thomas Carter went to her.

'I'll take you to your room. You'll feel better about things in the morning.'

He put an arm round her shoulders and eased her out of the chair. She didn't resist. Standing, she was almost as tall as he was. She took her hands from her face and, sobs subsiding, roughly rubbed at her cheeks with a table napkin.

'I wish Ted were here,' she sounded as forlorn as she looked. 'He shouldn't have left me.' She looked directly at Bridget. 'I'm scared on my own,' she said.

'There's nothing for you to be scared of.' Thomas guided her gently towards the door. 'You just need some rest.'

In the open door she slipped from under his arm and turned, eyes finding Bridget's again. 'It would be better if you stayed here,' she said, 'in this house.'

'I like my hotel.' Bridget gave her a reassuring smile.

'I wasn't thinking about you. I was thinking about me.'

Thomas Carter, with a wry look Bridget's way, took Eleanor's arm and closed the door behind them.

'Looks like the show's over for the night.' Lindsay grimaced at her dessert plate and lit a cigarette. 'I'll give you a ride back to your hotel when you're ready.'

The traffic was a trickle at that time of night. The snow had turned to rain which was blowing sheet-like in the teeth of a growing wind.

'An inauspicious introduction to the family.' Lindsay drove fast. 'But you can't have been expecting to find the Brady Bunch.'

'Victor gave very few clues for me to build on.' Bridget hesitated. 'How true is Eleanor Munro's version of the family story?'

'All depends how you look at it.'

Bridget felt a surge of irritation. Was anybody in this family capable of a straight answer? 'How do you look at it?'

'I wasn't around for any of the stuff she was talking about,' Lindsay said, 'but the outline's true enough. My grandfather died after a stroke. Eleanor's mother was my grandfather's love child and lived with the family for a few years after her mother took off. The rest is a question of perspective. Truth is never simple.'

'Who is Ted Morgan?'

'He was a nurse engaged by my grandmother to care for my grandfather when he was dying. I'm told by my mother, and grandmother, that he was a kind man and a great help to everyone during bad times. He turned up with Eleanor the day before Christmas.' It was raining hard as they crossed the bridge, the windscreen wipers beating frantically. Lindsay didn't slow down. 'He took off at New Year without saying where he was going. Grandmother would like him to come back. I suppose he was someone to talk to about grandfather.'

It was odd, Bridget thought, the way people who became caught up with the Baldacci family disappeared without saying where they were going. Eleanor Munro had been right about that at least.

In her hotel bedroom she crawled under the duvet, burying her head under the pillow for good measure. She decided against phoning home. She told herself it was because she was too tired but knew it was because she didn't know how to tell Anna, or Fintan, what she'd learned about their father's family.

She lay for most of the night without sleeping. In the small hours of the morning, with distant hotel sounds indicating another day beginning, she slept and had a dream in which Eleanor Munro and Anna together scattered Victor's ashes at the feet of broken, classical statues.

A hammering on the bedroom door at 8 a.m. took a while to waken her. It took a while too to separate the sound of Eleanor Munro's voice calling to her from the Eleanor in her dream.

'Open the door, Bridget.' The hammering sounded like a fist. 'I have to talk to you. Please open the door . . .'

Chapter Seven

The Eleanor Munro who pushed her way through the door was urgent and purposeful. She stood in the middle of the room with her hands in the pockets of a long, black coat.

'God, this is small. Didn't you want to stay in your husband's old home?'

'I wasn't invited,' Bridget said crossly, 'and you weren't invited here this morning either. I haven't had a lot of sleep.'

Now that she was fully awake she felt terrible. She'd had too much wine the night before and a heavy, dull hangover wasn't helping her mood. A sudden, miserable loneliness filled with an ache for Victor made her wish she could somehow hold his hand and tell him she was beginning to see and to understand.

But there was only the casket, out of the drawer and sitting on the desk. Seeing it gave her some comfort.

'I don't feel great,' she admitted.

'Sorry,' Eleanor Munro didn't look it, 'but we have to talk.' She picked up the casket with Victor's ashes. 'Cute. What's in it?'

'My husband's ashes.'

'Baldaccis not interested, huh? I could have told you that. They don't want his ashes and they didn't want you to come here either.' She put the casket down again, gently. 'Look, Bridget, I want you to understand that all of that stuff last night was me trying to force the issue, to get Veronica and Magdalena to open up about what happened in the past. I've been staying in that house since a couple of days after Christmas and last night was the first time I'd spent more than a half hour with any of them. You and me have got to team up, get things sorted.'

'We don't have to do anything of the sort. We're coming from different angles at this thing.' Bridget sat at the dressing table and began brushing her hair. Eleanor Munro remained standing, kept her hands in her pockets. 'My situation really is different to yours.' Bridget's face in the mirror looked to her like that of a stranger, belonging to a woman too uncertain to be the person she knew herself to be.

'You're wrong. You couldn't be more wrong.'

Eleanor Munro caught and held Bridget's gaze in the mirror. Everything about her was black: the scarf under the coat was black and so were her boots, her black hair was loose to her shoulders and the likeness to a vulnerable witch was even more pronounced than the night before. 'We're both in the same situation here. They don't want either of us around. Alone we're not safe, but by sticking together we give each other protection, even up the odds—'

'Stop, Eleanor, just please shut up. I want you to understand something.' Bridget turned round in the chair. 'Sit down,' she commanded, 'on the bed will do.'

Eleanor Munro looked mulish for a minute, then shrugged and sat on her hands on the bed. 'So far I've only heard your version of events,' Bridget said. 'I want to hear both sides. I want to know Victor's story.' She paused. 'In fact Victor's story is all I *really* want to know. I understand why your grandmother disappearing is a big thing in your life. But that was more than forty years ago and, apart from Veronica, the people involved are all dead. It's a different—'

'Nothing's different, nothing's changed.' Eleanor Munro

closed her eyes and began to rock back and forth. A deep furrow ran between her eyebrows and her voice rasped edgily. 'The poison was never got rid of, it's still there, infecting everything that happens, a disease in all of them.' She opened her eyes and, before Bridget could say anything, grabbed one of her hands and held it with a neurotic strength. 'You think I'm over the top. Everyone does. You think because I'm a writer then I'm inventing this stuff, seeing bodies where there are none. Well, you're wrong. You're wrong, wrong, wrong.' She dropped Bridget's hand and threw herself back on the bed. With her eyes fixed on the ceiling she said, 'I can't convince you, but you'll see soon enough that I'm right. There's danger here for both of us. These people are not going to give up anything, their money or their secrets, without a fight. It won't be clean.' She sat up. 'And it certainly won't be played by any of the normal rules.'

'You may be right.' Bridget looked at her thoughtfully. 'But as you say yourself, I'll see soon enough. Why don't we leave it at that and go and get some breakfast?'

'If that's what it takes to get you to listen. We don't have for ever, this is not Disneyland you've wandered into. Don't you realize what you're into here?'

'I'm beginning to,' said Bridget.

The Seattle streets, that bright morning, were sharply alive to a new day. The snow clouds had moved on, no doubt to retrench, and the skies above the tall buildings were a cold blue. Walking with Eleanor Munro passing coffee houses in search of the perfect brew, Bridget began to feel better. At intersections, when she looked downhill, she could see the waterfront and further out the waters of Puget Sound, chillingly lovely and pure.

It felt, for that while, like a good place to be.

'He never told me about any of this,' said Bridget.

'Your husband? He didn't talk to you about Seattle?'

Eleanor Munro hunched into her coat. Her face in the daylight was a blanched white. Her morning lipstick was a deep, dark red. 'Can't say I blame him. Hype and a couple of films and an eco-friendly reputation don't make a city out of a hick town. Don't make city people out of backpackers either. All that water scares me. So do the mountains. They're too close, right on top of the place. I'm out of here as soon as I get what I came for . . .' She stopped in front of a set of smoky, curved glass windows, 'I know this place. It's good.'

She was right. Bridget knew as soon as they stepped inside that they were in more than just a coffee house. The air had a spice-filled welcome and there was an open fire, wicker armchairs, a scattering of morning newspapers and a gentle conviviality. She ordered herself a caffè latte and a helping of cinnamon and raisin focaccio. Eleanor Munro went for an espresso Americano.

'Don't you know anything about cholesterol?' Eleanor eyed Bridget curiously as she bit into the focaccio.

'I know about cholesterol all right. It was too much of it killed my husband.'

'What was he like?'

'He was a good man,' said Bridget and thought that, as an epitaph, this was perfect. Victor had been a good man, in every sense.

'He was entitled. His children are entitled—'

Bridget cut her short. 'Entitled to what?' she demanded.

'A share in the Baldacci millions.' Eleanor had taken off her coat and was sitting in a thin, black wool sweater and skirt in one of the wicker chairs. Her knees were jagged points from which she dangled her hands as she leaned forward.

'Inheritance rights aren't as simple as that,' Bridget said. 'Victor, in effect, disinherited himself when he abandoned his family. He did nothing to help accumulate those millions.

That's the way the law will see it, though I'm certainly not going to enter into battle about it.'

'Bullshit. Bullshit to him being disinherited and bullshit to you having to go to law about it. Once you establish the truth of why he left home and stayed away, you have them over a barrel. All you have to do—'

'Oh, shut up, Eleanor,' Bridget said tiredly. 'You go ahead and put the Baldaccis over a barrel and get whatever it is you want. And good luck to you. Just leave me out of it.'

'God, you're so fucking self-righteous.' Eleanor Munro ordered a second coffee for herself. She didn't order for Bridget. 'You're making a big mistake if you think just poking into the past and their secrets will let you off the hook. There's something scary and evil about that family. Ted came up against it. That's why he's gone. I know it is.'

'Tell me more about Ted Morgan,' Bridget said.

'Ted knows about the Baldaccis, knows a lot of stuff they'd prefer he didn't know.'

'Like what?' Bridget said.

'Like he knows about my mother, and the raw deal she got, like he knows about your husband and why he left—'

'Why?' Bridget, cutting in, held her breath.

'I don't know. He never told me. He wouldn't.' She paused. 'Just refused to. But he knows all right. Look, here's the story on Ted.' She took out a packet of cigarettes, extracted one, looked around, twirled it unlit between her fingers, sighed and put it away again. 'Don't want any trouble in eco-friendly land. Right. Ted. He nursed Frank Baldacci when he was dying—'

'So you said, last night.' Bridget was impatient.

'He's one of the good guys, which didn't stop him getting to know the family real well. Inevitable, really, given that he was around the family big time. Night and day, in fact. It took Frank Baldacci a couple of years to die. My mother had already left but Frank knew all about her. He *was* around for Victor's departure from hearth and home, so he knows what that was about too. After Frank died Ted went to live in New York.' She pulled a wry face. 'Funny how everyone puts as much distance as they can between themselves and the Baldaccis when they leave, isn't it? Victor, my mother, Ted – none of them exactly went to Oregon or anywhere close, did they?'

'No, they didn't. Go on.'

'Anyhow, in New York, Ted got in touch with my mother. He said what had happened wasn't right. He was a bit of a loner but he looked out for us, my mother and me, all down the years. He encouraged my mother to keep in contact with Veronica Baldacci; it was because of Ted that my mother asked her for help from time to time – help with medical expenses, with my education, she even asked for money for food, once. None of it ever came through.' She lowered her head so that her hair fell forward, covering her face. 'When my mother died Ted was there for me. He's been a sort of father and grandfather.'

'When did your mother die?'

'A little over a year ago. She overdosed. It wasn't the first time but that time it worked.'

Eleanor Munro raised her head and shook her hair back from her face. Her eyes were a hard, shining black, and unblinking.

'I'm sorry. So very sorry . . .' Bridget thought about offering Eleanor the comfort of a hug. But her grief was an enraged, bitter, off-putting thing.

'Ted kept in touch by reading the *Seattle Post-Intelligencer*,' Eleanor Munro went on slowly, as if putting order on events as she spoke them aloud, 'and there was a piece in there about your husband's death. Fluke really. Some journalist picked it up and did a paragraph along the 'prominent family member dies abroad' lines. Ted, being Ted, wrote Veronica a letter of sympathy. She wrote back and told him you were coming out to Seattle. That was when I decided to come too. I persuaded Ted to come with me. He didn't want to and I suppose that's why he's bailed out. I don't blame him. Veronica was all over him – wouldn't leave him alone. I don't know whether she was talking about the past or telling him to forget it. All I know is that he left the house more than a week ago. He phoned me, once, told me where he was, said he didn't want me worrying and that he'd be going back to New York when he'd sorted a few things out. But when I got down there, to the hostel he was staying in, he'd left there too.'

'And Veronica thinks he's coming back?'

'Yup. But he won't. I know Ted.' The anger in Eleanor Munro had wilted and her thin face looked in momentary desolation at Bridget. 'He says the past should be atoned for but not lived in.'

'He's not far wrong,' said Bridget.

Silently, in a mood of brief companionship, they watched through the windows as the glory of the early morning died in fast, low rain clouds.

'Tell me about the Baldacci millions,' said Bridget as the first rain drops fell. 'How'd they make them?'

'Why? You changing your mind about . . .?'

'No, Eleanor. Just curious.'

'I can tell you what's up front, in the public domain so to speak. They've built up a lot of real estate over the years but the front-line business is a financial outfit called Ultimate. Its main line of interest is insurance and it operates in property, life, health and business cover. The financial side has investment and property subsidiaries. Veronica's still the president – she took over the lot when Frank had his stroke and is not about to hand over until death makes that decision for her. Thomas Carter is the senior vice-president and Magdalena is on the board. John-Francis is on the board too and looks after some accounts. Lindsay, who's real keen, is president of Ultimate Properties. The revenue last year was sixty-three point one million dollars. Profit was three point nine million. Those are the basic facts and they're a matter of public record, which is how I got hold of them.'

'Impressive. Sounds like a lot of hard work has gone into Ultimate over the years.' Bridget all at once didn't want to hear any more. 'I'm going to buy an umbrella.'

She stood up. She didn't add the word alone, but on her own was what she wanted to be. Information, bitterness, pain, they were all coming at her too fast. She'd lost Victor somewhere in the middle of it all, couldn't visualize or feel the young man he must have been when he was at the centre of all she was hearing.

Eleanor got to her feet eagerly. 'I'll come with you,' she said.

The coffee and cinnamon smells followed them up the street to the drugstore selling umbrellas and on to the hotel. It's the low cloud, Bridget thought, it compresses everything, even smells. Makes everything more intense. She needed to get away from it all, out on to the bay or up a mountain to see and make sense of what she was learning about Victor's family.

'They don't even sell my books in this town,' Eleanor said as they passed a bookshop.

'What sort of books do you write?' said Bridget.

'Novels filled with romance and sex.' Eleanor's sudden smile was wide and wry. 'Camilla Kidman's my writing name and I'm big in the bodice-ripping game. It's a living. Ever heard of me?'

'No. But I'll look out—'

'I'm going to write poetry when I get my inheritance from the Baldaccis. You could buy your son and daughter the freedom to do what they want to if you—'

'Enough, Elenor,' said Bridget.

At the entrance to the hotel, without thinking and

93

because all at once the idea seemed so very plausible, she said to Eleanor 'Did you send a letter to me at the hotel?' She was half smiling and very watchful as she asked.

'I only write when I'm paid to.'

'That's a no?'

'Absolutely. But now I'm curious.' Eleanor pushed through the door and held it open for Bridget. She looked perplexed. 'Someone wrote you here and didn't sign their name?'

'That's right.' Bridget followed her in and together they climbed the flight of steps up to the lobby, Bridget worrying that Eleanor intended sticking with her for the whole day. 'It was delivered by hand.'

She stopped. She was inclined to believe that Eleanor wasn't responsible and was feeling a perverse loyalty to whomever had written the letter. 'It's not important,' she said.

'Mmm,' Eleanor waited, frowning, as Bridget collected her room key. 'Why'd you bring it up then? It must have meant something. What did it say?'

'Not a lot. It welcomed me to Seattle,' Bridget lied, 'told me to enjoy my trip.'

'And that was it?' Eleanor Munro looked sceptical. 'Look,' she spoke with sudden energy, 'you're going to have to regard everything that happens to you in Seattle as important, Bridget. Everything. You've got to remember that.' Her eyes had the staring, manic look of the night before. 'Promise me you'll be careful, keep yourself alert to everything that goes on around you.' She clutched at Bridget's arm. 'Promise me.'

'I'll be careful, but on one condition.' Bridget prised Eleanor Munro's fingers from her arm. 'I want you to promise you'll be careful too.'

She had no idea why she said this, nor why she waited so anxiously for the younger woman's reply. But wait she did, holding her hand until Eleanor nodded impatiently, and said yes, of course she'd be on her guard, she always was. Living in New York did that to you.

Bridget held up the key to her room. 'I'm going back to bed. I really didn't sleep last night.'

'I'll call you later.'

'Make it much later,' Bridget warned.

She was aware of being watched, of a pair of eyes on her back, as she headed for the lift. Convinced it was Eleanor she didn't turn. She pressed the call button and was resolutely facing the lift door when a finger tapped her on the shoulder.

'My, but you're the early bird.'

Magdalena Baldacci was wrapped in creamy-coloured cashmere and wore a fox-fur hat. She ignored Eleanor Munro, who'd followed and was standing just behind her. 'I've been hanging around here for an hour or more waiting for you.'

'If I'd known you were coming . . .' Bridget muttered, visions of bed and sleep disappearing in the face of the woman's determined, and quite sober, expression.

'I'll take you for a ride, show you a bit of the city. Perhaps you'd like to see the Space Needle?'

'Not just now.' Bridget was firm. 'I was planning a few hours rest. Later, perhaps?'

'Later's impossible.' Magdalena was petulant and glacial. 'I need to talk to you.' Her eyes assessed the lobby.

'Can't it wait?' Bridget asked but knew she herself couldn't wait. Magdalena Baldacci was here for a reason and she wanted to know what it was.

'Is there a bar in this place?'

'There's a bar down there.' Eleanor Munro stepped forward, indicating a flight of descending steps to their left. 'I found it earlier. I'll take you.'

'What I have to say concerns Bridget.' Magdalena's curt

tone became icy. 'What a busy early morning person you are today too, Eleanor. Up and gone before my poor mother had even woken for the day. Thank you for telling us where the bar is. We'll find it ourselves.'

'You're not going to get rid of me that easily.' Eleanor shook her head. 'Bridget and me have agreed to stick together, share our experiences while we're in Seattle.' She stood beside Bridget and took her arm. 'The bar's one of those dark, aspiring-to-be-intimate joints.'

Bridget allowed herself to be led by Eleanor Munro while Magdalena, lips compressed and controlled fury drawing the rest of her face into tight lines, fell into step beside them.

The bar was a low, oval-shaped room with no windows and dull roseate lighting giving it an uninviting, underground look. Apart from a couple of argumentative men at a table against a wall there were no customers. The barman, tall and languid and blond, looked at them wearily as they took stools at the bar – Magdalena's idea.

'What'll it be?' He managed not to focus on any of them.

'I'll have a gin Martini.' Magdalena's coat fell open as she crossed her legs. Clad in silvery opaque stockings and dark court shoes they, and Magdalena, looked very at home on the bar stool. She kept the hat on her head.

The barman waited with exaggerated patience for Bridget and Eleanor to place their orders.

'Glass of water, please.' Bridget heard the primness of her voice and coughed. 'With ice.'

'I'll have water, no ice.' Eleanor said and the barman stiffened, looking as if he would argue with this. Then he shrugged, turned and walked down the bar.

'Do you think he's actually getting us the drinks?' Bridget asked.

'He'd better be.' Magdalena drummed her fingers on the bar top and tapped a foot against the stool. If she'd made an announcement it couldn't have been more clear that she needed this drink.

'What did you want to see me about?' Bridget was gentler with her than she'd been in the lobby, but not a lot.

'My mother has given some thought about how we might, as a family, acknowledge Victor's death.' Magdalena's smile was for Bridget alone. 'A case of her conscience rearing its head once she'd met you. You weren't a real person to her until then.' She paused and delicately cleared her throat. 'Contrary to appearances, and even to what she may have said to you, Victor's death really knocked her out.'

'She's quite a performer then,' said Bridget.

The barman brought their drinks and Magdalena paid while Eleanor lit a cigarette and dribbled smoke down her nose.

'Mother feels that a memorial Mass is needed. It's been arranged for two days from now, in Our Lady of Lourdes, a parish church she's got a particular affection for—'

'A quiet church, is it? In another part of town? As far from Madison Park as she can get, is it?' Eleanor, between questions, took quick puffs.

'It's a church my mother has always supported, as a matter of fact,' Magdalena spoke to Bridget. 'She knows the priest there and he'll do it at short notice. Mother feels that if we do the Mass as a family you can go back to Ireland feeling better about things.'

'So this is for me?' Bridget looked sceptical.

'It's for all of us.' Magdalena met her gaze over the rim of her glass.

'It's a way of getting Bridget on side, showing her what a decent family this really is.' Eleanor Munro slipped from the stool and stood facing Magdalena. 'It's my guess you've got a story lined up to tell her about why Victor left.' Her voice rose. The men at the table stopped talking and looked up, the barman raised an eyebrow. 'It's all about divide and conquer, isn't it?' She stabbed with her finger at Magdalena. 'All about getting Bridget out of here before she finds out too much, in the way that Ted Morgan was persuaded to go—'

'You really are a crazy woman, Eleanor, you know that?' Magdalena signalled the barman, who came at a trot, his eyes fixed on Eleanor. 'I bet you believe in every conspiracy theory there is, like every other New York whacko.'

She indicated to the barman that he should bring her another drink.

'Crazy is drinking the way you do.' Eleanor became quieter. 'Crazy is convincing yourself lies are the truth. Don't talk to me about crazy, Magadalena.'

Magadalena, head to one side, examined her face in the mirror behind the bar. 'You don't have to come to the Mass, Eleanor. The invitation is for Bridget.' She spoke to her reflection in the mirror. 'To be honest, we'd probably have ignored Victor's death if Bridget hadn't come visiting. But she did and it's good that we're doing this thing. Good for everyone. Mother hopes, we all hope, that the Mass will bring you peace, Bridget.'

'Preferably the day after the Mass?' Eleanor slammed her empty glass onto the counter. It cracked and lay there in three pieces.

'New York manners?' Magdalena raised an eyebrow, 'or simply the way your mother taught you to behave in bars?'

'My mother, compared to you lot, was Mother fucking Theresa.' Eleanor's face was flushed. 'A church ceremony won't change anything. Not a goddamn thing. And Bridget knows that too.' She spoke through barely moving lips. 'The edifice is crumbling, Magdalena, it's all coming apart.'

Magdalena looked around the bar and shivered. 'I really don't know, Bridget, how you can stay in a place like this.'

'I'm not staying in the bar,' Bridget said.

Victor's sister slipped with a practised elegance from the stool. Her eyes were glazed and too steady and Bridget wondered how many drinks she'd had before arriving at the bar.

'A car will collect you at nine fifteen day after tomorrow,' Magdalena said.

Chapter Eight

Bridget went shopping the following day for Victor's memorial Mass.

In Nordstrom – the slogan 'I'd rather be shopping at Nordstrom' was pasted on every other car in town – she bought herself a coat which matched her hair and a chenille jumper in ochre. She decided against a hat. She'd never worn one while Victor was alive and saw little point in covering her head to celebrate his death. Let the Baldaccis do the hat wearing today. She had no doubt that they would.

The Baldaccis wore black, every shade of it, and some of them wore hats. Veronica, when she arrived in a limousine with Hugo Sweeney to take Bridget to the church, was regal and waxwork-like in draped, jet-black lace. Hugo Sweeney sat beside her in grey-black, a pair of ebony leather gloves across his knees. Folded between them on the seat there was an animate-looking sable coat.

Bridget climbed in and sat with her back to the driver, facing them. They seemed very far away.

'Very roomy car.'

She sat back as they moved smoothly into the traffic. She hadn't spoken to a Baldacci in two days. She'd been glad not to. Eleanor Munro hadn't been in touch either and about this she felt more equivocal.

She'd done the tourist thing for a part of the time, from the top of the 605-foot-high Space Needle (inherited from the 1962 World's Fair) to the underground tour of the original Seattle, and found that the city had a relaxed, nicely diffident sense of itself.

But all the time she'd been haunted by the young Victor, by images of him growing up in a family where incest and cruelty and power games were the everyday way of doing things. If all that Eleanor Munro said was true he was a survival miracle.

Generous, kind, dutiful; he'd been a miracle if only half of it was true.

In bed at night the ache for him got worse and she wondered if it was in spite of all that had happened to him, or because of it, that he'd been able to turn the world on its head when he'd loved her, for hours. On one of the nights she had wept for a long time for everything she hadn't been able to share with him, for everything he hadn't been able to tell her.

She had come to understand something else too, or thought she did. She could see now how grief for her mother's life had made Eleanor Munro come as a terrorist among the Baldaccis.

'I hope your hotel room is adequate. Have you been sleeping well?'

Beneath the black lace of her mantilla Veronica's lips barely moved. She seemed tired, to have lost some of the energy of two days before. Hugo Sweeney, staring out the window, said nothing.

'My room is fine and, yes, I sleep well.'

Bridget lied, knowing it was expected of her. Veronica's question was a polite formula, not an expression of interest.

'The sleep of the just.' Veronica's face went through the motions of a smile.

'The exhausted, more like,' said Bridget. 'I've done a lot

of sightseeing in the last couple of days. Places like Pike Market, the Space Needle, Pioneer . . .'

'What energy.' Veronica yawned behind a black, leather-gloved hand. 'I've almost forgotten those places existed. One's life becomes circumscribed as one gets older, one inhabits an ever-decreasing space.'

'That's a choice, surely,' said Bridget.

'Of course it is. I didn't mean to open a debate.' Veronica, courtesies at an end, waved a silencing hand. Hugo Sweeney hadn't moved.

'Good morning, Hugo,' said Bridget.

'Good morning.' He didn't turn from the window. 'Not a bad day for the occasion that's in it.'

It was a bright day with clouds on the horizon. Suitable, as Hugo had said, for a Mass for the dead.

They drove for a silent twenty minutes through a city and outskirts busy with Saturday-morning traffic. When high buildings gave way to tightly packed housing and streets became narrower and crowded Bridget knew they were in the vicinity of Our Lady of Lourdes Church. A continent might have separated it from the climbing, leafy environs of Madison Park but it was from such places that large congregations for small churches were drawn.

She was right. Victor would have liked the small, grey and blue church they drew up to.

'Did Victor know this church?' She looked from the building to Veronica.

While the driver opened the door Veronica studied the trim façade of Our Lady of Lourdes. 'He attended with me a few times as a child.' She was helped down and stood leaning on her cane while Hugo Sweeney clambered out with the sable. 'You will sit next to me,' she said to Bridget as Hugo helped her into the coat. 'I am not an invalid,' she snapped as he proffered an arm, 'I have my stick.'

Bridget followed them slowly. The church was about twenty feet back from the road, at the end of a path which went through a trimmed patch of grass. Its wooden frame was grey, the doors blue. Our Lady of Lourdes was not a rich church, but it was dignified and friendly in its lack of presumption.

A priest came to meet them. He had bulbous eyes of milky blue and round, pink cheeks. His voice, when he spoke, was thin and wavery and a lot older sounding than his appearance.

'It's good to have you here again.' He shook Veronica Baldacci's hand. 'Though the unfortunate circumstances aren't what I'd have wished for.'

'We are the first to arrive, I see.' Veronica walked impatiently past him to the church porch.

'Plenty of time still, plenty of time.' The priest followed her on his short legs. 'I won't start without them.'

'You will if I tell you to.' Veronica sniffed as he fussed round her. She look through the glass doors into the church and announced, a tone of satisfaction in her voice, 'Everything looks the same.'

'You won't find any changes,' the priest was reassuring. 'Things are the way you always liked them.' He bobbed his head to Bridget. 'You'll be Victor Baldacci's widow. We meet in unfortunate circumstances.' He gave a deep sigh. 'It's a sad thing when a man dies so young. A sad thing for a wife to lose her husband and a sad thing,' he turned lachrymose eyes Veronica Baldacci's way, 'for a mother to see her child die before her. But the will of God is not ours to question. I'm Father Bob Matthews.'

Bridget shook his plump, dry hand. 'My name is Bridget. It was good of you to say the Mass at such short notice.'

He bobbed his head again, smiling a little and showing small teeth.

'The poor man's mother is one of our more venerable parishioners. I'm glad I can do this for her. Will we go inside the church?'

Talking in low, confidential tones to Veronica Baldacci he led the way up the aisle to the front pew. The altar was quite spare, starched white linen and a couple of vases of white flowers breaking up its functional look. As they reached the front pew Veronica stepped smartly away from the priest.

'You can get on with things now,' she spoke loudly. 'We are capable of seating ourselves.'

The priest bowed and scurried across the altar to the sacristy, genuflecting with a flourish as he passed the tabernacle.

Architecturally, Our Lady of Lourdes was traditional, but as spartan as the altar was in style. The narrow pews were of the same polished wood as the vaulted beams and behind the altar there were two long, and quite lovely, stained-glass windows. One of these showed the Virgin during an appearance at Lourdes in northern France. The other was of Veronica, the kindly woman of Jerusalem who wiped the face of Jesus when He fell while carrying His cross to Calvary.

'My father attended this church.' Veronica Baldacci followed Bridget's gaze to the stained-glass saint. 'He had those windows put in when his God delivered him from poverty and gave him a daughter.' She squinted against the light spilling from the window. 'Too much blue. I've never really liked the face of Veronica either.'

'She's rather gentle looking,' Bridget said.

'She has my mother's face,' said Veronica, 'or so they say. She died giving birth to me.'

'Your father brought you up then?'

'Yes.'

And arranged for you to marry Frank Baldacci when you were a very young woman, Bridget thought, but didn't say so. She had a sudden rush of sympathy for the young Veronica. The older woman's critical expression, as she gazed at the work of the stained-glass artist, revealed nothing of her feelings about her father.

A blast of cold air preceded the march of footsteps and murmured conversations up the aisle behind them. When the rest of the family shuffled into the pew behind Bridget she didn't turn and neither did Hugo Sweeney – a church etiquette ingrained in Irish childhoods. Veronica Baldacci did a stiff half-turn, surveyed the occupants of the pew and said, loudly,

'Where are Magdalena and Thomas? I had wanted everyone to be on time. We are a small enough congregation as things are.'

'When I rang to coordinate things Dad said we should go on ahead,' John-Francis spoke in an exaggerated whisper. 'I think Mom was having a late breakfast.'

'In that case,' Veronica faced forward and joined her hands in her lap, 'the priest had better get on with the proceedings. They won't be coming.'

'They'll be waiting at the house when we get back,' Lindsay was defensive. 'This whole thing was very short notice, you know. It wasn't easy for people to make time—'

'Tell the priest we're waiting,' Veronica said, cutting her short.

Lindsay, in charcoal coat and beret, crossed the altar to knock smartly on the door of the sacristy.

'We're happy to be here, Mrs Baldacci,' Russell Segal's voice, murmuring close to Veronica's ear, was reassuring, 'we're all behind you on this one.'

'Thank you for coming, Russell,' said Veronica, 'but it does not mean you're getting that loan you've been looking for.'

It was five minutes before Father Matthews, followed by several altar boys, appeared on the altar to the sound of a plaintive organ playing from the back of the church. The priest was sombre and dutiful, saying a short Mass and giving a sermon which was to the point, for which Bridget gave thanks. Anything prolonged or sentimentally insincere and she would have left, or thrown up, or both. His voice, from the altar, had a clarity born of years of sermonizing practice.

'Victor Francis Baldacci,' he intoned, 'chose to live his life in a land far from where he grew up. It was a tribute to his mother's influence that he choose a staunchly Catholic country. In Ireland he lived what we now know was a good life, rearing a fine family of' – he consulted a sheet of paper – 'two children, a boy and a girl, Anna and Fintan, now sadly without a father. Our thoughts are with them today. They are equally with his widow, Bridget.' He opened his arms in prayerful entreaty. 'Let us pray now, together with Bridget, whom we are privileged and happy to have with us here today, for the eternal rest of the soul of Victor Baldacci.'

The Baldaccis bowed their heads and Bridget, doing the same, wondered how fast Victor was spinning in his casket, back at the hotel.

Eleanor Munro, flushed and breathless and wearing a cloche hat with an inky velvet rose on the side, was waiting outside the church. She grabbed Bridget's arm as their small group emerged.

'I wanted to be here,' she said, 'but . . . oh, what the hell. I didn't make it. Was it terrible? Are you OK?'

'Hello, Eleanor. It was fine. Short.' Bridget eased her arm from the other woman's clutch.

'I left you alone,' Eleanor said sotto voce, 'and I haven't called you. I thought it would be good for you to think, get your head round things. Did you?'

'I did some thinking,' Bridget said as Lindsay, stamping

her feet and blowing clouds of vapour into the cold air, moved between them.

'Grandmother's laid on food at the house. Second time in a week – you're certainly getting the treatment, Bridget. You want to ride back with me, Eleanor?'

'I'd have appreciated a ride over here,' Eleanor was surly. 'Veronica called a limo and left before I was out of bed. Anyone would think I wasn't wanted.'

'You've brought her grief and a lot of shit – what do you expect?' Lindsay said. 'Do you want a ride now or what?'

The Baldacci mansion, by day, had a worn, exhausted look. The columns supporting the portico needed painting and the sharp morning light showed the façade closer to grey than white.

The front door was open and there were five cars parked in front. Two of them were police cars.

'Trouble.' Hugo frowned and leaned forward as the limousine crunched onto the gravelled front.

'The police?' Veronica Baldacci narrowed her eyes. She can't see a thing, Bridget thought, and is too vain to wear glasses. The realization made Veronica all at once more human.

'It's the police,' she touched the older woman's hand, 'but that doesn't have to mean trouble, or that something bad's happened.'

'You don't know what you're talking about,' Veronica snapped. 'The police visit only for the worst reasons.'

Helped by Hugo she climbed from the car with the slowness of the very old. She knows something, Bridget thought, she's been expecting bad news and now it's come. She stood close to Victor's mother as Lindsay and John-Francis came together through the front door and walked toward them. Hugo stood on Veronica's other side.

'What are the police doing here?' Veronica asked as her

grandchildren drew near. She still wore the mantilla, its scalloped lace edges like gashes on either side of her face.

'It's not good news,' Lindsay spoke carefully.

'Of course it's not good news.' Her grandmother, moving forward, was harshly impatient. She passed the police cars, and their driver occupants, without a glance. 'Just tell me what it's about.'

'Come inside.' John-Francis put an arm about her shoulder. 'There's no percentage in us freezing to death while we talk about things out here.'

Veronica allowed his arm to stay where it was but stopped absolutely still. For a moment only she closed her eyes. When she opened them she fixed Lindsay with their implacable gaze.

'Tell me,' she commanded.

John-Francis's hand tightened on his grandmother's shoulder.

'They've found Ted Morgan,' Lindsay said.

'Found him . . .' Veronica removed John-Francis's hand from her shoulder and began walking slowly towards the front door. 'I thought that might be why they were here.' The policeman at the door stood aside to allow her enter. 'Is he alive?' Veronica asked.

It was as if, Bridget thought, she couldn't bring herself to say the word dead. When no one said anything she stood in the centre of the hallway and turned again to Lindsay. 'Answer my question,' she demanded.

'He drowned,' Lindsay answered. 'Looks like he fell in the water.' She moved closer but didn't touch her grandmother. 'The cops say it looks like he was in the Sound awhile.'

'Not alive then.' Veronica let go of a long breath.

'Dad's in the sitting room, and so's Mom,' Lindsay said, 'there's a couple of detectives here too. They say they want to talk with you.'

'Yes.' Veronica didn't move until Hugo Sweeney took her arm. Then she allowed herself be led towards the sitting room.

Inside, dwarfed by the great room and in a tableau parodying the group which had greeted Bridget on her first visit to the Baldacci home, five people were gathered by the fire. Magdalena, Thomas, Russell, a middle-aged, balding man in a navy overcoat and a very tall, very broad black woman in grey trousers and anorak all turned as Veronica and Hugo Sweeney came through the door. Eleanor Munro was nowhere in evidence.

Thomas, after a quick word with the man in the overcoat, came to meet them.

'They're saying it was an accident,' he was wearing a sharp navy suit and dark tie, 'that he was out on one of the old piers, alone, late, that he slipped and fell in . . .'

'Most unlikely,' said Veronica, 'he was not one for taking late night walks alone.' She looked past Thomas to the man in the overcoat, now standing behind him. 'I fail to see either how he could have slipped unless he was drunk. He wasn't a drinker.'

'These are the things we want to establish, ma'am.' Rubbing a pale moustache, the overcoated man stepped forward. 'I'm Detective Lessig and this' – he indicated the woman in the anorak – 'is Detective Jacklin. We apologize for disturbing what I understand is a sad occasion . . .' He looked briefly from Hugo to Bridget. He had small, nut-brown eyes in a round face. 'Thing is, we need to find out how Theodore Morgan came to drown in the Sound and we understand he'd been staying here over Christmas.'

'He was an old friend.' Veronica moved past him, Hugo by her side. She said nothing else until she was sitting in an armchair facing her daughter. Hugo, with a look that stonily disapproved of the police presence, stood behind the chair. 'Ted Morgan was an old friend,' Veronica again said. 'He worked for this family once, a long time ago, nursing my husband in his final illness. We had exchanged letters over the years, but I had not seen him since after my husband's death until just before Christmas. He stayed here for nine days and then he left, on January the first . . .' she paused '. . . that was also nine days ago. I have no idea where he went and there is nothing more I can tell you.' She closed her eyes and sat back, the mantilla partly hiding her face. 'His death is very distressing to me.'

'It's a distressing death.' Detective Lessig shoved his hands deep into his pockets. 'We—'

'When did you find him?' Veronica didn't open her eyes.

'He was found two days ago, ma'am, discovered by a couple of kids went down one of the old piers to fish. He'd been in the water for the guts of a week—' He stopped, cleared his throat and rephrased the sentence, 'He'd been in there about five days, from the looks of things—'

'Please don't give me the details.' Veronica opened her eyes. 'So,' she sat looking straight ahead, 'he was here, in Seattle, all the time. I thought—' She stopped.

'You thought what, ma'am?' the detective prompted.

'That he'd returned to New York. Where he lived.'

'Far as we've been able to ascertain he was in Seattle all of the time between leaving this house and dying.' Lessig sighed and thoughtfully smoothed the thin moustache drooping from his upper lip. 'Stroke of luck, tracing him. We wouldn't have known any of this, or even who he was, if we hadn't been on the lookout for another guy went missing from the same hostel—'

'Hostel?' Veronica stared. 'Are you telling me Ted Morgan was staying in a refuge? Are you quite sure we're talking about the same person?'

'Absolutely.' Lessig became brisk. 'The details were all there in his personal belongings. Identity's been confirmed with a fingerprint check. He was staying at the Bible Mission

Refuge. Told them he expected to stay on awhile too.' He paused. 'That's why we're looking at an accident as the probable cause of death and not suicide. Either it was an accident or he was pushed in.'

'Pushed? As in murdered?' John-Francis sounded sceptical.

Thomas coughed. 'Ted Morgan was a well-meaning, inoffensive kind of guy. Not the type who made enemies. Why would anyone . . . push him in the water?'

'We don't know that he was pushed,' Detective Jacklin, in sharp, clipped tones, spoke for the first time. 'It's been hard to tell anything, way the fish got to him.'

In the silence Magdalena began to weep. Nobody else moved or spoke except for Detective Jacklin who, after a slow look round the faces in the room, produced a notebook.

'I'll just take the names of everyone here. Then I'd like to know who was in the house at the time of Theodore Morgan's visit and who the last person was to speak with him before he left.'

She took names and information meticulously over what seemed to Bridget an agonizingly long ten minutes. Magdalena sobbed quietly throughout. Thomas perched on the arm of her chair. Lindsay smoked. John-Francis paced. Russell Segal stared at the mock flames. Veronica sat rigidly unmoving with Hugo behind her.

'You've no idea why he left your home, ma'am?' Detective Lessig looked apologetically at Veronica as his colleague closed her notebook.

'None.'

'And he didn't say where he was going?'

'No.'

Lessig looked from Hugo to the others in the room. 'Did anyone here know where he was staying?'

'No one had any idea,' Lindsay said firmly. 'My grandmother had been enjoying his company. They'd been recalling events of way over thirty years ago, before my grandfather died. He knew he was welcome to stay on in this house.' She hesitated, looking at Veronica. 'My grandmother had been expecting him to return.' She turned toward the garden where a radiant, lit-up Christmas tree still shone. 'She'd even been holding out on taking down that thing because he liked it.'

'It seems I am no longer needed here. I will go to my room.' Veronica gave her hand to Hugo Sweeney and he helped her out of the chair.

'Thank you, ma'am, for your help,' Detective Lessig extended a hand which Veronica ignored.

'I want to say something,' Hugo Sweeney looked up at Detective Lessig, 'and it's this: there's nothing Mrs Baldacci can tell you about the dead man. Ted Morgan was his own person. He left here all those years ago when it suited him and he didn't come back again until it suited him. When he went off nine days ago it was for reasons of his own too. You'll not find answers in this house. The man himself was the only one had the answers to what you want to know.'

'Thank you, Mr Sweeney.' Lessig nodded. 'There's nothing you yourself might have to tell us?'

'I've given you my observations,' said Hugo, 'and that's all I have to say on the subject.'

The door hadn't closed behind Veronica and Hugo before Detective Jacklin, as precise as before, said, 'We need to see Miss Munro. Could one of you people bring her back in here, please?'

'I'll get her.' Thomas gave his small cough and stood. 'But as you saw earlier she is very upset. She and Mr Morgan came to Seattle together.' He paused. 'A nostalgic trip.'

'We need to talk to her,' the detective said.

'Won't take long,' Detective Lessig assured him. Thomas coughed again and left the room.

'Christ, I don't think I can take an Eleanor scene right now.' John-Francis faced the detectives. 'Do you need me here for this?'

'We'd prefer if you stayed, yes,' Detective Lessig said. John-Francis, after a look at the man's face, shrugged and sat down.

'Way I see it,' John-Francis stretched his legs in front of him and studied the toes of his shoes, 'Ted Morgan could have done anything, gotten into all kinds of trouble, made all sorts of enemies, in the thirty-five or more years since he was last here. Are you people looking at the rest of his life?'

'We'll be looking at everything,' Detective Lessig assured him.

Bridget decided to sit down too. She chose the seat vacated by Veronica and had a clear view of Magdalena's ravaged face. Tears had ploughed through her make-up, mascara washing into the furrows created on her cheeks. She looked up and lifted her glass to Bridget.

'Happy holidays,' she said.

The Eleanor Munro who came into the room with Thomas was chillingly subdued. She stood a few feet from the door looking in silence from one detective to the other. Her hands hung by her sides and she was still dressed in the long black coat and cloche hat she'd been wearing outside the church.

'We need to ask you an initial couple of questions,' Detective Jacklin's tones were surprisingly gentle. 'Maybe later, when you feel able, you'd come down to the precinct and talk with us some more?'

'Maybe I will,' said Eleanor. 'What do you want to know now?'

'Just if Theodore Morgan said anything to you about why he moved out and into the Bible Mission Refuge?'

'No. He didn't tell me he was going.'

'But you were travelling companions. You'd known him in New York. Had you expected to travel back with him?'

'We'd made no arrangements of any kind.'

'Did he get in touch with you after leaving here?'

'No.'

'Thank you, Miss Munro.' Detective Jacklin look at her colleague. 'I guess that's it, then. Unless you got anything you want to clear up with the people here?'

'Seems to me we've about covered things.' Lessig began to button his overcoat. 'Except to ask if Theodore Morgan made contact with anyone in this house after he left? Or if any of you know who else he might have looked up in Seattle? No?' He finished buttoning his coat. 'We've got information says he took a couple of calls at the Refuge. Since none of you knew where he was staying they can't have come from this house. Still, I'd appreciate it if you would all think things over, see if there's anything you might have forgotten to tell us.' He hunched into his coat. 'We'll be in touch.'

In the garden the lights went out on the Christmas tree.

Chapter Nine

The house closed in around Bridget, smothering and claustophobic.

'I need a walk and some air,' she said.

'I'll come with you,' said John-Francis. She couldn't think of a way to stop him.

For their walk, along the pathway between the classic sculptures, John-Francis favoured a white, Aran-style sweater. He stayed close to Bridget, attentive and kindly.

'You didn't have to come with me,' Bridget said.

'I'm glad to keep you company.'

He took her arm as they came to a step. When they reached level ground and Bridget tugged to free her arm he smiled and held on.

'Don't want you slipping on frosty grass,' he said.

Bridget ground her teeth and walked faster. John-Francis kept pace.

'Shame you getting mixed up in all of this,' he said and, when Bridget didn't reply, he added, 'I liked Ted Morgan.'

'You got to know him well, then?'

'I wouldn't say that, exactly. But he spent a lot of time with Veronica – he'd a way of making her feel good. Eleanor was more relaxed when he was around. More, uh, sane, if you know what I mean.'

'He seems to have been a sort of father to Eleanor,' Bridget said.

'I suppose.' John-Francis shrugged. 'He was the right age, in his sixties. Too young to die, that's for sure.'

'He was a lot younger than your grandmother then?' Bridget asked, surprised.

'Yeah. A good fifteen years or so younger. He saw her through grandfather's death. I reckon that was the bond.'

'She's taken it badly . . .'

'Yeah.' John-Francis was impatient. 'But Veronica's tough, a survivor. Eleanor's more the problem.'

Bridget agreed about Eleanor. After the departure of the police the younger woman had taken herself back to her room. Her subdued air had had an edge of dementia about it. She's got no one now, Bridget thought, her mother and father-figure both gone.

'Will Veronica look after Eleanor?' Bridget asked. 'See she gets some money?'

It was the first chance she'd had to put the question to one of the family directly. John-Francis, still holding her elbow, hesitated only slightly before answering.

'I don't have the complete story because it wasn't something my parents or my grandmother ever discussed with us.' He gave a half smile. 'The past is another country and all that.'

'So what are you saying?'

'That I don't know what Grandmother will do. We never know what she'll do.'

It was cold in the garden, the grass underfoot already crisp with an early afternoon frost as they skirted the phlegmatic Roman senator.

'Did Ted Morgan nurse Veronica's husband for long?'

'I don't know that either.' John-Francis looked rueful. 'I'm not a lot of use to you, Bridget, on these questions. Do you want to go back to the house?'

Bridget didn't but rounded the last statue with him and they began to retrace their steps. She was studying the statuary as they passed, thinking how humourless it was and how it fitted the mood of the house, when John-Francis said, 'You're in luck. My father's coming to join us. You can put your questions to him.'

Thomas, coming towards them along the path, looked harrassed and more than usually stooped. When he reached them Bridget added tired and apologetic to the way he looked. He rubbed a hand across his forehead.

'I want you to take your mother on home, son. I need to stay here awhile, sort some things.'

'Will do.' John-Francis Baldacci elegantly raised and air-kissed Bridget's gloved hand. 'I leave you in the wiser company of my father.'

'He's a charmer,' said Thomas as his son jogged down the pathway and out of the garden, 'but his sister's the worker in this family.' He sighed. 'Eleanor is back downstairs and is looking for you. She's . . . pretty excited.' he hesitated. 'I'm glad we have this chance to talk, even for a few minutes.'

'I am too. I've a few questions I want to ask.'

'Go ahead.' Thomas gave an unconvincing half smile.

'Tell me about Victor, how you remember him.' A spiteful gust of wind made Bridget's eyes water and she dabbed at them while Thomas framed an answer. He took a while.

'I remember your husband as a troubled teenager,' he said at last. 'I wasn't a lot older than him, four or five years I suppose, but, God, how I envied him his good looks. Handsome and brooding was how I saw him.' He pulled a wry face. 'Did he stay that way?'

'He was handsome,' Bridget said, 'and serious. He developed a few other traits too though. People don't change so much as add experience to the skeleton of what they are.'

'Yes . . .' He looked at her doubtfully. 'You know, you could say that I took Victor's place in the family. After his father died and he left' – he pushed his glasses higher up his nose – 'I became the male family figure for Veronica and Magdalena.'

'I can see how that would have happened. About Eleanor's story – is it all true?' Bridget stared at the ground and willed him to tell her no, that Eleanor Munro had exaggerated, some of what she had said was true but not all, not the incest, not the shocking cruelty.

'It's true,' Thomas's tone was neutral, 'but it all happened a long time ago and to another family, you could say. Everything's been rebuilt.'

Rebuilt. The word struck Bridget as bizarre and she wanted to ask him about the foundations for this rebuilding. What about seepage? Did not some of the rot from the family's cankerous bedrock work its way through, even exist still? But she didn't know quite how to put it so she asked him instead about Victor. 'Why did my husband leave?'

Thomas was gentle. 'That's between him and his mother. She'll have to tell you that. I don't know.'

Bridget didn't believe him. He knew. They all knew.

Lindsay was circling the hallway talking into the mobile phone, controlled frenzy in her voice, when they got back to the house. Hers were the only sounds in the echoing quiet. Bridget, listening, for no reason that she could pin down, knew all at once what she was going to do with Victor's ashes.

'I'd like you to call me a cab to take me back to my hotel,' she said to Thomas. With something like relief he produced a phone of his own and made the booking.

'I'll wait outside,' Bridget said, remembering the stranglehold effect of the house. 'Will you tell Eleanor?'

Thomas nodded, mute and pleasant still.

Bridget was leaning against the paint-peeling portico, thinking the day was as bleak and cold as the unfolding facts of Victor's family life, when Eleanor Munro came to her.

'Don't leave, Bridget.' She looked distraught. 'Don't go

back to your hotel. Move in here with me. I'm scared. I don't want to be alone in this place.' Her eyes had a glittering intensity in a face which was blue-white and drawn.

'You're not alone.' Bridget shook her head. 'Veronica and Hugo will be here. Veronica shares your grief for Ted, in spite of everything. But do call me whenever you want—'

'What I want is you here.' Eleanor clutched at Bridget's arms and shook her. 'I've got no one else now. I want you to be with me. Ted won't be coming back. You heard what they said. He's dead.'

'Oh, Eleanor, my poor Eleanor.' Bridget shook herself free and then pulled the younger woman into her arms. 'I'm so sorry about Ted.' It was exactly like holding Anna; same texture to her hair when she stroked it, same fragile, bony body. 'You'll feel better about things tomorrow, not much, but you'll begin to cope.' She held the younger woman at arms' length. 'There's a cab on the way here to take me back to the hotel. There's something I have to do.'

'I'll come with you. I'm not staying here.'

In the taxi Eleanor folded into herself and was silent. She was silent too as she followed Bridget to her room in the hotel and mutely watched while Bridget lifted Victor's casket from its spot on the desk.

'You can come with me,' Bridget held the casket in her arms, 'or you can wait here until I get back. The choice is yours.'

'I'm coming with you,' said Eleanor.

Bridget got directions from the woman on reception, who was more cheerful today for some reason, and made her way to the waterfront via Post Alley, a cavern of endless steps between high buildings. Eleanor Munro walked beside her in silence. Bridget carried Victor's ashes in her arms, the casket in a canvas hold-all.

On Pier 55 Bridget was told the next cruise of the bay and harbour area wouldn't happen for thirty minutes.

'We've got time for a hot drink then,' Bridget said and led the way to a waterfront bar and restaurant.

'Spiced cider,' she said to the overweight, bearded barman, adding, 'two glasses,' when Eleanor, slipping wordlessly into a window seat, refused to make a choice.

'You ain't going to like it.' The barman, looking at them, shook his head.

'Try us,' said Bridget.

It was sweet and overspiced and he was right, Bridget hated the cider. Eleanor didn't even try it. 'Why do you sell it?' Bridget asked.

'Some folks'll drink anything.' The barman grinned. 'You're taking a trip out on the bay, right? I can truly recommend the Northwest Fish Stew we do here. Call in on the way back. Ask for Stanley. That's me. I'll look after you myself.'

It was the last trip of the day and there were four other passengers on the boat. Bridget and Eleanor were the only two people on the open deck as it swayed gently out along the wooden pier. Was it under a pier like this, Bridget wondered, that Ted Morgan had been found?

She turned her face from the city, held the hold-all tighter and faced the wider waters ahead. The captain, over the tannoy, assured them these were a hundred feet deep in parts.

'That's a lot of water, folks, moving in and out on two high tides and two low each day.' He made this sound unusual. 'The whole thing carved out by glaciers.'

Fifteen minutes out the waters were a penetrating, icy blue. Victor would be at peace here, if anywhere.

Bridget balanced the bag with the casket on the ship's rail; not an easy thing to do since the rail was narrow and the bag a lot wider. She unzipped it and looked at the casket, insignificant in its towel padding. All she had to do now was unscrew the top and scatter the contents.

'Is there something I should know about?' Eleanor spoke for the first time since leaving the hotel.

'No. Nothing,' Bridget said. 'You can go below decks and wait for me. Keep warm.'

'Those are your husband's ashes, right?'

'Right.'

'And you're really going to do this? You're really going to dump them here in the bay?'

'I am.'

It was hard to let him go. The boat was moving fast and there was all of the Puget Sound to choose from. One hundred miles or more of it, the captain had said. Such a lot of water, such a great silence. Ted Morgan had died in these waters and they were telling nothing.

Spray stung her face and she blinked it from her eyes. They'd travelled a long way together, she and Victor Baldacci.

The boat began to swing round, sea birds skimming the waves ahead as it headed back for the harbour. It rolled with the tide, then heaved.

Bridget lost her balance. Clutching at the rail for support she could do nothing but watch as the bag slipped and turned, falling in a wide, slow arc before it splash-landed in the water. She went on watching as it sank, lazily, beneath the waves, until hold-all and casket were gone, for ever she hoped, beneath the water of the Puget Sound.

Ted Morgan hadn't stayed in the water. She added a prayer to her hopes that Victor's ashes would.

Letting go of the breath she'd been holding she thought that some things never change. As so often in her life with Victor a decision had been taken out of her hands. She felt rudderless, and very cold.

'Are you OK?' Eleanor touched Bridget's face, timidly.

'I'm fine, really I am,' Bridget said.

Stanley's Northwest Fish Stew was fishy and it was warm

and for the latter, at least, Bridget gave thanks. She and Eleanor sat close together at a small, round wooden table in curved-backed chairs. A fan whirred in the ceiling and Stanley, in a green striped apron, hovered with a two-foot-long pepper mill.

'I made that stew myself. It all right for seasoning?'

'No,' Eleanor pushed her bowl aside, 'I can't eat this stuff.'

Stanley's hold on the pepper mill took on a whole new aspect.

'There's a lot of cold water out there,' Bridget said hurriedly, 'does much fishing go on?'

'Depends what you mean by fishing.' Stanley turned his broad back on Eleanor and placed the pepper mill safely on the table. 'We get a lot of dead bodies fished out of those waters. One pulled out not more than a couple of days ago.'

'At this pier?' The fish stew's appeal diminished and Bridget stopped eating. She avoided looking at Eleanor.

'Further down. A lot lonelier place than here. Sort of place a man might go to end things, or be dumped by someone doing it for him. It's the kind of thing gives the place a bad name, stops people coming to the waterfront to eat.' Stanley folded his arms and looked contemplatively through the window and along the pier. 'Course there are others come because of the murders and suicides. There's always a lot of talk, people are interested in that sort of thing.'

'What are people saying about this latest . . . drowning?'

'See what I mean?' Stanley winked at Bridget and gave a chortle. 'You're interested. Knew you would be. It's human nature to be curious about death, and how it happens.'

'Well? What happened this time?' Bridget put a warning foot on Eleanor's under the table. The younger woman stayed silent.

'Word is he was helped into the water. Way the guys

down here heard it, he was caught in the struts and eaten mostly by rats, torso and head, not fish. Way they figure it was high tide, he was dead going in and was swept immediately onto the struts to become a meal for those rodents—'

'Stoppit! Just shut the fuck up! . . . I don't want to hear any more of this—' Eleanor's chair crashed to the ground as she stood gagging, a napkin to her mouth.

'Sensitive digestive system, have we?' Stanley removed her plate and turned, businesslike, to Bridget. 'That'll be eight dollars twenty, when you're ready.'

Outside, it was getting dark fast. Post Alley lost a lot of its appeal on the long climb upwards but the effort drained Eleanor of much of the explosive anger she'd built up on account of Stanley.

'Fucking jerkoff,' she panted as they emerged from the alley and hit the streets again. 'Fact that he may be right doesn't give him the right to talk like that.'

'We don't even know that he was talking about Ted,' Bridget said.

Eleanor said nothing while they crossed two intersections and headed uphill again towards the hotel.

'I know he was talking about Ted,' she said and then, 'And I know Ted didn't end his own life.'

'The police will—'

'Like hell they will. The cops'll toss it around for a week or two and then forget it. Ted was a nobody, a vagrant, a refuge inhabitant – that's all they want to know about him. No one's going to make a fuss, no one's going to scream to have his murderer brought to justice.'

'We don't know he was murdered—'

'*We* don't,' Eleanor's mimicry was acute, 'but I do. And I'm going to make a lot of noise. I'm going to keep asking questions.' She stopped, looking up and down the street. Her eyes were manic, and frightened. 'Someone has to. They can't be allowed to get away with it.'

Chapter Ten

At some point during a sleepless night Bridget decided she was going home. She would change her flight. Go for an earlier date. Be out of Seattle in twenty-four hours. Hopefully. The idea helped her sleep. But it was a sleep full of nightmare corridors without end, with still, bottomless waters and, everywhere she turned, the same headless figure.

When she woke she knew she wouldn't be leaving. She couldn't run away as Victor had done. She had to stay until she knew all there was to know about Victor's past, about his family's past – and present.

Because the first two were increasingly, and frighteningly, becoming a part of the second.

It was the reason she'd come. It was what had kept her going in the months since she'd become a widow. If she went home now she would never come back to Seattle, any more than Victor had. She would never really know, never be sure what exactly had so damaged the man she'd married.

But it was more than that, now. Something had changed since meeting his family; a dimension had been added to her reason for being here.

She wasn't in Seattle for herself alone anymore: she was now here for Victor too. She now knew that she owed it to him too to get to the bottom of the whole sorry mess. He hadn't been able to, he'd run away and kept running until he'd found a safe haven. He'd never had justice: he'd lost his childhood and young life and any rights he might have had within his family.

She would put things right for him, see him vindicated. It was the least she could do now she was here. It would be a small return for the happy years, a sort of acknowledgement of all he'd meant to her. She would stay until she'd found out everything possible. The circle of his life would be complete then, the past understood and, hopefully, put to peace.

His children would really know him. She would too.

If even half of what she'd heard was true then Victor's young life had to have been a confused and deeply unhappy one. But it was the straw which had broken his back and driven him from home that she wanted to know about.

It was Sunday. A day of peace and rest. She would take this day, at least, for herself. She would walk and puzzle things through and look at the waters everywhere. She would work on detaching herself from the Baldaccis – it was the best way to see things clearly.

She rang Fintan, then Anna, but told them nothing except that she'd been to dinner chez the Baldaccis. She just didn't know where to begin telling them all what she'd discovered. She had breakfast delivered to the room and sat with it on the bed, channel hopping through endless dissections of Sonny Bono's life and death, weather forecasts, further flashes of Fergie. Nowhere was there news or comment about the discovery of the half-eaten body of a man found at the waterfront. Probably, as Stanley the fish stew maker had said, bodies came ashore there all the time.

She was watching a talk show in which obscenely fat people discussed the virtues of flesh in bed when the call came. She'd never considered the pleasures of burying her head in a billowy stomach, or between smothering thighs, and her mind was distracted when she picked up the phone.

Too distracted to be adamant about keeping the day for herself.

'I hope I didn't get you out of bed.' Veronica Baldacci didn't introduce herself.

'Only in a manner of speaking . . .'

'I would like to talk with you. A car will pick you up in about thirty minutes.'

'I have plans for the day.'

'You need to hear what I have to say. I will be as brief as possible.' The line went dead.

Hugo Sweeney opened the door to her, his narrow eyes taking her in without enthusiasm. The house behind him was so silent it could have been empty. If Eleanor Munro was around she was keeping very quiet.

'Mrs Baldacci is waiting for you,' said Hugo, 'and you might as well know that she's a bit under the weather. She's settled on a death wish and there's nothing to be done but wait now and see if she comes out of it.'

He walked ahead of Bridget up the stairs, his small feet laced into black leather shoes, his white hair limp on his collar. She could feel his resentful energy with every step.

The landing walls were covered with heavy landscape oils, most of them of mountains and lakes. Hugo straightened one and spoke without turning around.

'She's been at the drink – though in her day she could drink more than any man I ever knew. It's different now. Doesn't agree with the insulin.'

'Veronica's a diabetic?'

'That she is.' He stepped back from the picture. It was still lopsided.

'Let me. Sometimes a fresh eye . . .' Bridget angled the picture until it came right.

'A fresh eye. So that's what you think you are,' said Hugo.

'That, Hugo, is what is called a loaded comment. What exactly are you saying?'

Hugo frowned at the mountains and lake. 'Maybe I'm saying that people can only tell you how things look to them and they've all got different ways of looking. The eye can be wiser or it can be foolish in the way it sees things.' He began to walk along the landing. 'Whatever you hear there's only the one truth. You'd do well to remember that, while you're here.'

Bridget followed him. 'I don't suppose you'd care to tell me how you see that truth?'

'I would not' – Hugo gestured at the landscapes – 'she thought that was what Ireland was like. That was why she bought the lot of them. But all of those paintings are of England. She never would believe me when I told her.'

'Hugo, is Veronica dying?'

Hugo Sweeney didn't reply immediately. He smoothed a hand over his thin, white hair and crossed the landing to stand by a door.

'She might be,' he said, 'and then again she might not. She's not a woman who goes by the ordinary rules.' He pushed open the door.

Veronica Baldacci sat in a wooden rocking chair by a long window whose partially opened shutters gave the room its only light. She was dressed in black, a wool dress with pearl buttons to the neck and a silk wrap over it. Her stick lay across her knees and her heavily made-up face was clown-like above the elegant black.

'Sit there.'

She indicated a second chair by the window and Bridget sat. In the murky light she could make out a large, lace-covered bed and, along one wall, a wardrobe and chest of drawers. A functional bedroom with a comfortable bed was how it seemed to her.

A low table between herself and Veronica held carafes of whiskey and water and a glass.

'Help yourself,' said Veronica. She already had a drink in her hand.

'It's a bit early for me,' Bridget said. 'What did you want to talk about?'

'To the point. I like that,' said Veronica. 'I was never keen on the superficialities of life.' Her stare, through the blue-black of the eye make-up, was hard to read.

'In that case, Veronica, perhaps you would begin—'

'I prefer Mrs Baldacci.' Veronica was curt. 'But since we both share the name I suppose I must make an exception. You may call me Veronica.' Turning her head slowly she looked round the room, her eyes picking out objects, resting on them, moving on. After a few minutes she said, 'I have found peace in this room, many times.'

She's playing with me, Bridget thought, she demanded I come here and now she plans to amuse herself and tell me what she has to say in her own time. She got up.

'I have plans for the day,' she said, 'but I'll call to see you before I leave Seattle.'

She was almost at the door when Veronica's voice, subdued and almost pleading, made her stop. 'Death is never pleasant,' she said, 'any more than life is, a lot of the time.'

Bridget turned, slowly. 'Life has its moments,' she said, 'though I'm not so sure about death.' She paused and said what she'd already said to Hugo, 'Are you dying, Veronica?'

'We are all dying, all of the time,' Veronica, eyes on the light through the gap in the shutters, didn't turn, 'but I am probably closer to death than you are.' She sighed. 'Please sit down, Bridget.'

It was the Bridget that did it. She went back to the armchair.

'I have come to a decision,' Veronica said, 'and when I tell you what it is I want you to leave here, go home to your

128

children and your life in Ireland. I do not want you to discuss what I am about to tell you with Eleanor Munro, or with anyone. Do I have your word?'

'You cannot seriously expect me to make a promise without knowing—'

'Yes, I can.' Veronica's expression became one of distaste. 'Please don't lecture me. I've no liking for high-toned moral speeches.' She turned her face from the window and looked briefly and coldly at Bridget. 'I will expect you to do as I have asked and not talk to anyone here, especially Miss Munro.'

'I cannot promise,' Bridget said. The older woman said nothing for a minute, then shrugged.

'And I cannot force you. I will simply warn you that Miss Munro is a woman to whom it is neither safe nor prudent to give information. It would be dangerous to talk to her of the things which we are about to discuss in this room.'

'Secrecy is a way of life in this family,' Bridget said slowly. 'You cannot expect me to go along with a way of behaving I fundamentally disagree with.'

'I do. Some things are best left unexamined. You are, after a fashion, a member of this family and it would be best, for everyone, if you—'

'Obeyed the rules?' Bridget cut her short. 'I'm sorry, Veronica. I would prefer to maintain the detached status I've had all these years.'

For a while it seemed to Bridget that Veronica Baldacci either hadn't heard or registered what she'd said. The older woman was silent, sighing a little and playing with the rings on her fingers. But when she spoke again she was businesslike.

'There is no legacy, no share in the family wealth, due to you or to your children. I disowned my son when he left home. However, despite the fact that neither you nor your offspring are entitled to anything from this family, I am making arrangements for shares in the company to be made over to you. Substantial shares. I am not doing this because of any affection for Victor. On the contrary. I am doing this as an expression of my gratitude to you for keeping him away, for ensuring I did not set eyes on him for thirty years. They will give you a degree of power and a role in this family. It is important for a woman to have power. I doubt you had any in your marriage.'

'Our marriage wasn't about power . . .'

'Of course it was. All marriages are.' Veronica leaned forward. Her breath smelled sweet, and whiskey laden. 'I intend making an allowance payable to Eleanor Munro. It is more than she deserves and will get rid of her.'

She really is dying, Bridget thought, and she's squaring her conscience. She's getting rid of me as well as Eleanor. The surprise was that Veronica Baldacci *had* a conscience. A flutter she recognized as panic started up in Bridget's stomach. She didn't want this. She was being sucked into things.

Aloud, she said, 'Why are you doing this now?'

'Because what has happened has made it inevitable. You are here. Eleanor Munro is unfortunately here. The family needs new blood,' she gave a cold smile, 'and I wish to decide what that blood will be while I am still capable. You will do. Eleanor Munro will not.'

'Ted Morgan—'

'Yes. Ted Morgan helped me see things . . . differently. He is . . . was someone whose judgement I respected. He thought it right that I make arrangements such as these. His death is a great sadness.' Her voice dropped. 'I wish to honour him.'

'I did not come here looking for money.'

'You've already pointed that out.' Veronica's face closed again and she waved an impatient hand. 'Consider this a recompense for the years spent with my son.'

'I was happy with your son. We were happy together.'

'I don't believe you,' Veronica said.

'I would like to know why Victor left home.' Bridget poured herself a small amount of whiskey and a lot of water. 'That's what I came here to find out.'

'We have already spoken about Victor's early years,' Veronica's voice rose angrily, 'I do not want to go over it again . . .'

The door opened. 'Everything all right here?' Hugo Sweeney looked from one woman to the other.

'Pour me a drink,' Veronica said. 'No water this time.'

Hugo poured whiskey into a glass. 'You shouldn't be upsetting her,' he said quietly, to Bridget.

'Leave us, Hugo.' Veronica downed half the whiskey in a gulp. 'We have things to discuss.' She was irritable, but calm.

'I won't be far.' Hugo Sweeney closed the door softly after him.

Bridget walked to the window and through the small opening in the shutters looked down at the curve of the avenue and the slow rain beginning to fall there.

'Why don't you tell me the whole truth about this family, Veronica?' She opened the shutters a little, 'or at least give me your version of the whole truth?'

She turned. In the light from the window, and despite the make-up, Veronica's skin had a decaying look to it. The icy, pale blue alertness of her eyes was unchanged.

'As you please.' Her mother-in-law finished her drink. 'Pour me another.' She held out the glass. 'Do it,' she said, raising her voice as Bridget hesitated. 'The truth is that though my marriage to Frank Baldacci was an arranged one it was also a love match.'

Love. Veronica said the word gently, shocking Bridget, making her aware how little she knew of the nature of love, of the nature of hate.

'Frank had indeed been involved in a liaison with a

131

young woman called Grace Munro.' The gentleness disappeared from Veronica's voice. 'He was unaware she was under age. Immediately our engagement was announced she revealed her pregnancy and claimed Frank as the father. She threatened blackmail, and a lot more besides, and Frank came to an arrangement with her about financial support for her and her child.' Veronica sighed. 'He provided diligently for fifteen years until Grace Munro one day disappeared, leaving her daughter behind.'

'Is it true that Grace Munro was never heard of again?'

'It's true,' said Veronica after only the slightest hesitation. 'It is my opinion that she left the state with a man.'

'Her daughter was Shelley, Eleanor Munro's mother?'

Veronice was silent for a moment, as if remembering. 'Yes, yes,' she said eventually and impatiently. 'And we took her into our home and cared for her as one of our own children. She was a strange, demanding child. Her mother's loss affected her badly and she became neurotically possessive of Frank. She couldn't be persuaded to go to school, nor to do anything else. The time came when she refused even to go outside.'

Veronica looked from Bridget to the bed and then the darker corners of the room. She gave an involuntary shiver. 'One day, just as her mother had done, she left. It was a difficult time. Frank was not in good health. There were business problems.'

A nerve began to tick at the corner of her eye and she rubbed at it with the back of her hand. 'We nevertheless hired a private detective because, though Shelley was twenty-one years old, she was an immature young woman and we worried that she might not be able to look after herself.'

She took the hand away from her eye. In rubbing she had smudged the make-up so that the clown look had become lop-sided and slightly tragic. 'She'd been gone several months when she was found in New York. Frank, though unwell, went to bring her home. She was living with a man and wouldn't leave. She was drinking. He thought it likely she was abusing drugs too. From being devoted to Frank she now wanted nothing to do with him and refused all help, financial or otherwise. The man she was with was her new life, she said, she was finished with the old.'

She stopped. When she went on it was after a deep breath and more slowly.

'Frank left her there and came home. But the trip had exhausted his reserves of strength and within weeks he suffered a stroke. He lived, what was left to him of life, paralysed and an invalid. I was obliged to take his place in the business. I found I had a flair for it. I have been involved ever since.' She shrugged. 'I had no choice in the matter.'

Yes, you did, Bridget thought, watching the other woman as she raised her glass and slowly sipped. There were always choices. Veronica Baldacci had run the business because she liked control. Maybe that wasn't all she liked though. The sad, clownishly smudged eye above the rim of the glass gave her an oddly vulnerable look. Maybe there was a neediness there too. Maybe that's what her love for Frank Baldacci had been.

'Thomas took Victor's place in the business,' Bridget said, 'he told me as much himself.' She sat in the armchair again. The room was uncomfortably hot and she longed to open a window but didn't dare. 'Maybe it's time you told me what it was finally decided Victor to leave home.'

Veronica closed her eyes. It was as if she hadn't heard.

'Was it because,' Bridget raised her voice only slightly, 'his father was having a relationship with his half-sister, with Shelley Munro?'

'A relationship?' Veronica's lips barely moved.

'Did he rape her?'

'Of course not. All of that is a fantasy of Eleanor's sick mind.'

Veronica opened her eyes and looked directly at Bridget. 'She is exactly like her mother – diseased of mind. Shelley Munro wasn't even a particularly attractive-looking woman. She had a bad complexion.' Veronica gave a slow smile and held up her empty glass. 'I'll have water this time.'

'Bridget took and filled the glass and gathered her thoughts the while. Veronica's version of the family history was plausible and more acceptable than Eleanor Munro's because it was less cruel. But did that make it any more true?

'Why did Victor leave home?' She handed Veronica the glass.

'You are a persistent woman,' Veronica's voice had become slightly slurred. She gave her a cold smile. 'Such persistence must be rewarded. Victor left because he judged and condemned me, his mother. It had to do with Ted Morgan. Ted was a young man when he came to nurse my husband. Just thirty-two years of age. I was a woman of forty-five but I came to rely on him totally in matters relating to Frank and, eventually, the house. He managed things here while I looked after the business. He looked after me too. He was a good man. We became lovers.'

Bridget nodded. It made sense. If Veronica was capable of hatred, which was what she seemed to feel for Victor, why not of love? She'd already shown neediness.

'Victor knew this?' she asked. Veronica ignored the question.

'I was a middle-aged woman. The man I'd married was gone from me in a wasted body which waited for death. Ted and I kept our affair secret. I did not trust my children to understand, though they were young adults. I was right not to.' Her voice became rough. 'Victor discovered us together. From then until the day his father died I lived with his hostility and disapproval, both of them ferocious, malignant forces in this house. He made me suffer—' She stopped abruptly. After a minute she went on. 'Victor had been groomed for the family business. It would be his place, as his father's son, to take over one day. He drove Ted away, forcing me to choose between my son or my lover. I chose my son, as I had to, and Ted left as soon as Frank died. And then, within three months, so did Victor. Once his father died he denied me completely and then he deserted me. He had been given everything, all his life. He took it all and he gave nothing back. He abandoned this family when he was needed. We, in turn, abandoned him to his choice.'

Bridget was glad when Veronica stopped talking. Seen from the older woman's perspective Victor's leaving had indeed been an abandonment. She herself felt that his decision had been that of a young man unable to deal with his mother's betrayal of his dying father. But there was something missing, still. The Victor she'd known would have been able to forgive his mother's need for love.

'Ted Morgan didn't visit over the years?' she asked after a while.

Veronica gave a small shake of her head. 'Too much damage had been done. It was a . . . shock when he arrived before Christmas.' She patted her hair in an oddly self-conscious gesture. 'He didn't say so but I'm sure he was surprised to find me as old as I am. I had lied to him about my age, all those years ago.'

'You're still a fine-looking woman,' Bridget said.

It wasn't a complete lie. Veronica was faded, withered even, but the formal, cold beauty she'd noticed the first day in the garden was as pronounced as ever. The loneliness there Bridget thought she understood too. To have loved and lost Ted Morgan once was bad enough. To have found and lost him again, the second time to the finality of a violent death, was infinitely cruel. This, then, was what Hugo Sweeney had meant when he'd spoken about Veronica having a death wish. Veronica was bereft – and had all the appearances of a woman winding down her affairs.

The room felt smothering, as well as hot. Bridget stood and went back to the window. The evergreens were brooding, the avenue bleak.

'What an awful waste,' she said aloud.

'Yes,' said Veronica in the room behind her. A sense of loss was everywhere between them.

It was several minutes before Veronica, her voice sounding remote, broke the silence. 'I will be taking care of Ted's burial as soon as the police release his body,' she said, 'I would like you to attend at the funeral.' It was a command.

'Of course,' said Bridget.

'You will arrange to go home then, I presume?'

'I would like to go home.'

It was true. She was suddenly lonely, missing her garden, the house, Anna and Fintan, the friends she'd known for a lifetime, the life she'd built with Victor Baldacci over thirty years and which was still there, even if he wasn't. He wasn't here either, she knew that now. Even so, she would leave when she'd done what she came to do, not before.

'Arrangements are being made for your shares. There will be some paperwork—'

'Please hold things for a day or two,' Bridget said. 'I'd like time to think.'

'What's there to think about?' Veronica's voice held a controlled outrage.

'What it will mean,' said Bridget.

It would tie her to the Baldaccis in all sorts of ways. Victor had escaped them. It could be argued that by accepting Veronica's offer she was undoing his life.

'I will give you a day. One day,' said Veronica. 'I intend meeting with my attorney tomorrow morning. You have until then.'

She closed her eyes and, with surprising force, banged three times on the floor with her walking stick. Hugo

Sweeney came instantly through the door, filling Bridget with an uncomfortable image of him hovering on the other side all the time she and Veronica had been talking. He crossed wordlessly to the shutters and closed them so that only the original sliver of light came through. He looked at his watch and then at Bridget.

'Mrs Baldacci needs to sleep now,' he said. 'You'd best be going.'

Bridget went slowly down the stairs. The rest of the house, after Veronica's bedroom, was refreshingly cool. It was silent too, just as it had been when she arrived, not a sound of Eleanor Munro anywhere. She hoped the younger woman was all right and immediately reminded herself that she wasn't her responsibility. Even so, the worry niggled.

In the hallway she stood, uncertain, wanting to be gone, wishing she'd hired a car, hating the trapped, compromised feeling of having no transport. She would walk. To hell with the rain and the distance. A walk, time alone to think, was what she needed. She opened the front door and saw that the rain had stopped.

'It's not a good idea to let the cold, wet air into the house,' Hugo Sweeney came down the stairs and into the hallway. 'I'd be obliged if you would close the door while I get your outdoor garments.'

Bridget closed the door and Hugo, after disappearing off to the end of the hallway for several minutes, reappeared with her coat and scarf.

'Mrs Baldacci's asleep now but I'm not at all pleased with the way things are looking.' His small face was set in tight, disapproving lines.

'She's very upset about Ted Morgan's death.' Bridget tried to read between the tight lines, but got nowhere.

'Indeed she is. Seems to believe she should have known the man was dead. Complete nonsense. She can't be aware of everything that goes on.'

'What did you mean about a death wish?' Bridget took her coat from him and shrugged into it.

'She's sick in herself,' said Hugo.

'The diabetes, you mean?'

'There's that. And there's the loss of heart for the battle. Still, she knows herself what has to be done and she's always been a woman lived by her own lights.' Hugo handed her the scarf. 'You'll be going now then,' he said.

'Is Eleanor Munro around?' Bridget couldn't help herself. She had to know. The niggle had become an irritating nag.

'Miss Munro left early this morning,' said Hugo.

'Left? As in went away? Packed her bags?'

'Any one of those descriptions would fit. She packed her bags, left her room and went away in a cab. I have no idea where. I didn't ask.'

'And you were the only one saw her go?'

'Mrs Baldacci was not abroad at that hour. If Miss Munro hadn't disturbed me in the kitchen, where I was having a bit of breakfast, I wouldn't have been aware of her departure either.'

'What time was this?'

'Not more than a half hour before you arrived yourself.'

Bridget compromised on the walk. She took a cab from the house to the other side of the bridge, then paid off the driver and walked from there. It took her an hour to get to the hotel but she felt invigorated, as if she'd reclaimed something of herself and a freedom.

But she wasn't prepared, at all, to find that Eleanor Munro had moved into the room next to hers at the Hotel Pacific Nights.

Chapter Eleven

There was a note pinned to the door of Bridget's hotel room. She saw the sheet of folded yellow paper as soon as she left the lift and, if the vehicle hadn't already moved on a floor, she would have got back in and moved on herself, gone anywhere it was peaceful, uneventful. She didn't feel like any more news, good, bad or indifferent.

The words on the yellow paper were written in purple ink.

> I'm at the end of the corridor. Come visit me when you get this. You know what they say – if the mountain won't come to Mohammed then Mohammed must come to the mountain.

Eleanor Munro had signed only with a significant E.

The niggle of worry about the younger woman's safety was replaced by a healthy annoyance. This amounted to stalking. But she couldn't be ignored.

Bridget banged loudly with an open palm on the door at the end of the corridor. The act gave her a sense of being in control of things. She knew this was purely illusory but enjoyed the feeling for the minutes she waited for the door to open anyway.

'Well – where have you been? I've been waiting hours.' After a darting, conspiratorial scan of the corridor behind Bridget, Eleanor pulled her into the bedroom. 'I moved in as early as I could, hoping we could have breakfast together but you weren't here and I've been hanging about ever since.'

She dropped Bridget's arm and cleared a chair for her to sit on. It was late afternoon, and still bright outside, but the curtains were tightly closed and the only light came from a reading lamp on the desk. In the shadowy gloom, not unlike the gloom she'd just left in Veronica Baldacci's room, it seemed to Bridget that clothes and towels were strewn everywhere.

Eleanor was wearing a scarlet, kimono-style wrap and her hair was wet. In the air was the dense, muskily herbal smell of cannabis. Bridget would have known it anywhere.

'Tell me where you've been.' Eleanor sat on the bed and watched Bridget's face. She was palely animated in the murky light and puffing on the joint.

'What're you doing here, Eleanor, in this hotel?'

'I told you, in the note. You read it, didn't you?' Eleanor offered the joint to Bridget, who refused. The lie about them being conspirators, a team, had to be nailed somewhere.

'It's a free world,' Bridget stood up, 'and you're free to stay wherever you like. But we are not a team, Eleanor, and I don't want you involving me in everything you do.' She stopped. She'd made the point and hoped it was enough. 'I'm so sorry about Ted Morgan. It's a terrible—'

'You still don't get it, do you?' Eleanor got off the bed and leaned into the mirror, examining her face. What she saw there made her grimace with distaste and sigh.

'Maybe I don't.' Bridget leaned against the wall with her arms folded and watched the other woman in the mirror. 'Or maybe I just can't accept that you and I are in the danger you say we're in from the Baldaccis. I can't accept it because what would be the point?'

'The point,' Eleanor turned to face Bridget, 'is that we

have rights, both of us, and those people do not want to give them to us, to allow anyone in. Ted saw that. Ted was working on Veronica. He was bringing her round to his way of seeing things, which was that the past had to be put right. Ted, for reasons he never did tell me, felt bad about whatever happened when he worked for the Baldaccis. Him feeling like that was one of the reasons he agreed to come to Seattle with me.'

She stopped, pulled on the last of the joint and stubbed it out. 'Now he's dead and you're telling me there's no danger and that we don't need to stick together?'

'I'm just saying that I don't quite see it like that.'

Which was becoming less true every minute. Bridget could see how Ted Morgan could have felt he'd been to blame for Victor's leaving home. Problem was – if Ted hadn't told Eleanor about his affair with Veronica then Bridget didn't feel right about telling her now.

There was a case to be made, however, for telling Eleanor just how successful Ted had been in convincing Veronica to, in some way, atone for wrongs done to Shelley Munro and Victor; even if it had taken Ted's death for Veronica to see things his way.

'What is it?' Eleanor frowned. She'd shifted her position and now, sitting directly in the light from the desk lamp, her face was drawn and distressed and close to tears.

'There's something you should know,' Bridget said, gently. To hell with Veronica's admonitions to secrecy. Bridget hadn't made any promises. 'Ted actually did get through to Veronica. She intends making over an allowance to you.' Bridget paused, wondering briefly about the wisdom of telling all, before plunging ahead. 'I'm to get shares, though I'm not sure I want them.'

'She told you this? Veronica told you this?' Eleanor stood and began to pace.

'Yes. This morning. She said she was doing it for Ted,

that he'd wanted her to do it. To honour him was the phrase she used—'

'But no one else knows, right? And she told you to keep quiet about it?'

'Yes. I'm taking a day to think about it. But look, Eleanor, I think—'

'Don't think, listen.' Eleanor jumped up and began to root convulsively through a black travel bag. 'Veronica's taken unilateral action. It's the way she's always done things but she's not in control anymore and she doesn't even know it. Sure, she has the authority to do it – to do what she wants with her own shares. But the others aren't going to like it and they're going to try to stop it happening, one way or another. Only we're going to be ready for them.'

From the bag she produced a small pistol.

Bridget stared, moved back and told herself the gun wasn't real, that Eleanor was acting out some sort of melo-dramatic joke. Myth and legend and Hollywood all said that every full-blooded American owned a gun but she'd never believed it. She still didn't. Eleanor had no business waving one about. When she felt the door at her back Bridget stopped.

'That's not funny, Eleanor,' she said.

'It's not meant to be,' Eleanor snapped. 'It's going to help me look out for us, for you and me.' She held the gun with dangerous familiarity. 'They're not going to get us the way they got Ted. They're not going to pawn me off with some fucking miserable allowance either. No way.'

'I don't want anything to do with that gun,' Bridget felt for the door handle, 'and I'm getting out of here if you don't put it away – now.'

She was aware she sounded cross and motherly. She couldn't help it; she was terrified. Eleanor heard the motherly tone too and half smiled.

'Relax,' she said. 'It's not loaded. You don't know much about guns, do you?'

'I know nothing at all about them,' said Bridget.

'They're a necessary evil, and we need this pistol. Believe me,' she held and stroked the gun in the palm of her hand, 'I know what I'm doing.'

'It seems to me that all you're doing is looking for trouble.' Bridget was curt. 'I'm not at all convinced we're in danger. Ted Morgan's death was an awful accident, something to do with his reasons for going to stay in that Refuge. It was a truly terrible thing to have happened—'

'But you think I'm going over the top?'

'Yes. No one's going to do anything to harm either you or me. There's no way they'd get away with it. It would draw too much attention to the family and the past and the business. Now, please put the gun away. I don't want to see it and I don't want to know about it.'

'Ok, ok.' Eleanor stuffed the pistol back into the bag. 'It's not a Pershing missile, you know.'

Bridget didn't move from the door. Eleanor straightened up and her voice was harsh when she said, 'You seem to forget, Bridget, that my grandmother disappeared from that house and was never seen again, that my mother had to leave to save her life, that Ted Morgan left and turned up in the Sound, dead.' Her voice shook. 'You may be able to take all of those things on board but I can't overlook them. There's something else you should know. I'll tell you when the time is right. At this moment I get the feeling you're not really ready to trust me.'

'If you know something and you're frightened why don't you go to the police? Why don't you ask them for protection?'

'God, you think everything's so simple and straightforward, don't you? Thing is, I've been in trouble a few times with the cops. Nothing much. A couple of small narcotics offences – caught partying with the wrong people, so to speak. It's better if I do my business here without involving the cops. Ted thought so too . . .' Her frenzied energy fizzled and died as she said the dead man's name and all at once she became forlorn and drab-looking. 'Christ, I'm tired,' she said. 'I'm really tired. I haven't been sleeping in that house. Not since Ted left. I'll be able to sleep here, I know I will. All I need is someone on my side of the divide. That's all I ever needed.'

'Sleep is what you need,' Bridget said. 'Get into bed and give it a try. We'll talk again.'

But not that day, if she could help it. She'd heard enough, didn't want to hear another word. The something Eleanor thought Bridget should know about might be revealed from her bags as a grenade or an automatic rifle, or worse. Eleanor was a mess. Vulnerable, needy, bitter, obsessive and taking God alone knew what by way of drugs. But for all that Bridget couldn't find it in her heart to dismiss or dislike her.

Partly this had to do with her obvious vulnerability, but a larger part, she knew, had to do with how very like Anna she was to look at. There was a lot of Anna too in her single-minded campaign to get what she saw as her Baldacci inheritance. But Anna – confident, bright, achieving Anna – had been surrounded all her life by tender, loving care. Who was to say that Eleanor might not have been the same, or at least more similar than she was, if her life had been different? Eleanor's mother had died just a year ago from an overdose: she must be feeling raw about that too.

In her room Bridget grabbed money and a guidebook before leaving to head for a half decent restaurant she'd spotted several blocks away. Afterwards she went to see the film *Titanic*, which took up several hours and did nothing to raise her spirits. Back in her room she phoned home again and then briefly phoned Eleanor to say goodnight. She slept a full eight hours before the younger woman woke her, at 8 a.m., with a rhythmic knocking on the door and an invitation to breakfast.

Bridget would be glad she had the sleep, and the distancing break from Eleanor Munro.

'Did you tell Veronica you were moving in here?' she asked as they went down in the lift.

'I left a note for her in my room,' said Eleanor. 'She should have got it by now.'

Veronica had got the note all right. They were eating in the small breakfast room, Bridget packing in cereal and muffins and juice, Eleanor managing a couple of strong black coffees, when a po-faced hotel porter arrived at their table.

'There's a cop in the lobby wants to speak to Mrs Baldacci and Miss Munro. That's you two, right?'

'I don't want to talk with any cops.' Eleanor gripped Bridget's arm as they followed the porter. 'It is not a good idea for me to be around the cops. Oh, God, I wish this wasn't happening.'

The cop in the lobby was young and impressively polite.

'I hope you took time to finish your breakfast, ladies.' He was blond and had a wide smile. 'I'm here because Detective Lessig of the West Precinct asked me to call.' He made it sound as if forcing him to intrude on their morning was extreme bad taste on Lessig's part. 'He wants to talk with you, both. I'm to give you a ride to the Precinct.' He paused. 'Right away, he says.' He sighed and shook an apologetic head.

The West Precinct was on the third floor of the Public Safety Building at Third Avenue and James Street. Detective Lessig was waiting for them in a small, bright room filled with files and a couple of desktop computers. There was a Pirelli tyre calendar on the wall, a large photograph of the

Space Needle and Detective Jacklin working on one of the computers. She gave them an indifferent nod.

'Mrs Veronica Baldacci told us you'd moved out of her home,' Detective Lessig said to Eleanor. 'Is there something that discourages guests from staying too long in that house?'

'It's a bit out of town,' Eleanor said cautiously. 'I moved because I wanted to be closer to the centre of things.' She hesitated. 'And to my friend Bridget.'

'You've known each other a while then?'

'Not really. We've got a lot in common though.'

'This won't take long.' Lessig sat on the desk, smiled and stroked his moustache. It was thin but the hairs were impressively long. 'We need to clear up a few points about the late Theodore Morgan. You're both vacationing in Seattle, I understand from Mrs Baldacci senior. In your case, Mrs Baldacci, you've only been here a short while?'

'A little over a week.'

'Which means that you did not, in fact, have contact with Mr Morgan while he was in Seattle?'

'I never at any point in my life met Ted Morgan. I'd never heard of him until about a week ago.'

He nodded and looked away from them through the window. There was a lot of bustling noise from the rest of the building.

'You've been in Seattle a while longer, Miss Munro?'

'Since before Christmas,' Eleanor said.

Detective Lessig turned from the window with a tired smile. 'Our talk here this morning is informal. We won't be requiring statements, yet. That way *we* get everything wrapped up nice and quick and *you* can get back to spending your money in the city.' He picked up and consulted a notebook. 'You are the widow of Victor Baldacci?' he said to Bridget.

'Yes.' Bridget's patience began to wear thin. 'I don't see what my husband's death—'

'Just filling in a picture, Mrs Baldacci, just filling in a picture.' Detective Lessig, interrupting without looking at her, made a note with a black pen. 'You've never been to Seattle before? Never met your late husband's family?' His look was questioning, manner sympathetic.

'No. Victor had severed contact with his family.' She hesitated. 'I came to see for myself what they were like.'

'Understandable.'

He helped himself to a drink, but didn't offer anyone else one.

'Was it your opinion, Mrs Baldacci, that members of the household were upset by Mr Morgan's disappearance?'

'I couldn't really tell . . . Veronica Baldacci was upset . . .' Bridget stopped. 'I don't feel right about this, Detective Lessig. I'd rather not answer questions which involve my giving an opinion.'

Detective Jacklin turned from the keyboard with a loud, resigned groan. 'This could turn into a homicide investigation, ma'am, and we are not taking a statement here, merely looking for your assistance.'

'Homicide? As in murder?' Bridget asked. Beside her Eleanor made an odd, gurgling sound before burying her head in her hands.

'Homicide, as in murder,' Detective Lessig confirmed. 'Further examinations seem to indicate that Theodore Morgan could have been dead before going into the water.' He paused. 'Though a conclusive examination may never be possible—'

'The fact of the head and part of the torso being eaten away,' Detective Jacklin's interruption was crisp, 'is making things difficult, but not impossible.'

Eleanor dropped her hands onto her lap and stared straight ahead. Detective Lessig sighed gently.

'Miss Munro, I'd like you to fill me in on a few points also, if that's possible . . .'

'I'd like a drink of water,' Eleanor said.

Lessig frowned at the water cooler and sighed less gently and looked at the unmoving Detective Jacklin. 'I'll get it myself,' he said.

Detective Jacklin, tapping assiduously on the keyboard, didn't look up as he fiddled with plastic cups. When it looked as if she was also going to ignore Bridget and Eleanor until he'd finished, Bridget asked,

'Does the need for . . . examinations mean you'll be holding onto Mr Morgan's body for a while yet?'

'That's right. Just a little while longer.' Detective Jacklin nodded.

'It's just that I've promised to stay for the funeral,' Bridget said. 'You've no idea when a burial might be possible?'

'Give it a week.' Detective Jacklin turned from the screen to look at Eleanor. 'You came to Seattle with Theodore Morgan?' Her eyes were bored.

'Yes.'

'You were friendly in New York?'

'Yes.'

'What is your connection with the Baldacci family?'

Eleanor, her voice flat and language businesslike, repeated everything she'd already told Bridget. She made no accusations and said nothing about coming to Seattle for her share in the family wealth.

'Why did you and Mr Morgan come to Seattle, Miss Munro?' Detective Jacklin asked when Eleanor had finished, resting her elbows on the desk.

'Ted Morgan read that Victor Baldacci had died. He wanted to come see Veronica Baldacci again. I came with him out of curiosity. I really don't know why he left the Baldacci home and I didn't see him after he did. Why don't you ask Veronica Baldacci about this? She's the one had most contact with him—'

'We tried to this morning,' Detective Lessig, turning with two plastic cups of water, cut across Eleanor. 'She was too unwell to talk with us. We'll be getting to her. And to the rest of the family.'

He handed Eleanor one of the cups and, when Bridget refused the other, drank from it himself.

'We're just about finished here,' said Detective Jacklin.

'Right. Let me ask one more thing.' Detective Lessig turned to Eleanor. 'The last time you saw Theodore Morgan was in the Baldacci home, is that how it was?'

'Yes.'

'We've a small problem needs solving . . .' Detective Jacklin got up. Standing she filled a lot more space than sitting. 'The people at the Bible Mission tell us Mr Morgan took some phone calls. They say he made some too. Did he by any chance call you, Miss Munro, or did you call at any time while he was staying there?'

'No, I didn't. On both counts.'

'Well, that's about it then.' Detective Lessig sighed. 'We're grateful for your help.' He fiddled again with the moustache, making Bridget wonder if it was a new addition to his face. 'Enjoy the rest of your stay in the Emerald City.'

'That's it?' Eleanor said.

'For now,' Detective Lessig opened the door.

Eleanor refused, for both of them, the offer of a police car back to the hotel. Walking along the hectic, early morning streets in the new boots she'd bought for the funeral Mass, Bridget lodged a resigned complaint.

'I would have been glad of that police car to the hotel,' she said.

'I've seen more than enough cops for one morning,' Eleanor was surly.

'You've certainly got a way with the truth when it comes to talking to the police.' Bridget, choosing her words carefully, stopped walking and, catching Eleanor's arm, stopped her too. 'Why did you lie back there? Lie number one: why did you tell that detective you came to Seattle only out of a curiosity to see the family?'

Eleanor turned her head and stared down the street. As she began to speak she walked on. Bridget walked with her, watching her agitated profile as she spoke. It was filled with a rigid, stony anger.

'I told Lessig I came here out of curiosity because once you talk money to the cops they start looking at your life and I don't want them investigating me.' Eleanor hugged herself as she went on, 'They turn up that narcotics violation in New York that's all those Baldaccis need to cut me out for ever. I'm entitled. This is my chance for a new life. All I've got to do is keep my head down.'

'And get what's yours at any cost?' Bridget took Eleanor's arm again as a sudden rush of people threatened to separate them. 'Even denying Ted Morgan?' She stopped and turned the younger woman to face her. When Eleanor tried to free her arm she held on, tight. 'Your second lie back there was when you denied knowing where Ted Morgan went after he left the Baldacci home.'

'They asked if I'd seen him after he left and I didn't, so that was the truth.'

'Stop being so bloody disingenuous.' Bridget shook Eleanor, hard. 'You know what I'm talking about. You spoke to him, you told me so yourself. He phoned you. He told you where he was, gave you the address so as you could go to him if you needed to.'

'I don't have to tell you anything.' Eleanor yanked herself free.

'The fact is, when I phoned to say I was coming to see him he was already gone.' She looked mulish. 'So, I didn't actually *see* him.'

'No, you didn't. But you still lied and you certainly

denied Ted Morgan. If he was . . . dead before going into the water then someone murdered him. You, Eleanor, have information about his last movements which could help the police find the person who did it. Ted Morgan's entitled to have his death accounted for – are you going to help?'

'I can't right now. In a few days I'll tell the police everything, I promise.' Eleanor, anger gone, looked at Bridget from a white, pleading face. 'There's another way of looking at things, you know. Ted wouldn't have wanted me to blow this thing now I'm so close. I just have to hang on, do things my way for another few days. Stick with me, Bridget,' she caught Bridget's hand, 'please, and trust me. Just for a few days more.'

The red, message light was flashing on the phone in Bridget's hotel room. She said a hurried goodbye to Eleanor and closed the door before she could see it. She didn't trust her.

The message was from Thomas. She phoned him back immediately.

'Veronica's not good,' he said, 'and she's been asking to see you. Says there's something she needs to discuss with you.'

Bridget could hear him waiting, wanting to know what possible business she had with Veronica. That Veronica was keeping him in the dark about the shares didn't surprise her. The Baldacci family code, if it had any, was about secrecy and deceit and playing all sides against the middle. On the other hand, maybe Veronica had good reason and maybe it was better not to say anything to Thomas, for now.

'I'll come out to visit her this afternoon,' she said.

'That sounds good,' Thomas said. 'But, uh, I need to ask you to, uh, come alone—'

'Without Eleanor, you mean?'

'Right.' Thomas sounded relieved. 'Veronica doesn't want her around the place.'

Visiting the Baldacci house without Eleanor Munro was a lot easier said than done. She phoned as soon as Bridget finished the call to Thomas and, in spite of Bridget's plea for time alone, arrived at the bedroom door ten minutes later.

'Let's go eat,' she said, 'I never ate at breakfast. I'm starving.'

'I don't want to.' Bridget knew she sounded petulant. Anna sometimes had the same effect on her, usually when she tried to organize Bridget's life, as Eleanor was doing now.

'You going to stay in this room all day?' Eleanor looked disdainfully at the repro desk and unmade bed.

'I thought I'd go to see *Titanic* in the cinema. Alone. I want a break from all that's been happening.'

How easily the lie came, how quickly she was fitting herself to the Baldacci way of doing things, how lucky she'd seen the film already and could give an account of it if necessary.

'I've seen it,' said Eleanor. 'You won't enjoy it. Unrealistic love story between an actor who's still a boy and looks it and an actress who looks like a full-blooded woman. I'd never have written a romantic coupling so fundamentally unsexy myself. Why don't you and me go to—'

'I want to see *Titanic*. Alone.'

'Fine. Waste an afternoon. It's your life. If watery special effects and simpering boys are your thing then go ahead, go—'

'Oh, shut up, Eleanor,' Bridget said.

Eleanor sniffed, tossed her hair back and turned on her heel. 'I'll be in my room,' she said. It was another Anna-like performance.

*

Thomas opened the door to Bridget, his usual benign courtesy blighted by a distracted air.

'Good of you to come, especially in the circumstances.'

He led her to the dining room where he stood looking out a window and talking over his shoulder in quick, short sentences.

'Veronica's clearly not well. Magdalena's – oh, let's not talk about Magdalena. I'm worried about Veronica. I don't like her being on her own. She won't hear of a nurse. There's Hugo . . .' He coughed. 'I dislike being away from business during the day, from the office I mean. I worry things will collapse without me, which they won't, of course.' He coughed again. 'Couldn't get either of my offspring to come over here when their grandmother called. Don't get me wrong. They're good kids,' he sounded defensive, 'especially Lindsay.' He gave Bridget an apologetic look. 'She puts so much damn time into the business.'

He made an imperceptible adjustment to the curtain and gave another throat-clearing cough.

'Veronica's waiting for you,' he said.

'How is she, really?'

'Well . . . she's . . .'

Thomas looked for a minute in silence at the straggling line of conifers along the avenue. He looked very neat in his grey suit and silver-grey tie.

'Her fire seems to have gone out. She's acting like . . . her mind was going. Only thing she seems sure about it that she wants to talk to you.' He turned, leaned forward a little. 'Please remember Bridget, that she is old. And powerless.'

He smiled. It was not a nice smile.

Veronica's bedroom was, if anything, murkier than it had been the day before. She was sitting in the same chair by the window, staring through the same barely opened shutter at the falling darkness outside. Bridget sat again in the chair opposite and looked as closely as the gloom would allow at the older woman. Veronica seemed to her much the same as she had at yesterday's visit, even to the glass of whiskey cradled in her lap. She was pale and freshly made-up and wearing the same high-necked, pearl-buttoned dress. The room was still hot but there was an additional something. Bridget tried without success to pin it down. Thomas's smile had unnerved her.

'Have you thought about what I said?' Veronica demanded after a while.

'I have,' said Bridget.

There was a smell, that was what was different and additional to the day before. It was of nail-varnish remover, or at least of something with a strong acetone base. Veronica, along with making up her face, obviously manicured her nails on a daily basis. The smell was oddly pervasive.

'Well?' Veronica was querulous.

'I don't want the shares, Veronica, though I appreciate the offer.' Bridget hesitated, then leaned forward and touched Veronica's arm briefly. 'Whatever way I say this will sound ungracious and rude. The truth is that I don't want to be involved with this family on an ongoing basis. It would be a denial of Victor, of his decision to make a life apart for himself and his children . . . and me.' She took a breath, let it out. 'I couldn't do that to him. I don't want to.'

Veronica's silence crackled in the room for several minutes.

To break it, Bridget said, 'I will keep in touch, though. I will write.'

By the time she left she would know everything so an occasional letter, on her terms, would not be a betrayal of Victor.

'You are telling me that you will not accept my gift?'

In the gloom, Veronica turned her head toward Bridget. Her face appeared to be still and expressionless.

'I don't want the shares, Veronica. I don't want to be involved in the family business.'

'You are a fool. I might have known that only a fool would have married Victor Baldacci.' Veronica made a harsh sound which came close to being a laugh. 'I have been saddled with a fool and a madwoman, both of them alive and troublesome while a good man like Ted Morgan lies dead and rotting.'

She stopped. Bridget said nothing. Grief needed its outings, however irrational, she knew that. After a few minutes she said, firmly,

'You've put me in an awkward position, Veronica, asking me not to discuss your plans for shares and an allowance for Eleanor with the family, with Thomas and Lindsay, in particular. These things concern them too.'

Maybe Thomas already knew. Maybe that was what he meant when he said Veronica was powerless.

'They do not. They will know about my plans when they need to know. How I choose to distribute my majority shares is my own affair. I hold control until the day I die and I am not dead. Yet.' Veronica stopped, fingering the buttons at the neck of her dress as if too hot. 'I will also decide on the shape the company will take after I am gone.' She stopped again and frowned as if clearing her thoughts. 'You have been hasty. You are confused by all you have found here and you are not, in my opinion, capable of making a clear decision. I want you to give my offer some more thought.' She placed her elbow on the arm of the chair and rested her face in the palm of her hand and it seemed to Bridget that she smiled. Or maybe it was a grimace. The acetone smell was quite strong and her nails looked newly shining. 'It is not so easy to walk away, Bridget. It is not an easy thing to do at all. You will be glad, in time, for what I've done. You will thank me, in time.'

'How are you feeling?' Bridget asked.

'Tired . . .' Veronica sipped her drink.

'Maybe you should get into bed,' Bridget suggested.

'Don't patronize me,' Veronica snapped. 'I will get in bed when the time comes and not before.' She nodded toward the shutters. 'You might close those for me, if you please. The wind forecast by the meteorologists is blowing up the avenue. I've seen enough of it.'

Bridget, after a look at the icy rain whirling in the gathering winds outside, saw the older woman's point and closed the shutters.

'There's snow promised across the Cascades and for the southern Washington Cascades,' Veronica sounded dreamy. 'I haven't been in any of those mountains since I went with my father as a girl.'

'Seems a shame, when they're so close,' said Bridget.

'My son-in-law tells me your hotel is small, noisy. The description,' she held up a hand as Bridget began a protest born of a perverse loyalty to the Pacific Nights, 'is my daughter's but Thomas nevertheless thinks it would be a fine thing if you stayed the night here, with me. He is being pragmatic, of course. He has no desire to spend the night with me himself, my grandchildren are too busy, my daughter, his wife, is drunk. So you, Bridget Baldacci, are being used. They merely want you to act as watchdog for the night.'

'I'll stay if you need me to,' Bridget said, 'but what about Hugo?'

'Hugo is about, somewhere.' Veronica waved vague fingers and her voice developed an unpleasantly wheedling note, 'You can tell me about your children. My grandchildren.'

'I'll stay a while,' said Bridget, 'but first I need to make a phone call.'

Thomas, more obviously anxious than before, was

waiting for her downstairs. Hugo Sweeney hovered within earshot as they spoke.

'I'm glad you're staying,' Thomas said when she told him. He looked it. 'You'll have seen by now how she is. It's a ludicrous situation, you having to . . .' he trailed off. 'I'll get you a drink. Veronica may pull out of this melancholy, or whatever it is. She's gone down before and recovered, Phoenix-like. She's immortal, in her own way. If you could just stay until she sleeps . . .' He hesitated, then said, 'Or even the night?'

'I'll do that. I'll stay the night.'

When she asked for a phone Thomas led her to one in Veronica's small library. Bridget didn't even try to fathom her own reluctance to tell him she wanted to let Eleanor know where she would be spending the night, she put it down to an inability to trust anyone, even Thomas.

'Take all the time you want.' He smiled, closing the door discreetly after him.

There was no reply from Eleanor's room and when Bridget checked with the reception the woman there was adamant.

'Miss Munro is not in her room,' she said. 'She went out a couple of hours ago. I saw her go myself.'

'Did she say when she would be coming back?'

'That is not the sort of thing we ask our guests.'

'Was she alone?'

'She seemed to be, yes.' Frosty didn't describe her tones.

'Put me through to Miss Munro's voicemail, please,' Bridget said.

She left a message asking Eleanor to phone her at the Baldacci house when she got in. That way she would at least know when she was safely back in the hotel.

Chapter Twelve

Thomas was waiting for Bridget when she got back to the hallway. He took her hand for a minute, saying nothing, looking very much like a man wishing he were elsewhere.

'I appreciate all that you're doing for us.' He dropped her hand and rubbed her arm in an awkwardly appreciative gesture. 'Staying here tonight – well, it's a big help in the present situation.'

'I wasn't exactly turning down dinner invitations,' said Bridget and wished she hadn't when Thomas blinked and looked startled.

'You could have been invited somewhere else?' He stared at her. 'You have friends in Seattle?'

'No, I don't. Unfortunately.'

All at once she would have given anything to have someone to phone, to have a link to life outside this house. Even Eleanor had gone missing. No one in the world knew she was here, except the Baldaccis. Thomas's relief that she'd agreed to stay was palpable, she'd wanted to stay herself so why, now, was she feeling manipulated? As if she'd been set up?

Thomas reached for an overcoat lying across a heavy, wood-carved armchair.

'Would it be all right with you if I left right away? I've been out of my office a lot lately and one or two things need attending to.'

He shrugged into the coat. His head, buried in the

collar, looked remarkably small. He looked slightly lost and she warmed to him all over again.

'No need for you to stay.' She smiled. 'I presume Hugo is around if I need anything?'

'Hugo is here, yes.'

Thomas buttoned the coat neatly and carefully. A man used to looking after himself, Bridget thought; not much chance that Magdalena had ever mothered him.

'He'll get you whatever you want.' He stood with his hands by his sides. 'This is not the ideal way to spend your vacation,' he said, 'but it's certainly a way of getting to know your late husband's mother.'

'How ill do you think she really is?' Bridget asked.

'I've seen her like this before.' Thomas took his gloves from his pocket. 'It's as if her spirit just goes right down. Understandable, when you know about the rough times she's had. Ted Morgan dying the way he did . . .' He pulled on the gloves, smoothing the fingers carefully. 'She'll come round. She always does.'

There it was again. The family belief in Veronica's immortality. She's eighty-two, Bridget wanted to say, she mightn't 'come round', she could very well die.

'As long as I've known her,' Thomas went on, 'she's been independent in all things. Like I said earlier, she's refused the doctor, says she won't let him near her. Isn't that right, Hugo?'

'She's quite adamant.' Hugo Sweeney, appearing from the end of the hallway, had clearly been there all the time. 'Her diabetes is controlled and there's no moving her on the matter of seeing a doctor.'

With small, busy steps he walked past them to open the front door. He stood there with his back to them.

Thomas, unexpectedly, leaned forward and kissed Bridget lightly on the cheek. 'As with everything else in her life Veronica will not die until *she* decides,' he spoke close to her ear. 'Believe me, Bridget, I would not leave you here if I thought there was anything seriously the matter. Hugo was wrong to think she has a death wish. He realizes that now. That sort of thinking comes from being too close to her – and Hugo's always been close to Veronica.'

He stepped away and handed Bridget a card. 'My number, our home number too, Magdalena's and mine, in case you need us.' He left then, quickly, Hugo Sweeney stepping aside to let him through the front door.

Outside, where the sky above the trees was unrepentantly sullen, an early frost had settled on the roof of Thomas's waiting car.

'Good night.' Bridget waved the card as he slipped into the driving seat. Thomas, head down, didn't respond. She waited until the car's tail lights disappeared round the bend in the avenue before turning to face Hugo.

'Looks like you're stuck with me for the night.' She gave him a wry grin.

'It's looking that way,' Hugo, not disposed to be humoured, was unsmiling, 'so we'd best put up with one another. I'll get you a drink. Coffee or tea?'

'I'll have a gin Martini,' said Bridget. She needed it.

'I'll bring it to you in the sitting room,' Hugo said. 'Mrs Baldacci's sleeping at the moment so there's no good you going up to her right now.'

He was a long time getting the drink. Bridget studied the paintings and the furniture in the big room and spent a while at the window looking at the darkened Christmas tree. When the silence and the claustrophobia became too much she wandered out and into the hallway. Hugo's voice, low and confidential, came from behind the half-open door of a nearby room. Bridget hesitated, wondering if Veronica had come downstairs, and was about to push open the door when Hugo said goodbye and hung up a telephone.

Deciding on discretion as the better part of valour she slipped back into the sitting room.

When Hugo reappeared minutes later he was carrying a tray on which he'd arranged what amounted to afternoon tea. Along with a silver teapot there was a selection of miniature sandwiches, pastries, milk and sugar.

'Looks good.'

Bridget searched hopefully for her drink as Hugo fussed and laid the contents of the tray out on a table. There was no gin Martini.

'It is always my task to prepare tea in the afternoon for Mrs Baldacci. She wasn't up to taking it today and there's no point in letting good food go to waste.' He poured tea into a delicate pink china cup. 'Milk? Sugar?' He placed a chair beside the table. 'I'll leave you to it then.'

Bridget sat on the chair and eyed the food. She didn't want sandwiches and she certainly didn't feel like pastries. A gin Martini was what she felt like. She sipped the tea.

'Why don't you get another cup and join me?' she said to the still hovering Hugo.

He shook his head. 'I'm too old a dog for new tricks. It's my custom to eat on my own.' He moved the plate of sandwiches closer to her on the table. 'I was talking to Father Bob Matthews on the phone just now. You'll have heard me when you were out in the hallway?'

'I heard you on the phone, yes,' said Bridget, 'though not what you were saying or who you were talking to, obviously.'

The man missed nothing. He was watching her now.

He said, 'You'll remember Bob Matthews from the memorial Mass?'

'Yes, of course.'

'Well, he's on his way over here now.' Hugo consulted a pocket watch. 'Should arrive in about fifteen minutes.'

'An official or social visit?' Bridget tried and failed to catch Hugo's eye. Could Veronica have agreed to the last rites? Or was Hugo organizing a priestly blessing on his own initiative?

'A social visit,' said Hugo. He went on hovering.

'If there's something you want to say, Hugo, then for God's sake say it,' Bridget said briskly, putting down the tea cup.

'You don't want the sandwiches then?' Hugo nodded at the plate. 'Nor the pastries? More tea?'

'No. Thank you.'

'Well, then . . .'

Hugo locked his hands behind his back and began to rock on his heels.

'I'll be brief about what it is I want to say. It's this: for the past while I've been wanting to put a few things in order around here. I was the one sent you the letter you'll have found in your hotel room when you arrived. I thought it would be best if you didn't stay long in Seattle, didn't add to the trouble brewing here.' He paused. 'I was thinking along the lines of maybe bringing about a bit of damage limitation.' He stopped rocking on his heels long enough to align a pair of silver candlesticks on an inlaid table beside him. 'You can always tell when Mrs Baldacci's not around,' he muttered, 'place goes to the dogs.' He looked critically around the room before beginning to rock on his heels again. 'I was sure you'd be the powder which would ignite the situation but I was wrong. I see now that you weren't really the one who was going to do that. Not on your own anyway.'

'What situation? What trouble?'

So Hugo had sent the letter. Bridget was surprised how easily, and with what small degree of shock, she accepted this. Of course he'd sent it. Hugo was one of those insidiously manipulative people who were always trying to control things.

She looked at him steadily while, with obvious care, he put together the words to answer her question.

'I'll tell you something of my story,' he said at last. 'It'll explain a lot of things to you. Bob Matthews has other things to tell you when he gets here. Between the two histories you can make up your own mind about things.'

'Why not?' Bridget was curt and, all at once, feeling bitter. 'I've been given the other versions of family events. Why not yours, why not Father Matthews'? Go ahead.'

Hugo gave a quick, small shrug and sat, with fastidious care, on a spindle-backed Windsor chair.

'You, no doubt, see a controlling old woman when you look at Veronica Baldacci,' he began. 'I see a beautiful woman, in the prime of her early middle years. I always will. That's my cross and that's my salvation. That was the age she was, with the looks of a Grace Kelly, when she rescued me from a life that would have surely ended in jail or the gutter, and that's the simple truth of it.' He stopped and met Bridget's eyes, briefly. 'It's not too fanciful to say that she has been my mother, my wife, my sister, my friend ... my redemption.' He stopped again, this time to spread his hands. 'And there you have it.'

'There I have what?' Bridget's patience gave out. 'You've got a great turn of phrase, Hugo, and you've got a sad story to tell. But so what if Veronica rescued you from a bad situation and you've lived here, worked for and been beholden to her ever since? That doesn't tell me anything much about what's going on here today. You've given me the bones of your story. Now,' Bridget stabbed a finger at him, 'give me the flesh.'

'I don't at all care for your metaphors,' Hugo said huffily. 'I'm inclined to leave it to yourself to put two and two together—'

'You do that and I'm going up to drag the story out of the priest – out of Veronica if I have to!'

'You don't need to know—'

'I'll decide what I need to know from now on,' Bridget snapped.

Hugo, with a long, raspy sigh, rested his narrow, veined hands on his knees.

'I've never put my story into words before,' he said, 'so

you'll have to bear with me while I tell it my own way now. I was in serious trouble with the law when Veronica Baldacci took me in. I arrived in Boston from Cork and from day one got myself in with the same sort of company I'd left behind me.' He gave a small, irritated shrug of his shoulders. 'I got out of Boston with the cops on my tail about some matters involving thieving and arson and the like. I was staying in a boarding house close to Our Lady of Lourdes when I got myself into another spot of bother. Bob Matthews, who was a young curate there at the time, talked the parishioner I'd robbed into not pressing charges. I gave back the money and I talked to the priest. I hadn't an intention in the world of staying on the straight and narrow but in the church with him that day I met Veronica Baldacci.' His expression was tired and sour. 'I was a young man, still. Bob Matthews was a young man too, about my own age, and he was bent on a mission to save souls. He set about saving mine.' He gave a thin laugh. 'It was a bit late for that, but when he got Veronica Baldacci to give me a job looking after the gardens he at least saved me from jail.'

Bridget nibbled on one of the sandwiches. In the dry heat of the room it had begun to harden and go stale. 'Frank Baldacci was still alive when you first came here then?' she said.

'He was.'

'And my – Victor was still living here too?'

'Victor Baldacci was in his late teens.'

'Was he very unhappy?'

'I wouldn't have called him a happy young man. He didn't confide in me. I didn't think a lot about him.'

'Do you know why he left?'

'I do. And so do you. Mrs Baldacci's already told you the reason why . . .' His voice tailed off and he looked, for a minute, both very old and very sad.

'Tell me,' Bridget said changing the subject, 'what made you give up a life of crime to work as a gardener?'

Hugo Sweeney contemplated the tips of his shoes and spoke with dispassionate fervour.

'Love. You could say it was love turned me around and you wouldn't be far wrong. When Veronica Baldacci stood in front of me and said she was of Irish stock and would I look after her gardens, it never occurred to me to refuse her.'

He folded his arms and leaned back and looked at Bridget. He seemed to her to have grown smaller in the days since she'd met him.

'What I was thinking about was that I would hide out here for a few months and then be on my way. Well, the months stretched on and I got to like the gardening and the day came when I didn't know how to leave either the gardens or the woman.' He paused. 'Of course I was a drinker then and the drink is a great man for dulling the feelings. There was never any shortage of drink around here.

'My health went and things got to a stage where it was easier to stay than to go. It was only as I grew older, and the drinking got less, that I was able to face the reasons I'd stayed and the feelings I had for her. She knows, of course. She's always known, from the first day, and she's used it. She needed someone she could trust in this house and she got someone in me. She had a power over men, in the way that icy women have. I never wanted her the way other men did, and that's the truth. I wanted only to be where she was.' With an air of finality, he said, 'So now you know.'

Bridget could think of nothing to say. Or do. She sat in silence with Hugo Sweeney in the vast room for long minutes, the emotions and loneliness of the story just told resonating about them.

When sounds came of a car coming up the avenue, and its lights shone across the closed curtains, she broke the silence.

165

'You knew everything that was going on in this house, didn't you, Hugo?'

Hugo Sweeney didn't answer, just shook his head slightly from side to side, the colour of his face almost exactly matching the still, cold grey of his eyes.

'You knew about Shelley and Frank, about Grace Munro.' Bridget made her voice firm. 'What happened to Grace?'

'All history, but not my history,' Hugo said. 'There's no good to be served going back over things that're dead and done with.'

'What about Ted Morgan? He was a part of that history but he came back and—'

Bridget stopped. Dead and done with, about described what had happened to poor Ted Morgan.

'Ted Morgan's part in all of this is something you need to know about.' Hugo stood and moved quickly across the room as the front-door bell chimed. 'The priest will tell you about him. He's the one with the first-hand information.'

While Hugo attended to the priest's arrival, taking his coat and explaining that Veronica was still sleeping, Bridget found a phone and called the Hotel Pacific Nights. There was still no answer from Eleanor Munro's room. The receptionist, when she got her on the phone, was disinterested.

'Miss Munro has not returned,' she said, 'would you care to leave a message on her voicemail?'

Bridget didn't. A message wouldn't adequately explain what she was doing in the Baldacci home. She tried to ignore a nagging unease about Eleanor's whereabouts as she put the phone down and went to greet the priest.

He was waiting for her in the hallway, the rosy skin of his choirboy's face stiff and anxious-looking. A benign, practised smile split his cheeks as she came towards him. Hugo was disappearing quickly up the stairs.

'Keeping well, I hope?' The priest shook Bridget's hand formally. 'It's kind of you to stay. Mrs Baldacci is far too often on her own in this house. I have prayed that she be sent company.' He looked around the hallway as if expecting a legion of angels to appear. 'It would appear that God has listened.' He smiled hopefully.

'I am only staying for one night. You will need to begin praying again tomorrow. Surely Magdalena or Veronica's grandchildren—'

'Busy people, all of them.' The priest, interrupting, waved a gently dismissive hand. 'It must also be said, however, that Veronica can be a difficult woman.' He fell silent, the smile fixed on his face.

'Hugo's been talking to me,' Bridget said carefully. 'You've known each other a long time, it seems. That there are things you might explain to me . . .' Bridget waited.

'Call me Bob,' the priest said.

'Bob. Please tell me what's going on. I need to know.'

The priest clasped his hands in front of him and studied them. 'I understand. Hugo has been talking to me too. He thinks you should know what was happening with Ted Morgan before he died. I guess you should.' He pursed his lips. 'What I am about to tell you is confidential.'

'Of course,' Bridget said. But this was not a confessional and she would not be bound with oaths. There were too many secrets which needed to be outed.

She was aware, as the priest began to talk, of Hugo Sweeney coming back into the hallway.

'Mrs Baldacci wanted to marry Ted Morgan.' Bob Matthews shook his head. 'She wanted, she said, to put right their relationship of years before. Also, she wanted a companion and she trusted Mr Morgan. I was to marry them.'

'What did Ted Morgan want?'

'Primarily, not to offend Mrs Baldacci. He said he wanted to put the past to rights but wasn't sure that marriage was the way to do it. He left this house to have time alone to think things through.'

'Who else knew this?' Bridget said.

'I don't know. Mrs Baldacci didn't intend telling the family until everything had been settled. Things were by no means settled when Mr Morgan disappeared – died.'

Bridget took a deep breath. 'Do you think Ted Morgan's death was in any way connected with Veronica's marriage proposal?' She stopped, thought quickly and went on, 'Could it have had to do with someone not wanting him in the family? Resenting his influence with Veronica?' Possibilities piled up in her head. 'With fears that he would outlive Veronica, have too much control—'

'Mine is not to judge,' said the priest.

'Oh, for Christ's sake,' Bridget exploded, 'yours is to help where you can, surely. And I need help here.' She looked the priest full in the face. 'I need to know because I am spending the night in this house. I need to be sure I'll be safe. Who's to say I'm not resented in the same way? Now tell me.'

'I have thought long and hard,' Father Matthews pressed the palms of his hands together in a pleading gesture, 'and the most I can say, even to myself, is that there's a possibility his death may be connected to family fears such as you describe. I do know,' the choirboy face sagged, 'that Ted Morgan was uneasy about things. He told me so. "This plan of Veronica's is not welcome within the family" was how he put it. I said to him that it would be a strange family which would welcome the matriarch taking a husband at eighty-two years of age. He said . . .' the priest paused, frowning as he tried to remember exactly the words spoken to him, 'that the Baldacci family was stronger than most and that he was trying to talk Veronica out of the idea of the marriage. He left this house the next day. I did not see him again.'

'Did Veronica know how he felt?'

'If she did she said nothing to me about it.'

'Did you talk about any of this to the police?'

The priest cleared his throat and shook his head. A nerve twitched at the side of his eye and he raised a hand to stop it.

'Things are not as simple in this country as—'

'They are not simple in Ireland either. Why didn't you tell all of this to the police?'

'You have to understand,' he moistened his lips, 'that Veronica Baldacci has been good to Our Lady of Lourdes. She has donated generously for many, many years.' His expression pleaded for understanding. There was fear in it too. 'She saw to it too that I was given Our Lady of Lourdes when my time came to be made a parish priest.' He squared his shoulders. 'Her secrets are safe with me.'

Bridget stared at him, putting the pieces of what he'd told her together out loud. 'You're obligated to Veronica . . . you know about things which happened in the past . . . you're afraid they might come out in an investigation . . .' She took a deep breath and let it out again. 'So you didn't go to the police because you're protecting Veronica's secrets.'

'We're both of us, Father Matthews and myself, beholden to Veronica Baldacci,' Hugo said. 'She's saying now that she wants to see the two of you. You first, Father.'

Bridget, waiting for the priest and Hugo to return, paced twitchily between the hallway and dining room. The urge to tear upstairs and be a part of what was going on was a physical thing.

But Veronica was old and not well and the two men in her room with her were old too and, in the priest's case at least, frightened.

Father Matthews didn't stay long. In less than ten minutes by Bridget's watch she heard him on the stairs again with Hugo, his voice low and insistent. Hugo, except for the barest of monosyllables, was silent. Bridget stood at the bottom of the stairs waiting for them.

'I'll be back in the morning,' Father Matthews spoke hurriedly from the bottom step. 'She's asked me to visit again.' He looked panicky as Hugo left them. 'It's a good thing you're staying the night.' He didn't look at Bridget.

Hugo reappeared with the priest's coat and together, pointedly ignoring Bridget, they walked to the front door. When he had closed it Hugo turned to Bridget.

'She'll see you now,' he said. 'You can go on up yourself. I've things to be doing down here.'

Veronica was sitting in bed with a silver-grey shawl around her shoulders. She had loosened her hair so that it lay yellowy gold on the pillow. Her tightly stretched skin seemed held together by the glue of a fresh make-up job and she smelled strongly of a sweet, musky smelling scent. The room itself still smelled of acetone.

'How are you feeling?' Bridget said.

Veronica ignored the question. 'You've been talking to the priest?'

'Yes. And to Hugo.' Bridget stood at the end of the bed. 'You'd planned to marry Ted Morgan.'

'I would most definitely have married Ted, had he been allowed to live. I'm old.' She spread, and looked at, her hands on the white of the bedcover. The rings, grotesquely shining, sat just below the knuckles. 'I am often alone and I don't care for it. Ted and I understood one another.' She folded her hands and the rings, even more grotesquely, bunched together. 'I've asked Hugo to make up a bed in the room across the corridor. It was your husband's room as a boy.'

Bridget held a breath until she was reasonably sure the sudden, shaky feeling had passed.

'Thank you, Veronica,' she said, 'that was thoughtful.'

Victor's mother nodded. 'I wish to sleep now. You should do so too.' She reached toward a bell in the wall by the bed.

'Hugo will show you to your room.' She smiled. The effort at agreeableness seemed to Bridget both sad and cynical. 'Sleep well.'

'Thank you.'

Bridget stood and put a hand over Veronica's where it was poised on the bell.

'There's no need to call Hugo. I'll make my own way to Victor's room.'

It was not a big room. The dull green of the walls were splattered with faded squares and rectangles where, long ago, pictures, or posters, had hung. The wardrobe and drawers were empty and the brown wool cover on the single bed hadn't been turned down. There wasn't an echo of Victor anywhere in his room. Even so, the white lawn nightdress lying across the bed looked out of place. When Bridget lifted it from the pillow to her face it had a sweet, musky smell.

In bed Bridget coaxed and pounded the single pillow until she found a way of lying that was bearable. For a long time she tried to imagine the teenage boy who'd become the man she'd married. It was enough to visualize him; he would have been dark-eyed and bonily thin. Trying to make sense of how he must have felt about the loveless cruelties of the family he'd grown up in was more difficult.

Around her the old house was silent, the wind beyond the shuttered window a small rustle of sound. Had Victor lain in a silence like this and heard Ted Morgan with his mother in his father's bed across the corridor? Had he heard his father too, engaged in incestuous couplings with his half-sister Shelley Munro?

Listening as the house whispered its sad horrors she cried a little, for herself, for the injustice Victor had done her by not trusting her with his secrets.

After a while she slept, but restlessly and for only a short time before the rustling sounds awoke her.

They had become louder and smotheringly close . . .

Chapter Thirteen

Veronica Baldacci's silky grey shawl brushed gently over Bridget's face.

'Wake up, Bridget Baldacci, I want to talk with you.' The old woman's bony fingers were on her shoulder, shaking her. 'Wake up . . .'

'Bridget, fully conscious, pulled away from the stifling effect of the silk on her face and sat up. Even then she could smell, rather than see, Veronica; the familiar smell of acetone mingling with the musky perfume.

'What is it? What's wrong?' Bridget pressed herself against the wall. Veronica was too close; she could feel the dryness of her, a sense of her withering.

'I am restless. I cannot sleep,' Veronica's voice was disembodied, somehow apart from the slightly weaving rest of her. 'I cannot talk to Hugo. He is not the kind of person one talks to. But you are here and will have to do.'

Bridget could see her more clearly now, hair floating loose on either side of the pale shape that was her face.

'I'll turn on the light . . .' she began.

'No!' Veronica hissed the command. 'There is enough natural light for our purposes.' She lifted her walking cane and pointed. 'I want you to open the shutters. The worst of the night's dark has passed and there's a moon, of sorts.' Her laugh was like glass splintering. 'We will talk by its light.'

She sat in an armchair not far from the bed and waited while Bridget opened the shutters.

For just a minute after she'd done so, watching the wild sky and fitful moon, Bridget stood and gathered her thoughts. Then the armchair in the room behind her creaked impatiently and she went back to the bed, pulled the covers around her and sat facing her mother-in-law. The moon, suddenly free of the clouds, spilled into the room and by its light Veronica's mouth became a purple slash, her eyes dark sockets in a skull.

Hugo Sweeney knocked sharply on the open door.

'I heard movement,' he said, 'so I thought you might like some sweet tea.' He came into the room with a tray and spoke directly to Bridget. 'You probably need a cup, after being woken up like that.'

He ignored Veronica as he put the tray on the bedside table, poured and handed Bridget a cup.

'You needn't offer me any of that,' Veronica said dismissively.

'I wasn't going to.' Hugo sniffed. 'You've got your drink.'

Bridget took the tea gratefully and smiled at Hugo as he left.

'Tell me about your children,' Veronica said.

'They're children no longer.'

Bridget pulled the bedclothes more tightly about her as a sudden and unexpected flurry of loss went through her for the time when Fintan and Anna had been small and needy and the world had had a focus.

'Fintan is twenty-five, Anna twenty-eight. Fintan is a sculptor and lives in the west of Ireland. Anna is in law and very like her father.' And she missed them, all at once and with an intensity that stopped her breath.

'Go on.' Veronica was impatient.

'Anna looks astonishingly like Eleanor,' Bridget was off-hand, 'even down to some mannerisms. She's got the same hair, same eyes . . .'

'But not, I hope, the same craziness.' Veronica's snappiness lacked energy. 'It would indeed be a tragedy if your daughter were inflicted with a similar insanity. Eleanor Munro is a dangerous woman. Stay away from her.'

'She's a damaged person,' said Bridget, 'of more danger to herself than anyone else.' She paused. 'I feel sorry for her. In a way I even like her.'

'Appalling judgement on your part.' Veronica rapped the floor with her walking cane. 'She's unstable and she's an operator and you,' she lifted and pointed the cane, 'are a fool to be taken in by her. But that,' the cane jabbed, 'is your problem. You chose to come here on your voyage of discovery and you must live with the consequences. I have done what I had to do and my conscience is clear where you are concerned. You have refused my offer of shares but . . .'

Her voice tailed off and she shrugged. When she spoke again her voice was less uneven.

'You meet me at the end of my life. I am grotesque.'

The word, as she said it, had a plaintive edge. It was as if she could see how, with the moonlight on her thin, thin limbs, her cavernous eyes and death-pale skin, she was a parody of faded beauty.

'I was not always so . . . physically feeble.' Her voice became dreamy. 'I want a good death. I'm not sure what happens after I go, in spite of all the church has told me and in spite of the faith of the good Father Matthews. I've always suspected that when we die, we die, and there is nothing else.'

She paused, seeming to lose the thread of what she was saying. After a minute she shook herself, frowning, and went on.

'But I fear I have been a daylight atheist. Now that the light is dying, I want my fears to be wrong. Now I want there to be somewhere else and for Ted to be waiting there for me. Do you hope to meet with Victor again?'

Bridget stared at her. 'I don't know. Maybe,' she said eventually.

'I don't want to live anymore.' Veronica didn't seem to hear her. 'I have given up on nothing in my life. I am not giving up now either. It is simply that there is no longer anything to give up, nothing to live for. My life has run its course. I want to move on to whatever's next.'

'There is your family,' said Bridget, 'they are something to live for—'

'Don't be ridiculous.'

'You make it sound as if death is imminent.' Bridget took a couple of deep breaths, trying to keep the panic in her stomach at bay. The room was beginning to seem like a grey tunnel with Veronica at the end of it. If she had really decided to die, if all of this wasn't simply histrionics and some game she was playing, then Bridget didn't want to be a part of that death.

'Death is always imminent,' said Veronica, 'yours, mine, everyone's.'

She plucked at the shawl around her shoulders and Bridget felt an all-consuming chill. She had seen that same fretful fingering before: her mother had plucked in just such a way as she lay dying in a hospital bed.

'We have lived with a lot of secrets in this family,' Veronica's voice was low but the words were clear enough. 'It was how we functioned. Every family has its way of being. Every family has secrets. The family, by its nature, is a secretive institution. I'm sure our secrets were no more shameful than most.'

'You're overtired,' said Bridget, 'I'll take you back to your room.'

She slipped from the bed and stood beside Veronica's chair. She felt desperately in need of sleep herself. Even her legs felt leaden. She'd probably got out of bed too quickly, been sitting in the same position too long.

'I'm tired myself,' she said.

'I was glad when Frank became ill,' Veronica again seemed not to have heard her, 'glad when he became a dumb, useless thing in the bed, glad to see the end of him as a person.'

She spoke in sighing pauses, hands plucking all the time at the shawl as if it were a great weight against her body.

'I was happy to be loved by Ted Morgan.'

She brushed uncertain fingers across her face, as if there was a cobweb there. Or a tear.

'Leave me,' she said and her voice was stronger. 'Go to my room and ring for Hugo. Tell him I would like to be helped back to my room.'

'You need to see a doctor.'

Bridget's tongue felt thick, her mind foggy as it tried to deal with what she knew was going on.

'Give me a number and I'll call her . . . him . . .'

'I will send for him myself,' Veronica said, 'in the morning.'

'Now . . .' Bridget said.

'I will not see anyone tonight.' Veronica's face closed. 'I want Hugo to help me back to my room. No, you will not do,' she said as Bridget caught her arm. 'I want Hugo.'

From the door of Victor's room Bridget called to Hugo. When she called for a second time and failed to get a response she remembered the bell beside Veronica's bed. She would ring from there.

The other room seemed very far away; tiredness forced her to hold on to the wall as she made her way there. But the movement helped liven her up and she was reasonably awake by the time she found and pushed the button by Veronica's bed. The tiredness came back, waves of it, as she waited for Hugo to answer. Sitting on the bed she had to resist fiercely an urge to sink into the bank of lace pillows.

'Hello,' Hugo's voice was brisk and clear on the intercom.

'Veronica would like you to help her back to bed,' Bridget spoke slowly and carefully.

'I'm on my way.'

'I don't like the look of her, Hugo. I think her doctor should be sent for.'

'You just leave things to me,' said Hugo. 'I'll look after her. Go on back to your room.'

Bridget, making her way along the corridor, stumbled twice. To keep herself awake she squeezed her eyes tight shut and opened them quickly. She squeezed and opened, squeezed and opened . . .

'Victor's coming . . .' She stood in the bedroom doorway at last, propping herself upright with a hand on either side.

'Victor's . . . dead,' Veronica's voice was indistinct and distant, 'and Ted's dead and so is Frank.'

Bridget reached the bed and sat there. Veronica was a wraith in the chair.

'There was something in the tea,' Bridget knew she was forming words but wasn't sure how they were coming out. 'Hugo put something in the tea he gave me. I can't stay awake.'

'Why . . . would . . . he . . . do . . . that . . .' Veronica's response came slowly, long pauses between the words.

Bridget, not sure the other woman had understood, was beginning to explain again when Hugo Sweeney quietly appeared by Veronica's side. He helped her out of her chair and she stood, leaning on him and on the cane.

'I don't forgive anyone.' Standing seemed to have given her a return of strength and her voice was clear again. 'I have forgotten nothing.'

Bridget slept after that, only vaguely aware of Veronica and Hugo slowly leaving the room and of the door closing behind them with a small click.

She slept until the blue light of morning and a bitter wind through the open window brought her groggily awake. The bedroom door was open too and there was something else, a sound . . .

The sound, a phone shrilling unanswered close by, brought her fully awake. The siren-like ringing didn't help a needling headache. She lifted an arm and, as the embroidered cuff of the lawn nightdress fell away from the face of her watch, remembered where she was, how she'd felt before falling asleep, all that had happened the night before.

'God, oh dear God' – her head reeled – 'Hugo's tea . . .'

It was eight o'clock. She'd slept for eight hours or more. It was years since she'd slept more than six. Even the sleeping tablets she'd taken after Victor's death had only knocked her out for that long. Whatever he'd put in the tea Hugo Sweeney had intended it to knock her out until morning. But why?

And where was he now? Why wasn't he answering the damned telephone.

Standing, she didn't feel too bad. Apart from the headache, and a dryness in her mouth, she was reasonably intact. Alert enough to be certain she hadn't opened either the window or door. The room was like an ice-box; someone had meant her to waken.

Closing the window she saw car coming quickly towards the house through the avenue of trees. She watched until it came to a stop in front of the house and the driver got out. Lindsay, in a business-like coat and gloves, didn't look up as he strode toward the front door.

Veronica's grey shawl was on the floor by the chair. Fallen there, most likely, when Hugo had helped her out of it the night before. Bridget picked it up and wrapped it round her shoulders before stepping into the corridor. The telephone was still ringing, coming clearly through Veronica's open bedroom door.

Bridget knew, the instant she stepped into the room, that Veronica Baldacci was dead.

Victor's mother lay against the pillows, her hands gracefully resting on the bed, one either side of her. Her white, lawn nightdress had been buttoned, nun-like, to her neck and her hair, a dusty ochre in the morning light, fell so carefully across its rucked shoulders that it had to have been arranged that way during the wait for death. Under the make-up her parched face had a garish peace, lipsticked mouth gentler than Bridget had ever seen it in life.

The room was thick with the smell of acetone, nothing now to disguise it for what it was; the smell of death and whatever had killed Veronica.

Chapter Fourteen

The ringing phone was on a table beside the bed. Bridget picked it up as Lindsay came into the room behind her and made a small, choking sound.

'Hello.' Bridget kept her eyes on Veronica as she spoke into the phone.

'Mother? Is everything all right? I've been calling and calling . . . Mother?'

'This is Bridget.' It was hard to think what next to say.

'Bridget? Where is my mother? Why . . .'

'Your mother's dead, Magdalena,' Bridget said and listened to the silence on the phone. She turned and saw Lindsay, hunched and hugging herself as she stared at her dead grandmother.

'Are you sure?' Magdalena's voice came at last, precise, in a way Bridget had never heard it before.

'Quite sure,' Bridget said. 'She died in the night. You should call her doctor and . . .' she paused, 'I think she planned to die, Magdalena, so maybe you should call the police too.'

Lindsay pulled up a chair and touched one of Veronica's still, waxen hands. She went on staring at her dead face.

'Where's Hugo?' Magdalena asked.

'I don't know. He doesn't seem to be about . . .' If he was in the house surely he'd have answered the phone?

'Of course he's about. Hugo is always about. Call him. I

must speak to him...' Magdalena's voice was losing its precision.

'I think it would be a good idea if you and your husband came over here,' Bridget said. 'Hugo Sweeney's gone.'

She knew, as she said it, that this was true. Hugo had aided and abetted Veronica, his last and most loyal act, and now he was gone. He had put Bridget to sleep, sat with Veronica while she died and then taken himself off.

'Her insulin... Oh, Christ, the godamned insulin... Can you tell what happened to her?' Magdalena asked.

'No. But she doesn't look to have suffered pain before she died.'

'Thank God for that,' Magdalena said. 'She didn't deserve any more suffering...' she stopped to listen to someone in the background, then added, 'We'll be there immediately,' and abruptly hung up.

Arriving ten minutes later with Thomas, Magdalena was surprisingly in control of herself.

'She was alone when it happened?'

She climbed the stairs with Bridget. Thomas followed behind. He was withdrawn and silent. We all deal with shock in our own way Bridget thought. To Magdalena she said, 'I don't think so. I think Hugo may have been with her. I was asleep.'

In her bedroom Magdalena kissed her mother's forehead and touched her lips and left her exactly as she'd arranged herself, or been arranged, for death. Lindsay, visibly pulling herself together, asked if Veronica's doctor had been called.

'He's on his way with the medical backup. I called the priest too.' Magdalena studied her mother's face. 'You were right, Bridget, when you said she didn't seem to have suffered pain. She looks peaceful enough.'

Thomas stood with his back to the window and looked around the room.

'It's hard to take in,' he said.

'I often wondered how it would happen,' Magdalena said, 'but my wondering was always in the nature of a fantasy. Something that would never really happen.' She touched her mother's forehead again, smoothing a furrow there. 'She'd given up. That was another thing I never thought she'd do. Her being strong and in control allowed the rest of us . . . to be what we are . . .'

Lindsay came and stood by her mother and took her hand. After a minute she took Bridget's too and together the three women stood in what would be the only peace surrounding Veronica Baldacci's death.

The house became crowded with death's hectic aftermath. Thomas took efficient charge as ambulance people and Veronica's doctor filled the hallway. Father Matthews, an uncontrollable shake in his hands, set candles and oils about Veronica's bed.

'I can't take this stuff,' Lindsay said.

'Then you'd better go downstairs,' said Magdalena.

Bridget knelt with Magdalena while the priest administered the last rites of the Catholic church.

Hugo's disappearance was complete. The bed in the room in which he'd lived for most of his life hadn't been slept in and everything he'd ever owned had been removed from the rest of the house.

'He was a miserable shit, but he was always here,' Lindsay's anger was diluted by a confused concern. 'You'd have thought he'd have wanted to, well, be around for the funeral and all that. He gave his life to grandmother, after all.'

They were in the kitchen, everyone gathered together in a tight group by a worktop by a wide window. It was as if, Bridget thought, the overpowering size of the other family rooms had driven them to herd together in this relatively small corner of the house.

No one was saying much. John-Francis, looking the worse for wear and unshaven, sat slumped in a chair with his eyes closed. Bridget recognized a bad hangover when she saw one. Russell sat a little apart, cracking his knuckles. Magdalena, Thomas by her side, stood stiff-backed with a drink in her hand and contemplated the view of the garden and plastic Christmas tree from the window.

Only Thomas, grey-suited and shaven, seemed in control of himself and the situation.

Upstairs, in the bedroom, Veronica's doctor was with her. The priest had been put out of the room and was waiting to go back in.

'Hugo may come back,' Thomas's voice was cool. 'Veronica dying spooked him, that's all. When he comes to himself and calms down he'll come right back . . .'

'I don't think he will and I don't think it happened like that,' Bridget spoke loudly, and slowly. Lindsay was the first to turn to her but she waited until she had Thomas's attention too before going on. 'I think Hugo aided and abetted Veronica's suicide.'

'What makes you so certain it was suicide?'

Magdalena didn't turn around and nor did she raise her voice. She sipped her drink and went on staring through the window.

'Things she said to me,' Bridget said. 'She'd been talking fatalistically for days. Ever since Ted Morgan's death. I can't have been the only one to notice, surely?'

'I noticed. I didn't pay a lot of attention. Veronica hated being old. She hated the way she looked and she often spoke like that, as if her life was over.' Lindsay, irritation on her blanched features as she dragged on a cigarette, stopped and frowned at the sound of Russell's cracking knuckles.

'Fact is, it was nowhere near over. She had more instinctive business knowledge in her head than anyone I know. She knew it too . . .'

'We all hate being old,' said Magdalena.

'Bridget's right,' said Thomas, 'it was different this time. I've had the feeling for a while that her mind was going. She'd come up with a few crazy plans for the business and didn't seem able to keep her mind on other things . . .'

'She was upset about Ted Morgan was all,' said Lindsay, 'and Eleanor Munro being here and bringing up all sorts of shit didn't help, nor did Bridget's arrival help much.' She gave Bridget a carelessly apologetic look. 'Sorry, but it's true.'

Thomas cleared his throat, 'I think Bridget's right, that Veronica had decided to end things. I had a sense that things weren't right.' He turned to Bridget. 'I was wrong to ask you to stay last night.'

'I doubt it would have made any difference who was here. Veronica planned what happened and more than likely got Hugo to help her.'

'Why are you so sure?' John-Francis, speaking for the first time, massaged his forehead with two fingers.

'Because he gave me something to make me sleep – put it in the tea he brought up to my room late in the night. Veronica was there too, only she refused to have anything to drink. He made sure I didn't oversleep, that I found Veronica this morning, by leaving my window open so that the cold air would waken me early.'

'You could be right,' Thomas said, 'all she had to do was mess around with her insulin dose – and Hugo could have helped her there. I always thought,' he took Magdalena's free hand in his, 'that she would die when she wanted to die. Looks like I was right in that and that she made the choice.'

Magdalena took her hand from his and smoothed her

hair. 'How simple you make it seem, Thomas. But then you always were a simple man. My mother was not a simple woman.' Her thin body shuddered involuntarily. 'I wish I'd been with her.'

'I wasn't aware of Grandmother making any business plans recently, crazy or otherwise.' Lindsay's expression had sharpened. 'What sort of plans were they?'

'Nothing that had got beyond the ideas stage.' Thomas shrugged. 'Nothing I thought worth bothering you with.'

'You did know she was making shares over to Bridget?' Lindsay's tones were neutral.

Thomas nodded. 'She told me about that plan. It was a good one, and fair. I approved.'

'But?' Lindsay raised an eyebrow.

'No buts.' Thomas shook his head. 'I was completely for it.'

'I know you, Dad,' Lindsay said. 'There's a big, fat *but* written all over you.'

'Not about the principle of Bridget getting shares, there isn't,' said Thomas. 'What you're picking up is a worry about the legal end of all this. She was being secretive about it and so I'm not exactly sure what Veronica had arranged for Bridget but if—' He stopped, took off his glasses and pinched the bridge of his nose.

'You're stalling,' Lindsay said calmly. 'But if *what*?'

'Well, *if*, and this is only an if as yet, Veronica took her own life then we may have a problem. The law's funny about suicide, takes the view that it's the act of someone whose judgement was unsound, mind unhinged. It would have been better if Bridget hadn't had those meetings with Veronica. Bridget being in the house the night she died is going to look bad too. The legal people are going to ask questions about undue influence and that kind of thing. That's all I'm saying . . .'

'If that's all, we'll deal with it.' Lindsay was offhand. 'The legal people don't need to be told anything that's not their business. Things'll be fine, Bridget, no need for you to—'

'I don't want shares in the company,' Bridget said sharply. 'I'd already told Veronica that, yesterday morning. This is all unnecessary and inappropriate.'

'You're right,' said Lindsay, 'we'll talk about it some other time.'

'There won't be any need for us to talk about it, ever,' said Bridget.

'How naïve you are,' said Magdalena. 'I'd have thought living with my brother would have taught you that things are never that simple.'

'Where's the New York flake? Anyone think of telling her the old lady's dead?'

Russell stood and stretched his large frame before bending over to touch his toes. Guilt and panic did a sickening double turn in Bridget's stomach. She'd forgotten to make contact with Eleanor that morning. Learning about Veronica's death, after everyone else, was going to reinforce her neurosis about a conspiracy to get her.

But then Eleanor hadn't returned the message Bridget had left for her. Maybe, like Hugo, she'd gone.

'Eleanor's staying in my hotel,' she said, 'I'll give her a ring.'

'No need. I called her a short while ago. She's on her way.'

So much for conspiracy theories; Lindsay and the family had thought to tell Eleanor when she, Bridget – her supposed ally – had forgotten.

Chapter Fifteen

Veronica Baldacci's doctor confirmed what Bridget had suspected and Hugo had known: Victor's mother had ended her own life. Veronica had ensured this would happen by not taking her insulin for three days. The smell in her room had indeed been of acetone.

More specifically, it had been of the keto-acidosis of the last stages of uncontrolled diabetes.

'No way you could have known this.' Dr Luke Kellerman patted Bridget's hand.

'Not what was causing the smell,' Bridget removed her hand, 'but I knew there was something wrong. She seemed to lose track of what she was saying from time to time, to grow feeble very quickly...' She looked away from the doctor's moist, overly understanding eyes. 'I should have been more insistent about calling you—'

She stopped. This, and the sleeping tablet, was a line best not pursued. It would be self-recrimination at its most dishonest since she knew in her heart that Veronica and Hugo had together conspired to prevent her getting the doctor to the old woman's bedside. They would have been altogether more ruthless if she'd gone against them.

Another thought came.

What right had she to judge Veronica if, at eighty-two, she wanted to die for love of Ted Morgan? Given the confusion of truths about the old woman's life she didn't feel at all equipped to join the chorus of righteous and disappointed disapproval.

Dr Kellerman sighed. 'I've been her doctor for many years, and Mrs Baldacci was not a woman who could be diverted from a path of action once she'd made up her mind.' He pursed his lips. 'Please be assured that she did not have a lot of pain.' His sad gaze roved over his small audience. 'Death would have come with a gradual drifting, a loss of sensation and final coma.' He selected John-Francis for a full-frontal focus and condoled with him directly. 'She was a remarkable woman and her death, if you'll forgive my saying so, became her as much as her life. She choose her time. She would have hated the slow decay of extreme old age.'

'That was still some years away,' Magdalena said icily, 'and if you've finished, Dr Kellerman, we would prefer to be alone, as a family.'

'Of course. If there's anything else I can do . . .' murmuring gently the doctor stood up, 'please call.'

A heavy man, he stood dolefully with his bag on the kitchen table. There was about him the air of someone used to attending on the very rich.

'She will need to be taken to the hospital but I will attend to the autopsy and to the legal details. They will be a formality, nothing more. There will be no need for you to concern yourselves.'

No one said anything. As a group, with Eleanor a recent, potentially explosive addition, they had uneasily occupied the kitchen for an hour or more. We're like geese, Bridget thought, scratchily circling one another while we make protesting sounds.

'Thank you, Luke,' Thomas said, when it seemed the doctor would stand indefinitely awaiting acknowledgement.

'No need to prolong the pain and upset of the living.' Dr Kellerman lifted his bag from the table.

'I blame myself,' Thomas said suddenly. 'I will not tolerate any blame being placed on Bridget.'

'I don't think that will arise.' The doctor looked surprised.

'Why should Bridget be blamed?' Lindsay said.

'She was here alone . . . I should not have allowed it to happen . . .' Thomas, who'd moved to sit at the table, beat a tattoo with his fingertips on its marble top. 'I handed over to her and left . . .' He put his head in his hands and leaned his elbows on the table. His short, greying hair stood on end as he massaged his forehead.

'Oh, God, Thomas, this isn't about you.' Magdalena knocked back her drink. 'We all know how caring you were of her. We just don't need to be reminded right now. I presume, Luke, that you will want to take my mother away immediately, or at least pretty soon.'

'It would be best.'

'Veronica dying had nothing to do with Bridget,' Eleanor watched the smoke from a cigarette circle in the air, 'so don't think, Thomas, you can lay that on her.'

'You're poisoning every one of us with that cigarette, you know that?' Russell, clutching his chest, opened a window wide.

'You are such a stupid jerkoff, Russell.' Eleanor dragged on the cigarette and blew more smoke in his direction. 'You're worried about smoke and nicotine inhalation while the fallout from the malignancy in this family is the real poison in the air around here.'

'This is not the time for anger, my child,' Father Matthews touched Eleanor's arm timidly. 'These things can be discussed another day—'

'Damn right they can.' Eleanor cut him short and fixed Bridget with a bayonet stare. 'And they damn well will be discussed too.'

'Death is a terrible business,' the priest murmured, 'it

reveals as much as it conceals. But the least the dead deserve is our blessing for a peaceful passing.'

'Just what the hell are you trying to say?' Eleanor, while the priest moved closer to the door and watched her with cloudy, remorseful eyes, got up and closed the window Russell had opened. 'People die from frostbite too,' she snapped. 'Now you,' she stabbed her cigarette at the priest, 'tell us all what you mean by death concealing as much as it reveals.'

'I was thinking that we take secrets with us to the grave and that that is a good thing,' Father Matthews said. 'I would advise you, Miss Munro, to let the past die with Mrs Baldacci. There is peace in letting go of unhappy events.' He spread his hands and fixed a look of appeal on his face. 'We should all of us see the passing of this good woman as a time for reconciliation and moving on—'

'Cut the crap,' said Eleanor. 'If there's something we should know then cough it up. Now.'

'I've said all I *can* say,' said Father Matthews. 'I am bound by an oath.'

'The confessional cop-out.'

'A man-made promise, which I am going to keep.'

'You hypocritical old druid.'

Eleanor advanced on the priest until she was standing over him.

'You got what you wanted out of her over the years. Your church was funded. It's easy for you to forget the past. It's even easier to deliver a righteous sermon to those of us who haven't got what we want. But why don't we do the hard thing here – why don't you tell us about those old secrets? The ones Veronica's taking with her to the grave? If you really want there to be peace and reconciliation then tell us what it is we're supposed to forget, and forgive.' She poked him in the chest with a long finger. 'The past needs to be sorted, so start talking.'

'Please. I entreat you.'

'No, Father, I'm the one doing the entreating here. Talk.'

'No.'

The priest drew himself to his full height and took a step back. He was suddenly a man with a mission.

'I will not reveal what the dead woman thought it best to conceal. I made the point only because to be forewarned is to be forearmed.' He looked round the assembled faces, his expression righteous. 'This family has had enough sorrow. With God's help we will rise above this situation too.'

'This family has lied and cheated and worse for three generations.' Eleanor stared at him in disbelief. 'You know it too. You took Baldacci money and forgave Baldacci sins and that makes you a fucking hypocrite—'

'That's it.' John-Francis, moving quickly, took Eleanor by the arm. 'This thing has gone far enough.' A muscle twitched in his jaw. 'I suggest you leave now, Eleanor, and cool off somewhere else. We can do without this shit here today. In fact we can do without it any day. So,' he shoved his furious face close to hers, 'are you going to leave or am I going to help you on your way out of here?'

'Mrs Baldacci would not have—' the priest's protest was cut short by a vicious aside from his defender.

'Shut up,' said John-Francis. 'If you'd kept your mouth shut in the first place this would never have happened. Are you leaving, Eleanor?'

'I'm leaving. But it would be a terrible mistake to think that I'm going to forget why I came here.' Eleanor Munro, straight-backed and shaking, looked around the assembled faces as the priest had done a minute before. 'The past hasn't died with Veronica. You could say, in fact, that it's just about to come alive again.'

*

Eleanor was pacing beneath the portico, shoulders hunched and head down as she waited for a taxi, when Veronica's body was carried from the house to the waiting ambulance. She kept her distance, leaning against a column, as Bridget and the rest of the family stood to see the stretcher loaded and the doors closed. Magdalena, the doctor and the priest all travelled with the body.

Bridget went to Eleanor as the vehicle moved off.

'Are you all right?' she asked.

'What's it to you? You abandoned me to play house with the Baldaccis as soon as I let you out of my sight. You—'

'I left a message for you on the voicemail in your room. You know I did: I don't believe you didn't listen to it. Where were you last night?'

'I decided it was time I had a night on the town,' Eleanor said offhandedly. 'Only I could have saved myself the money and energy spent.' She shrugged. 'This is one miserable dump when you get right down to it.'

'I was worried about you,' said Bridget, 'seems I could have saved myself the energy spent on that.' A taxi hove into view on the bend of the avenue. 'I'll get my things and come with you to the hotel. I need to shower and change.' She paused. 'And I really want to get away from here.' She caught Eleanor's hand and turned the younger woman to face her. 'Maybe at the hotel you'll be able to find your way to telling me the truth about last night.'

Eleanor was silent on the journey to the hotel. As they were crossing the bridge they got stuck in traffic. Watching the slow boats in the water below, she said,

'You wouldn't believe me if I told you the truth about last night. Not yet, anyways. I need to get it sorted in my head first.'

'Why don't you try me?' Bridget said.

'Because I need to think what I'm going to do about it.

Also . . .' Eleanor gave a quick, childlike smile and Bridget had a first, brief glimpse of a happier, free-spirited Eleanor.

'Go on.' she prompted.

'I don't want to be influenced by your opinion of what I should do. You're a persuasive lady and I don't care to have common sense decide things here. The situation needs . . . this needs a strategy. I'm good at strategies.'

'I've noticed,' Bridget said drily. 'Please tell me when you come up with one.'

After that Eleanor stayed silent until they got to the hotel. At the door to Bridget's room it seemed she would walk past, wordless to the end. But then she stopped and quickly caught Bridget in her arms and held her smotheringly tight.

'See you in a little while.' She let go and stepped back, her face glowing a little, almost happy-looking. 'We'll talk when you've had time to shower and change.' She pulled a playful grimace. 'And boy, is there a lot to talk about.'

Bridget's room, even to the tassels and repro furniture, had the calming reassurance of a port in a storm. She lay on the bed and contemplated the ceiling for several quiet minutes before ringing home and connecting with the blessed sanity of Anna's response to her grandmother's death by suicide.

'What a sad, sad end to a life. How terrible to have nothing to live for, poor old woman . . .'

Bridget heard her take a breath, then let it out slowly. She knew her daughter would be biting her lip and making her small, frequent frown. She envied the young woman her distance from Seattle and the Baldaccis.

'Are you all right?' Anna asked. 'Isn't it time you were coming home?'

'I'm fine. I'll leave immediately after the funeral. Should be home in a week, maybe less.'

'Great. It's raining here. Pissing cats and dogs, as a matter of fact. I called at the house the other day to check on things. The garden looks a bit lost.'

'I suppose it does.'

It wasn't until after Bridget had hung up, changed into a towelling robe and was on her way to the bathroom that she saw the envelope. Buff coloured and rectangular just like the first one, it was close to the wall and had clearly been shoved under the door. She'd been too preoccupied coming in to notice it.

She knew before opening it that it was from Hugo Sweeney. She read it while running a bath; the sound of the water was soothing. It was longer than the first letter, but then Hugo knew the person he was writing to this time. He'd been painstaking, writing carefully in blue ink with meticulous punctuation.

Dear Bridget Baldacci,

You would be wise to take my advice this second time: go home to your life in Ireland, now. By the time you read this I will be far away myself and Veronica Baldacci will be gone to her eternal rest.

There is no point in your staying in Seattle. You already know more than enough about your dead husband's family. Any more and you will know too much and that would do you no good at all. It would be more likely to bring harm to you. Knowledge will not bring an end to things either. The cycle is unending and will repeat itself. Go home.

Who knows, maybe we'll meet in Dublin one day.

PS: I will be slipping this under your door at the hotel. To leave it at the reception would betray our correspondence to the Munro woman. It would be dangerously unwise for you to discuss my letters with her. Look out for yourself and let Eleanor Munro and others look out for themselves.

He hadn't signed it. He was too careful for that. He hadn't put a date on it either but Bridget felt certain he'd written it in the hours before Veronica had died. Probably while packing to go away.

She wished, all at once and with a sense of foreboding stronger and fiercer than anything she'd felt before, that she had never come to Seattle. Events were building to something, she didn't know what. Victor's death had further destabilized an unravelling family.

Veronica's and Ted Morgan's deaths were not coincidences. They were merely a consequence of the secrets and struggles which controlled the family. Bridget didn't for a minute believe their deaths had resolved things, any more than Victor leaving or Grace and Shelley Munro disappearing had resolved things. The rot at the heart of the Baldaccis had taken over. Veronica knew this, had known since Ted Morgan died, if not before. She'd been unable to keep it at bay any longer and had decided she didn't want to go on.

A chain of events was in motion which could only end badly. There was too much money and power at stake, too much decay and corruption and far, far too many unspoken and unresolved secrets.

She could leave, of course, but knew that she wouldn't. She needed the resolutions she'd come for – justice for Victor, answers for Anna and Fintan, peace of mind for herself. She would wonder, later, whether the cost of those things had been too high.

But that morning she still believed she had a choice.

It was just after midday when she stepped out of the bath and got into bed. She slept for a couple of hours and woke feeling restless to a day which had turned moody and dark.

The ringing telephone, inevitable as the rain and probably Eleanor, dragged her unwilling from the bed.

But it was Lindsay Baldacci on the phone, brisk and almost cheerful sounding.

'I've decided the way to deal with Grandmother's death is to drop out of working for the day,' she said, 'to do the dutiful, family thing.'

'And this somehow involves me?' Bridget wasn't encouraging. She didn't want to see Lindsay, or anyone else just then. What she wanted was time alone to put the events of the previous night, and this morning, into perspective.

'Sure does.' Lindsay sounded upbeat. 'I know John-Francis offered, but none of us have shown you anything of the city—'

'I've done the tour on my own, thanks.'

'Not the same as getting a native's perspective on things. To be honest, my motives are entirely selfish. I want your company. I don't seem able to tolerate my own right now.'

'Where in the city had you in mind?' Bridget tried to keep the resignation out of her voice. She'd never been good at saying no when she felt needed but she made a half-hearted attempt to put Lindsay off. 'The weather's not promising – doesn't look as if it's going to be one of the five days a year it's said not to rain in Seattle.'

'That's the thing about Seattle, it's a real unpredictable place, so you just never know.' Lindsay's voice dropped. 'The autopsy's to be tomorrow morning and Grandmother will be buried at the end of the week. You'll be out of here after that and I may not have another chance to do something like this.'

'You don't have to do anything, Lindsay, I'm quite happy to—'

'But I want to. Please let me. You were with her last night and it seems to me right that I should spend time with you today. I need to talk about her. We'll go walkabout, take in Pioneer Square, maybe even do the sewer tour.'

'Sounds good,' said Bridget, and meant it.

Lindsay needing to talk about her grandmother changed everything. Lindsay was sharp and bright and not noticeably hung up on the past. She might be the one to make sense of things.'

'I'll even go beyond the call of duty and take Eleanor along,' Lindsay said magnanimously. 'I'll be there in thirty minutes. We'll have dinner on me this evening too.'

Funny the things people do when a loved one dies, Bridget thought, remembering her own midnight gardening forays after Victor's death, the long months during which she'd been unable to grieve. In the light of her own behaviour Lindsay's desire to act as a tour guide didn't seem at all unusual.

Eleanor was asleep. So deeply asleep it took three minutes of Bridget's knocking on her door to persuade her out of bed.

'Lindsay wants us to sightsee with her?' She gave Bridget a bleary, confused look. 'You're sure?'

'That's what she said, though needs might be a better word,' Bridget admitted. 'She's restless and upset about Veronica and wants to do something dutiful with the afternoon.'

'She said that?' Eleanor yawned, then frowned. 'Did she say what part of town?'

'Yes. She's talking about looking at Pioneer Square and the underground sewer tour.'

'Pioneer Square?' Eleanor shook her head as if clearing it. She took a deep breath. 'Well, that's a part of town I've already had a look at but maybe I should see it again. I'll meet you downstairs.' She gave another yawn. 'I need to have a quick shower.'

Lindsay arrived in exactly the half hour she'd promised. Dressed in sneakers and a bulky jacket she looked as if a cross-country trek was what she had in mind.

'Very noble of you, acting as a tourist guide like this,' Eleanor said as they went through the doors together into the street.

They walked quickly, three abreast with Lindsay in the middle setting a brisk pace and speaking in sporadic bursts. Bridget sensed a tension between the two yonger women which she hadn't noticed before. If she was lucky the day might yield more than the sightseeing trip.

'We're headed for one of the city's oldest neighbour-hoods,' Lindsay told them. 'It's got real character, it's full of squares, cafés and galleries. Crime's a bit of a problem there, but show me someplace crime isn't a problem and I'll show you a place that's dead to the world.'

'Yeah, right,' Eleanor said caustically. 'Nothing like a daily murder rate to make a neighbourhood interesting. I hear it's where the homeless and citizens like work-release prisoners hang out too.'

'It's a while since I've been to this part of town,' Lindsay admitted. A sharp wind at their backs hurried them along. 'The history of the square goes back to when Seattle was first settled and moves on to when it was destroyed by fire in 1889. When they rebuilt it they raised the sidewalks and streets a storey higher than before so as to avoid tidal flooding from Elliott Bay. The original streets are below-ground passageways now.'

'From what I've seen you could call some of the above-ground streets passageways too,' said Eleanor, 'as well as half the population of the place being derelicts.'

'Some of the area's like that,' Lindsay conceded.

When they came into view Bridget immediately recognized the red-brown nineteenth-century buildings of Pioneer Square. Along with the Space Needle they were pictured on the front of almost every brochure she'd ever picked up about the city. When they came closer and moved into the square she saw that it was both smaller and more homely than she'd imagined.

'What do you two say to starting off with a drink in Merchant's Cafe?'

Lindsay's cheer, as she led the way to an impressively worn and aged building, was unconvincing.

'It's the oldest restaurant we've got here, used to serve five-cent beer to miners during the gold rush while they queued for the upstairs brothel.'

'We've read the guidebooks,' Eleanor said carelessly as they sat at a long table. She drummed her fingers impatiently. 'Any chance of these guys bringing us a beer if we pay them today's rates?'

Lindsay ordered and they sat, the three of them, in a silence filled with unasked questions while they waited for the drinks to arrive. Why do I feel, Bridget wondered, that there is more to this outing than meets the eye? Is it because I've got used to things not being what they seem in this family – or because there is a real and root cause to the undercurrents I can feel between these two women?

'This part of town's seen a lot of misery, I'll hand you that much, Eleanor,' Lindsay broke the silence when their drinks came. 'Yesler Way, just across the square, used to be known as Skid Row, gave the nation a name for areas where the—'

'Down and out congregated. We know all that too,' Eleanor, interrupting, sounded peevish. She encircled her glass with her hands and turned it round and round.

'God, this town is sad. It looks sad and it feels sad and it's full of sad people. Now that we've had the word on Skid Row,' she arched an eyebrow at Lindsay, 'I suppose you think we should take the sewer tour?' She sipped from the glass and grimaced. 'Or maybe,' she spoke softly, 'you think it would be more interesting if we took a walk down by Second and Yesler to see where the homeless and the lonely live?'

'OK, Eleanor, OK – you can stop hitting on me.' Lindsay pulled her jacket round her as if suddenly cold. 'You're right about why I brought us here – but then you must feel the same or you wouldn't have come along. Why don't we go there now? I'll explain to Bridget on the way.'

'Why don't you explain to me before we leave?' Bridget said coldly.

'Because this way we save time,' said Lindsay.

'I'm not in any hurry,' Bridget said, 'and I'm not going anywhere until you explain what this is about.'

Lindsay took a deep breath and, making an obvious effort, spoke slowly. 'I want to see where Ted Morgan stayed when he left my grandmother's home. I need to see for myself where he went to. I sort of feel it might be easier to understand what happened – how it could have happened – if I see the Bible Mission Refuge. I didn't feel I could go there on my own and I thought if I asked you straight you wouldn't want to come with me. So I came up with this plan to' – she gave an apologetic smile – 'lure you two into coming with me. Only Eleanor guessed what I was up to because she knows this part of town and knows it's where Ted Morgan holed up.' Her eyes pleaded to be understood.

'So – now that you know will you walk that way with me?'

'Yes,' Bridget said, 'but you should have been honest with me.'

She should have been, but couldn't. Lindsay, like the others, understood only the devious.

'Veronica died because Ted Morgan died, because she didn't want to go on living with him dead. It's as simple as that and it's important to me to lay Ted's ghost to rest. Taking a look at the refuge will help.'

'Let's go then.' Eleanor Munro stood and pulled gloves from her pocket.

Bridget, crossing the road to Yesler and Second, wished she'd brought gloves too. She wished even more that she knew whether Lindsay had known about Veronica's wedding plans and if she believed that her grandmother's suicide had only to do with Ted Morgan's death. Given the Baldacci attitude to truth, and the fact that Bridget had been told about the proposed marriage in confidence, there didn't seem much point in asking.

But answers would have helped her feel a lot more comfortable about heading into the narrow, downhill streets on the wrong side of the square.

Chapter Sixteen

They walked three abreast again, this time with Bridget between Lindsay and Eleanor. The ground was uneven and when the footpath narrowed Eleanor stepped into the roadway and walked there.

There was no traffic, and there were no people. Rain began to fall lightly. It was very cold.

'Where to now?' Bridget stamped her feet when they came to the end of the street and arrived at a T-junction.

Eleanor raised her eyebrows at Lindsay.

'It's your city,' she said.

'Yes.' Lindsay frowned. 'I checked a map and by my reckoning we go one block along and then take a right. After that we should be close enough to see Ted Morgan's Bible Mission.' She stamped her feet on the ground as Bridget had done. 'It's cold. Best to keep moving.'

The right turn brought them into a narrow, dark street which was no more than an alleyway. The buildings on either side were for the most part unlit and unused and by the time they'd walked five hundred yards had become completely derelict. They looked like warehouses, tired lettering on some windows indicating they might at one time have housed shipping or other offices.

The ground underfoot became even more uneven as the street curved and got darker. The quiet was penetrating, and Pioneer Square and the main thoroughfare they'd just left might have been miles away.

There was nothing resembling hostel accommodation anywhere.

'You're sure we're heading in the right direction?' Bridget said.

'I'm sure.' Lindsay stared ahead, as if expecting a beacon to show the way. 'How in hell did he find this place . . . we must be almost at the waterfront.'

'He looked hard, that's how,' said Eleanor. 'He needed somewhere he could hole up and not be found. He needed it to be cheap too, in case he had to stay on a while. Ted wasn't a rich man.'

'He told you all this?' Bridget said.

'Yep. The other thing he told me was not to come down here. So I didn't, until now.' She looked around and for a moment it seemed as if she was going to turn tail and run. But she hunched her shoulders and kept going. 'I've a feeling I'm going to regret doing what he asked for the rest of my life.'

'Did he tell you precisely why he left the house?' Bridget tried, but failed, to see Eleanor's face. In the murky light and with her hair falling forward it was a whitish blur, nothing more.

'He told me that too,' her voice sounded strained. 'He wanted to get away from Veronica's talk of marriage. He cared for her but he didn't want that. But he did want to stay round for me.' She shook her hair back and looked sideways at Bridget. 'You know about Veronica's plans for them to marry, though, she had to have told you.'

'I know she wanted to marry Ted Morgan, yes.'

Bridget stopped and, a few steps ahead of her, the two younger women stopped too.

'You told someone in the family where Ted was staying, didn't you Eleanor? You think that person might have . . . harmed him, or caused him to be harmed, don't you?' She put the question flatly and waited, without moving, for an answer.

'Yep. I told someone.' Eleanor looked at Lindsay. 'I told two people, as a matter of fact.'

'I was one of them but you only told me last night, a bit late for me to get excited about Grandmother's plans to wed, given that the man involved was already dead. Why don't you tell Bridget who the other person was?'

'Good idea,' the strain had gone and Eleanor's voice had become flat and expressionless. 'I didn't tell Bridget because I didn't believe Thomas had anything to do with Ted's—'

'You told Thomas?' Bridget said.

'Yes – and he probably told someone else. I should never have told anyone where Ted was staying. Once you tell a secret it belongs to the world. God, it's cold. Can't we move on?'

They began walking again, close together, along the empty road. The rain got heavier. Bridget added a couple of things together in her head.

'And you didn't tell the police because you wanted Thomas on your side working on Veronica for your inheritance,' Bridget said. 'That's it, isn't it?'

'That's about right, yes,' Eleanor said.

'You trusted Thomas,' Lindsay said.

'I trusted Thomas,' Eleanor agreed.

What was left of the late afternoon light shone wetly on the road ahead. At a corner they turned right, into a slightly wider street where dull yellow street lighting made for shadows and not a lot more visibility.

'This does not look promising.' Bridget stopped.

Doors on either side were closed and bolted and a building not fifty yards away was propped up by scaffolding. The street curved and sloped downwards, the buildings high and close together, allowing only small amounts of the dying daylight through.

Lindsay was ahead now, looking carefully about her as she went.

'It's OK.' Eleanor's arm on Bridget's shoulder was a surprising comfort. 'The Bible Mission's got to be around here somewhere. It's not as bad as it looks and anyway,' she squeezed Bridget's shoulder, 'you'll be OK with this big city gal.'

'I've got a bad feeling about this,' Bridget confessed. 'Nothing rational, nothing I can put my finger on. I just feel we should get out of here.'

'Let's go then,' said Eleanor. 'This is Lindsay's thing, she can go the rest of the way alone. I don't feel all that comfortable about the set-up either.'

'We can't leave Lindsay here alone,' Bridget protested.

'Do you see her leaving because you want to?' said Eleanor. 'Or because I want to?'

'No . . .'

'Well, let's go then.'

'We can't leave her here,' Bridget repeated. 'Not just because of an irrational feeling of mine. Looks like it's too late now anyway. She's calling to us. Why don't we stick with her until we at least find the Bible Mission?'

Lindsay, when they caught up with her, pointed ahead. 'It's just along there,' she said, 'and there's a coffee shop opposite.'

The Bible Mission Refuge, the name in white letters on a green background, loomed out of the shadows a couple of hundred yards further on. The glass, double doors were at the top of a set of scrubbed granite steps and just inside it they could see a wooden desk and several deep, dark-brown armchairs.

'How far do you want to take this thing, Lindsay?' Eleanor asked. 'Do you want to go inside?'

'I don't know.'

Two of the armchairs were occupied by Bible Mission

residents. As the women stood watching in the street one of them, red-faced and straw-haired, gave them the two-fingered sign.

'Maybe we'll just go across the road, have a coffee and warm up a little before we head back.' Lindsay turned away.

The coffee house was in shades of yellow and black. They sat on black wooden chairs at a yellow table beside a black wall and had coffee from glossy, yellow mugs. They were the only people there.

'Poor Ted.' Eleanor traced a question mark in a coffee spill on the yellow table top. 'He was a good man who got caught in the wrong place a couple of times and tortured himself about it until he died. And that about sums up his life . . .'

When she fell silent Bridget, studying the punctuation mark, prodded her with a question of her own. 'The wrong place was Seattle?'

'One of them was. The other wrong place was New York.' Eleanor drew a circle around the question mark. 'The New York thing happened because my mother wrote to Veronica when she heard her father was ill. She wanted to come back, help nurse him. When Veronica got the letter, she sent Ted to New York with $25,000 to pay her off. Ted was persuasive. My mother took the money and stayed in New York and that was all she ever got. Ted never felt right about it and it was part of the reason he looked out for my mother. Me too, I reckon.'

'And in Seattle?'

Eleanor looked Bridget in the eye. 'Seattle was where Ted had an affair with Veronica and was caught, as the Romans used to say, *in flagrante delicto* by Victor, who was, by Ted's account, an impressionable young man. He left.' She paused. 'You knew this, didn't you?'

Bridget nodded. 'Veronica told me. In her account Ted

Morgan left before Victor.' She looked questioningly at Lindsay.

'That was the version I heard too.' She shifted uncomfortably in her seat. 'It's getting dark,' she said, 'and I've gone as far as I want to with this thing. I want to buy dinner to sort of make up for dragging you two down here. We're real close to the waterfront so why don't you two walk on down there in about,' she looked at her watch, 'say twenty minutes? I'll bring the car around and pick you up. No sense in all three of us going back to the car park and I'm at least dressed for a run. How's that sound?'

'Sounds to me like you can't stop organizing people,' said Eleanor, 'but since you were the one got us here you may as well get us out as painlessly as possible.'

'I'll get going then.' Lindsay stood and zipped up her jacket. 'Wait for me by the first pier you arrive at. I'll find you there.' She took a wallet from her pocket. 'Let me get this. See you in a while.'

Once in the street Lindsay started to run.

'She's got a different way of doing it,' Eleanor said, 'but she's just like her grandmother when you come right down to it. Lindsay Carter gets what she wants, same way Veronica did.'

'I've noticed,' said Bridget.

Eleanor looked thoughtful. 'We're here, where Lindsay wants us to be, while she's gone, running in the trainers she was so conveniently wearing. Right?'

'That's certainly the way it looks.'

'And we are going to walk to the waterfront to wait for her to pick us up by the waters of the Puget Sound. Why are we going to do this?'

'Because Lindsay asked us to.'

'Right.' Eleanor paused and pushed her hair back from her face in one of her Anna-like gestures. 'The trainers were so goddamn convenient.' She narrowed her eyes again. 'Do you think her wearing them was a coincidence?'

'Probably,' said Bridget, 'but only because I don't see why she would want us here.' What possible gain was there for Lindsay in having herself and Eleanor wandering the early evening backstreets and waterfront?

'Two coffees and two of our sticky pecan rolls.' A young man with a tray stood smiling by their table. 'Ordered and paid for by your friend who just left.' He hummed 'Lilli Marlene' as he arranged the food and drink in front of them.

'She's making sure we stay here,' said Eleanor.

Bridget touched the oozing stickiness of the roll and pushed it away. There was only so much her stomach could take.

'I lied to you about going on the town last night,' Eleanor said. 'I spent last night with Lindsay. She came to the hotel . . .' Edgily pushing aside the food she looked around, and said, 'Why don't we get out of here? Head on down toward the waterfront and look for a cab? I'll tell you about it as we go.'

The rain had become a dense, freezing drizzle that stung their faces and fell about them like millions of icy needles. It was dark too, the street lighting failing miserably to illuminate threatening corners and doorways. They stood briefly in the light thrown onto the footpath from the coffee house and the Bible Mission doorway opposite.

'Left?' Bridget asked.

'Left,' Eleanor confirmed.

They'd walked a bare twenty yards when a voice from behind hailed them.

'Bridget! Eleanor! Hold on there . . .'

They turned together, towards a figure hurrying in their direction from the other end of the street. His leather-soled shoes made neat tapping sounds as he called again and then he came close enough for both of them to recognize it was Thomas.

'Thomas,' said Eleanor, 'this is a real surprise.'

Bridget, close beside her, felt her go rigid. Oh God, she thought, this is not good. There's something else here I don't know about.

'Couldn't believe it when I saw you,' Thomas said.

'You didn't expect to find us here?' Eleanor asked.

Thomas, coming out of the shadows into the light from the coffee-house window, stopped a few feet away and smiled. 'I didn't expect to find you with Bridget,' he said.

'It's a surprise all round,' said Bridget. 'We didn't expect to meet you either.'

There was an ending here. She knew it as surely as she knew that the kind and gentle Thomas was no longer either of those things.

If he ever had been.

Chapter Seventeen

'Bad night to be out . . .' Thomas stepped closer.

Bridget tried to meet his eye but all she got was the coffee-house window reflected in his glasses.

'I'm long past believing in coincidences, Thomas,' Eleanor's voice was rough. 'What're you doing here?'

'It's an out of the way part of town for all of us.' Thomas looked around, then up and down the street, then back at Eleanor. His smile didn't waver. 'Maybe we should all explain what we're doing here.'

'We came with—' Bridget got no further. Eleanor, swearing under her breath, turned furiously.

'Keep out of this, Bridget.' She shook her by the arm. 'You haven't a fucking clue about what's going on here. I'll handle this.'

'Handle it? For God's sake, Eleanor . . .'

The fury in Eleanor died. 'Just do what I say. Please. For a little while, that's all.' Her voice was pleading and her eyes, fixed on Bridget's, had a manic desperation Bridget had seen there before.

'Fine. The show's yours,' she said.

If standing back would calm Eleanor down, ease the situation, then she would stand back. For the little while she'd asked for, at least.

'Why don't you let the woman speak?' Thomas, watching them, sounded icily amused. This was another Thomas. 'Tell me, Bridget, who was it you came down here with?'

Bridget shook her head. 'I really don't know what's going on here, Thomas, so I'm going to keep out of it.'

'Too late for that,' Thomas said. 'You're part of the family. You're involved.'

He rubbed his gloved hands together. The movement was strangely threatening, seeming to promise other, more violent movement to come. The benign, kindly air he'd worn as the concerned consort of Magdalena and indulgent paterfamilias to Lindsay and John-Francis had been replaced with a detachedly cold one. But there was a nervousness there too, and a feverish anxiety that no amount of icy detachment could disguise. Dear God, Bridget thought, I wish I knew what was going on, what games these people are playing.

The sane thing would be to walk away but she knew, with an awful certainty, that whatever was to happen would follow her.

Thomas was right. She was involved. She was family. And she couldn't leave Eleanor.

'First things first, Thomas Carter,' Eleanor's voice came so loudly beside her that Bridget jumped. 'You're not going to do a thing to make sure I get my due rights in this family, are you? You never were, were you?'

'Oh, Eleanor, Eleanor . . .' Thomas shook his head resignedly, 'you must learn to stop being so paranoid, to stop thinking about yourself.'

'Answer the questions,' Eleanor snapped.

'You've blown it.' With a sharp, hard laugh Thomas suddenly dropped the pretence of civility. 'I *was* willing to do something, see you got a decent pay-off, but not any longer. Not since you moved to that hotel and got this conspiracy thing going with Bridget.' His voice was as hard now as his laugh had been. 'There was a time when I thought I might take you on board, that you might be useful in the way a dangerous dog can be useful. Not any more. You've become a handicap. Things have changed now Veronica's dead. I've no fallback. I've got to take all the risks myself and you're a risk I'm not willing to take. Anyway, you're even crazier than I thought you were if you think I'm going to keep you around after the stunt you tried to pull here tonight.'

'What're you talking about?' Eleanor's eyes narrowed.

'You know what I'm talking about.' Thomas rubbed his hands together again. 'Let's clear up a couple of things here and now and you can be on your way. We can get out of this rain in the coffee house. But you should know that I'm willing to deal in a one-off payment, nothing more.' He shrugged. 'Once we've sorted things you can both get out of here.'

'You know your way around this area pretty well—' Eleanor began.

Without warning the pool of light around them disappered and they were standing in murky, near-black shadow. Bridget jumped and gave a short, hysterical laugh as the young man from the coffee shop appeared in the doorway and began to lock up.

'It's pretty dark around here when we turn our lights out,' he said, 'there's a problem with the street lighting. Should be fixed by spring, if you want to wait that long.' He looked at them curiously and jangled the keys in his hand. 'There's not a lot goes on after we close for the day.' He stuffed the keys into his jeans' pocket and zipped up his jacket. 'Unless you're planning on booking in across the road my advice to you is not to hang around.'

'Sounds like good advice.' Bridget moved after him as he jogged away up the street. 'I think we should take it.'

'Not just yet.'

Thomas's hand on her arm stopped her. His grip was tight and for a minute she thought about screaming. But years of self-control, thirty of them as a wife and mother holding fort and family together, stopped her. The young man from the coffee shop had jogged out of sight by the time she turned to Thomas, her arm limp and unresisting.

'Fine,' she said, 'but I think it's time you gave me a reason why we should stand here in the wet and dark and cold.'

'Because, like I said, we've got a few things to sort out,' Thomas let her arm go, slowly. 'Like the implication in what Eleanor's just been saying.'

He took a step closer to Eleanor. Bridget's eyes had got used to the murk now and she could see the tight, hard line of his mouth. Eleanor stood her ground but Bridget could feel an almost convulsive stiffening in her long body. It took all of Bridget's own self-control to stop herself running.

'No implication, more like a statement,' Eleanor's voice rose accusingly. 'I'm saying, straight out, that you had something to do with Ted Morgan's death and that I'm not going to keep quiet about what I think anymore. Don't ask me to believe in coincidences. I told you where he was staying and within days he disappears and the next anyone hears about him he's dead.'

'You told me where he was staying.' Thomas, repeating the phrase, nodded and stared at her. 'Listen to what you're telling me, Eleanor. You're saying that you knew where Ted Morgan holed up and that you told me. That's as far as any real knowledge on your part goes. Who's to say you didn't come down here and have some argument with him that ended badly?'

'That's bullshit and you know it.'

'Do I? What I know, Eleanor, is that you're one freaky lady. What I know too is that just because you told me where Ted Morgan was staying doesn't mean I came down to visit with him. Why would I do that? He was an adult, a fairly senior one at that. He knew his own mind. He wanted to stay over there.' Thomas's sudden jerk of his head toward the Bible Mission startled Bridget into a gasp and made Eleanor flinch. Thomas smiled. 'God knows why he moved lodgings,' he said. 'God knows why he came to Seattle in the first place. I don't know why he did these things and I don't care. I didn't ever care.'

Rain began to fall more heavily, the icy drizzle turning to heavy drops which bounced at their feet. Instinctively they moved closer to the shelter of the coffee house front, all three of them.

'This makes no sense, having this conversation on the sidewalk,' said Thomas. 'I'm parked a bit from here in a side street. Why don't we get into the car and drive out to the house and talk there?'

'I'm not getting into any fucking car with you,' Eleanor's voice rose. 'I'm not going anywhere with you, you murdering bastard.'

Bridget, with the detached part of her which was still rational, thought: murderer . . . is that what he is, this man who was once so pleasant and kind to me? Is the queasy lurching in my gut telling me that yes, this is a man capable of taking life?

She decided she'd been silent long enough.

'We've arranged to meet Lindsay by the waterfront.' She gave Thomas what she hoped was an apologetic look. 'Eleanor and I should really begin making our way there now. She'll be waiting for us.'

Thomas's eyebrows shot above the rims of his glasses but he said nothing, just looked past them, towards where the street sloped and curved down to the Puget Sound. His silence was deliberate and calculating and frightening.

'Christ, Bridget, why didn't you shut up like I told you?' Eleanor's voice was ragged. 'You've really fucked things up now.' She turned to Thomas. 'Lindsay brought us here,' she said, 'she said she needed to see the Bible Mission so as she could deal with Ted's death—'

'Cut the crap.' Thomas's eyes were narrowed and calculating. 'Where is the man you came to meet?'

This is the reason he's here, Bridget felt a glorious relief rush through her, it's all a misunderstanding, he thinks we're here to meet someone.

'We weren't meeting anyone,' she spoke confidently and clearly, 'so it looks as if standing here is a waste of everyone's time.'

She linked her arm through Eleanor's, tugged, took a step. Thomas stood in front of them, blocking the way. He ignored Bridget.

'Where is he, Eleanor? Where's your witness? Is he inside the Refuge? Is that where he is?' He was blinking fast, his hands clenching and unclenching by his side. 'Bring me to him, Eleanor, now.'

Bridget took a deep breath. 'Whatever this is about it can be sorted out—'

'Shut up, Bridget. Just shut up and keep out of this.' Thomas went on looking at Eleanor. 'It's too late to be polite. Way too late. Why don't you explain to her, Eleanor, exactly why it's too late?'

'Because I don't know what the fuck you mean or what you're talking about,' Eleanor yelled.

'Your witness, Eleanor, I'm talking about your witness, the guy you came down here to meet, the bullshit artist you were going to give the money you borrowed from Lindsay to. Where is he?'

'This is crazy stuff. I told you already; I didn't come down here to meet anyone and I certainly didn't borrow money from Lindsay. Coming down here was Lindsay's idea.'

'Eleanor's telling you the truth,' said Bridget, 'Lindsay wanted—'

'For the last time, Bridget, stay out of this,' Eleanor said more calmly. 'I'll handle it.'

She stepped away, separating herself from Bridget and Thomas by a couple of feet. She was breathing quickly and even in the bad light her skin was ashen-looking.

'The person who knows all about this is Lindsay. We'll talk it over with her.'

In her hand she held the small pistol she'd shown Bridget in her hotel room.

'Turn around and start walking towards the waterfront.' Eleanor held the gun steadily, close against her body. 'We'll all go together to meet Lindsay.'

Bridget, disbelieving, shook her head. 'This is crazy, Eleanor, this isn't going to—'

'Shut the fuck up. I really mean that. Don't say another word. I'm getting to the bottom of whatever's going on and I'm not taking any more shit from anyone. I can't trust you not to go AWOL so you'll just have to come along and do as I tell you. Now move, both of you,' she made a tight, small gesture with the pistol, 'and don't think I won't use this thing. I'm crazy, remember, a whacko. Why wouldn't I use it?'

She was close enough for Bridget to make out the small black hole of the muzzle at the end of the gun's barrel. It would be a very simple thing for Eleanor to pull the trigger, would take very little the way her mood was swinging.

Trying not to think about it she began to walk, with Thomas beside her, in the general direction of the waterfront. As they passed the glass doors of the Refuge she looked quickly across the street. One of the men in the brown armchairs had fallen asleep, the other stared blankly and without recognition as they moved on by. He doesn't see us, Bridget thought. Now, when we want him, he doesn't even notice us.

'Eyes front and move it. Faster . . .' Eleanor's voice was close, and hoarse-sounding.

Bridget looked ahead, at the rain on the uneven pavement slabs, at the diminishing light as the street sloped backwards. You were right not to come back to this place, Victor, she thought, right to believe that the evil men do lives after them.

Chapter Eighteen

It was all downhill. The rain got heavier and ran in gullies along the sides of the cracked sidewalks.

For a lot of the time they walked on the rough surfaces of empty, vehicular-only streets between high, disused buildings, an occasional rat scuttling out of sight as they approached. Eleanor, prodding them along, spoke only once and her tone was conversational.

'You forced this on me, Thomas, you left me no option.' she said. 'I trusted you. You said you'd look out for me and for that I was willing to go along with not saying anything about you knowing where Ted was staying. But I was wrong, wasn't I?' She was silent for a minute, thinking. 'You shouldn't have come after me and Bridget and you sure as hell shouldn't have come on all threatening like that. There's nothing for it now but to find out everything. When I have the whole picture I'll decide what to do.' She took a shaky breath. 'I want to know why you killed Ted and what the fuck you and Lindsay are up to. I don't know what witness you were talking about back there on the street but Bridget will be my witness when we get to talk with Lindsay.' Her voice lightened. 'You know something else, Thomas? No, don't turn around, just keep right on the way you are. That's it. You too, Bridget. Well, the something else is that I'm enjoying this. It feels good to be in control of things, to know I'm not going to be fucked around any more.'

'You've got this whole thing wrong.' Thomas kicked a

loose stone ahead of him. 'You're crazy if you believe I had anything to do with Ted Morgan's death.'

Eleanor, swearing under her breath, moved quickly to lay the cold, wet length of the pistol's barrel along Thomas's cheek.

'Don't use the word crazy when you talk about me,' she spoke so softly Bridget could barely hear her, 'don't do it ever, ever again. In fact,' she smiled and stepped back, 'don't open your mouth again until I tell you to.'

There was an inevitability about the strip of waterfront when it appeared, shining, ahead.

Encouraged by Eleanor they crossed a wide road onto a disused wharf. They stopped then and Bridget, looking out across the darkly heaving glitter of the water, thought she had never in her life been so wet, or so frightened. Her stomach, acknowledging the fact, had settled into a remorseless lurch.

'Thomas, standing beside her, cleared his throat.

'I'd like to clean my glasses,' he said. 'The rain . . .'

'Give them to me,' said Eleanor.

'I'd prefer—'

'Give them to me with one hand,' Eleanor said and Thomas, with infinite care and even greater reluctance, handed over the glasses. 'Thank you.' Eleanor dropped and ground them underfoot. 'Should have thought of that before,' she said, 'not too much you can try on now you're half blind.' She took a deep breath. 'Rain's easing and it's nice and private and sheltered here so we'll talk a little, before we head along to the pier to meet Lindsay.'

She leaned against a low building, resting the elbow of the arm holding the gun on a window ledge. Bridget didn't for a minute think she was as relaxed as she appeared. Nor did she think there was any way on God's earth, or on that piece of Seattle waterfront, that a scream of hers would have been heard, not with the noise of the traffic thundering on what looked like a flyover road behind them and the sound of the water against the wharf. Whether by accident or design Eleanor had chosen well. Bleak, abandoned, noisy, it was the ideal spot to hold two people at gunpoint.

'I want you to listen to me, Thomas,' Eleanor said. 'If I get answers that sound right we'll continue on down the waterfront to meet with Lindsay. If I don't' – she shrugged before straightening up to hold the gun with both hands – 'then it might just happen that I really will go crazy and use this thing. There's no knowing what a crazy woman with too much control will do in a situation like this. Are you willing to risk finding out by fucking me around Thomas?'

Thomas grunted and stared blindly as she poked the gun against his chest. His hands twitched by his sides.

'Tell me,' Eleanor said, 'why you followed me today.'

Thomas looked away from her and the gun, before he began to speak. His voice came in a flat monotone. 'Lindsay said you were meeting a man at the Bible Mission Refuge who was willing to swear he'd seen me with Ted Morgan about the time he died. She said she gave you money to pay him off. I wanted to see the guy for myself.' He turned to Bridget and his face twisted with distaste. 'I don't care to waste company funds.'

'Lindsay was lying,' Eleanor said. 'There was no man. Why do you think she wanted you to think there was?'

'I've no idea. Why do you want me to think there wasn't?'

'There wasn't any man,' Bridget corroborated. 'It was Lindsay's idea that we all go to the Bible Mission.' She pondered the implications. 'She set you both up, for whatever reason. Me too, I suppose.'

'Thank you, Bridget,' Eleanor said, 'for the support—'

'Do you have to keep pointing that thing at us?' Bridget gave way to a sudden surge of anger. 'You've got us here and we're talking. You don't need it any more.'

'I need it,' Eleanor was curt, 'and you're a fool if you

think you can take over control with sweet reason. I need to think about what's happening here and I don't want you to speak again either unless I say so. Got it?'

'Seems fairly clear.' There were a lot of things she could say; none of them would make any difference.

Eleanor became suddenly restless, jerkily looking around her. The gun wavered, but never enough to create a doubt that she would use it if anyone moved. Bridget watched her, carefully. She didn't for a minute believe Eleanor was a killer. What she did believe, with certainty, was that the younger woman was on a knife edge, likely to pull the trigger if pushed and to realize too late what she'd done.

In the circumstances, she might just as well have been a killer.

'What are you and Lindsay up to?' Eleanor spun suddenly on Thomas, the gun in front of her aiming at his stomach. 'Tell me, or by God I'll use this thing. I feel like using it. I feel like causing you pain. You killed Ted. I told you where he was staying when you asked me because I trusted you. Then you went there and you killed him. I didn't believe it before but I do now. I knew it when you appeared in that street tonight. I don't need any witness to tell me. You told me not to tell the police about you knowing where Ted was staying and I didn't tell them. You fucked around with my head, Thomas, you and Lindsay both.' Her voice, which had been rising as she spoke, dropped suddenly to a low snarl, 'Tell me, Thomas, tell me what went on, what's going on here.'

'I'll do a deal.' Thomas lifted his head and looked Eleanor squarely in the face. 'I level with you about the problems we've been having and we all go to meet Lindsay, get in the car and go home. Deal?'

'Depends on what you tell me,' said Eleanor.

She pushed her wet hair from her face with her free hand. The rain had eased back to a drizzle. Bridget was wet enough to have become indifferent to the condition, cold enough to be numb, almost. She supposed it was the same for the other two.

'What I want to know is why you killed Ted,' Eleanor said roughly.

'But there's something you should know before that, Thomas Carter, and it's this.' She took a breath. 'I had a very long talk with Lindsay last night. Your story better be the same as hers.'

'I didn't kill Ted Morgan.' Thomas cut her short and turned his head seaward, searching for words. Bridget was struck by the chilling stillness of his eyes, made unnervingly obvious now he wasn't wearing glasses. He shook himself, as if from a reverie, before going on. 'It is more accurate to say that I didn't kill him intentionally,' he said and Bridget caught her breath. 'Ted Morgan dying was an accident, something I'll spend the rest of my life—'

'I don't want to hear about your problems with your conscience,' Eleanor said. 'Tell me . . .'

'Veronica wanted Ted to marry her. She told me so herself.'

Thomas spoke into the wind, his head still turned away from where Eleanor stood.

'I went to meet with him to talk him out of the marriage. It would have ruined everyone, as well as everything I've worked for all these years. To be honest,' he lifted one shoulder in a shrug, 'I went to buy him off. But he said he was against the marriage himself, that he'd moved out of the house to get away from the pressure from Veronica. He'd had left town altogether, headed back to New York, if it hadn't been that he was worried about you, Eleanor, and wanted to hang around until you'd got things sorted out. That's what he said, but that was only part of it.' Thomas turned and looked again at Eleanor, his eyes squinting with the effort. 'He told you where he'd be staying so you could keep in touch with him, right?'

'He gave me the address, yes. He came here on my account and then he got killed. But you know what?'

With a sudden, violently stabbing movement she brought the gun to within an inch of Thomas's face.

'I'll feel a lot less bad about it when I get what's mine. That's what he wanted and it'll vindicate his death.' She gave an impatient shrug before going on, 'But what I want right now is some more explaining. Talk.'

The rain had eased again and the air had become colder. Behind them Bridget could hear the waters of the Sound give great, heaving sighs, as if it would haul itself up and over the wharf sides. She kept her eyes on the gun and didn't look round.

'You have to take some of the blame for his death,' Thomas spoke in his old familiar voice, soft and kind. 'As you say, he was in Seattle for you and he was staying in the hostel because he didn't want to leave you alone in town. The row which led on to the accident that killed him was about you.'

'Don't you try to lay Ted's death at my door,' Eleanor's voice had become ragged.

Thomas gave a sad smile.

'He said he wasn't going to marry Veronica. I didn't believe him. He'd have done it in the end. Veronica spent a lifetime getting what she wanted; she was going to have this marriage too. I offered him money and he laughed. I upped the price and he told me I was wasting my time. He didn't want to talk in the hostel. We walked down here, to the water. Just walking and talking. We were down the way a bit . . .'

Thomas gestured and Eleanor, with a small scream, shoved the gun in front of him again.

'Keep your hands by your sides,' she yelled.

Thomas shrugged and Bridget closed her eyes against the agonized confusion and misery on Eleanor's face. The other woman's mood had shifted; she wasn't enjoying her power anymore, her fragile control of herself was disintegrating.

'He wouldn't talk to me. Wouldn't listen.' Thomas, his hands by his sides again, went on relentlessly. 'He started to go back to the hostel.' Thomas hesitated. 'I tried to stop him.' He hesitated again, for longer this time. 'I've thought about how things happened then. Over and over. It's the same every time and it never makes sense. I grabbed him and he shook his arm free and I yelled at him and he stepped back and I grabbed him again. I shoved the money at him and he did something, sort of jerked, and I let go and he fell. As he went down his head hit the wall beside us. There was blood everywhere by the time he hit the ground and once he lay there he didn't get up, didn't move again. I looked at him for a long time. But I knew before I touched him that he was dead. It was deserted, like now. I kind of carried and dragged him along until I could tip him into the Sound.'

Bridget broke the long silence, raising her voice above the heaving water, the gulls and the traffic. 'Why did you do that?' She tried to keep the disgust and incredulity out of her voice. 'Why didn't you take him to a hospital, call the police?'

'Couldn't expose the family. Listen,' Thomas, turning short-sightedly her way, spoke with the air of a not-so-patient parent to a recalcitrant child. 'Ted Morgan was an old man with nothing much left in his life. He could've ruined all that this family's built – made of itself. He was not an important man, no one to miss him. He's already forgotten by everyone but us three. The cops don't care. As far as they're concerned he was a drifter, couldn't stay put anywhere. Why stay in a refuge if he was above board? That's the way they think.' He shrugged. 'On the other hand, if the family business was damaged, and it would have been, hundreds of people would be affected: they'd have been out of work and neither they nor their families would have had the luxury of forgetting the consequences. Put simply, the consequences of a collapse in confidence in the business would have been catastrophic for a huge number of people. It's a question of priorities.' He looked from one to the other of the blurred faces in front of him and settled his gaze on Bridget. 'You see what I mean?'

'Yes.'

Bridget saw what he meant all right. Ted had been a problem and Thomas had killed him. She didn't believe him that it had been an accident. She'd seen the other terrifying Thomas outside the Bible Mission Refuge, and he was a man in whom things she didn't understand were at work. Violent urges, evil intentions . . . all of them driven by a need to protect what he saw as the Baldacci empire.

Eleanor didn't believe him either.

'I don't believe you,' her voice was high, uneven. 'You're a murdering liar. You came down here to kill him and it had nothing to do with any marriage. Lindsay told me—'

'You told Lindsay I knew where Ted was staying?' Thomas sounded curious.

'I told her,' said Eleanor. 'She called at my room in the hotel yesterday and took me out to eat. We talked, about a lot of things. Family things. All of it while Veronica was dying, though we didn't know that at the time. Want to know what she told me, Thomas? You'll really want to know, Bridget. This is the big one they've been keeping from you.'

When she looked at her Bridget saw that Eleanor's eyes were bright not just from the wind. Eleanor Munro was crying.

'You killed him because you found out that Victor Baldacci wasn't Veronica's son.' She took a deep breath. 'Victor's father was Frank Baldacci all right, but his mother was Grace Munro, my grandmother. Veronica couldn't have

224

any more children after Magdalena and Frank wanted a son and Grace provided one. Money can do anything and it was made to look like he was Veronica's. Even the church took their cut and helped out – Father Matthews kept Veronica's secret until the end. But Veronica was losing it and she told Ted and Ted was going to tell me so you killed him.'

'None of that makes sense.' Thomas was gentle, soothing almost. 'Even if it were true, why would it be a reason to kill Ted Morgan?'

'Because the truth makes Victor my mother's full brother and makes Victor's children my full cousins.'

Eleanor was openly weeping now, her breath catching as she spoke. The gun in her hand had never seemed so dangerous.

'The truth makes the Munro-Baldacci side of the family numerically equal to the Langan-Baldacci side. There's me and my cousins on the one side; Magdalena, Lindsay and Jack on the other. You don't count, Thomas. You're nothing, just the boy brought in to marry Magdalena and take over what should have been Victor's role in the business. You're not a Baldacci and neither is Bridget. But the rest of us have the blood and we've got rights in law under a charter drawn up by Frank Baldacci. You knew I would line up with my cousins, you knew the power we would have once Ted told me—'

'You're a crazy! You can't prove any of this!'

'Don't call me crazy,' Eleanor hissed; hunched into the long coat she looked ominous. 'And you're wrong. I can prove everything. The old priest might want to keep Veronica's secret but there's no way he can hold on once a serious, legal investigation gets under way. If you ask me he'll be glad to get things off his chest.'

Thomas had become very still again. For several minutes the only sound was the pitiless sucking sounds of the water behind them. Bridget's hands, in her pockets, broke into a cold sweat as she looked quickly from Thomas to Eleanor and back again, and wished she hadn't. They both had the cold, hard look of people for whom there was no going back.

Thomas, without warning, began to shout, 'You've said your bit, you crazy bitch – now what're you going to do?'

He's calling her bluff, Bridget thought. She's going to have to use the gun, or walk away – forget this whole thing and admit she was bluffing. Very gently she eased her hands from her pockets, then flattened her cold, sweaty palms against her wet coat. For just a few seconds she closed her eyes against the scene.

She opened them with a squeal of heart-thumping fear as her arm was twisted viciously behind her back. Thomas's voice, behind her and very close, was rough and spitting. 'Shoot now, Eleanor, why don't you?' he said. 'Why don't you shoot the mother of those cousins you're so keen to tie up with?'

He jerked Bridget's arm and she felt a wave of sick pain. She wouldn't have believed a man so slight could have such strength. She doubled over, trying not to vomit. Thomas twisted her arm. She gave a low, agonized scream.

'Keep your head up.' She could feel his breath in her ear. 'You're going to be my protection, Bridget, so stand straight and maybe we'll all make a deal here. Depends on Eleanor.' He gave Bridget's arm a convincingly vicious twist. 'You want to shoot me, Eleanor, you're going to have to shoot Bridget first.'

'I don't need Bridget and I don't need you.' Eleanor took a step closer. 'The difference is, Thomas, that I truly hate you.'

Eleanor's face took on a dreamy look, and Bridget, held tight against Thomas, felt him tense. Then she was pitched forward, clawing the air as he pushed her from him and threw her bodily at Eleanor. She tried to stop herself from bringing the other woman crashing to the concrete with her. But she'd been thrown too hard and too fast, and even as she fought for balance Eleanor screamed, hit the ground beneath her, and lost her hold on the gun.

Bridget rolled free, on to her hands and knees, in time to see Thomas's feet step smartly after the clattering sound of the gun on the stone. There was nothing she could do to stop him when he bent to pick it up.

'On your feet.' Thomas caught Bridget by her hair. 'Up.' He jerked her to stand in front of him and pointed the gun at Eleanor as she struggled upright. 'I will shoot Bridget, dead, if you don't do exactly what I tell you to do. And do not think that my half-blind state will prevent me. At this range any one of the six bullets will most likely kill her. You too, in all probability. Now walk ahead of us, slowly.'

Eleanor began to walk. She was limping.

'Hurt your leg? Good.' Thomas put the gun against the back of Bridget's neck. 'Follow her, Bridget. You're going to be my eyes as well as my protection.'

They made their way to where the wharf narrowed and a disused pier stretched out over the water.

'Start along the pier,' Thomas commanded, 'and keep going.'

He prodded Bridget with the gun, casually cruel, as if the weapon was a part of the everyday paraphernalia of his life.

Wordlessly, Eleanor stepped ahead of them on to the pier and began to walk out over the water. Bridget, a numbness filling her with an unreasonable calm, followed.

'Where are we going?' she asked.

'Just a little further.' Thomas prodded her again.

Rain began to fall once more, carried in from the sea on high, whip-lashing winds. Under their feet the boards moved and sighed with the swelling motion of the sea. As they went it was clear to Bridget that he had been here before. He was too sure of things, too confident about where they were going for a man with limited vision. This had to be the pier along which he'd dragged Ted Morgan's body, off which he'd thrown it into the waters of the Sound.

Chapter Nineteen

'I'm not going out there.' Bridget jammed her hands into her pockets, clenching them until she felt a nail break through the skin of her palm. She turned to face Thomas. 'Whatever you're planning will have to happen here.'

Thomas rapped the side of her head, hard, with the gun. 'Keep going,' he said.

But Bridget, her head throbbing as if with the motions of the sea, couldn't have moved to save her life.

'You're going to have to shoot me here,' she said. 'I'm not going on.'

She didn't feel brave, just strangely calm. Images from her life floating through her mind. She had loved and been loved and she had children on the other side of the world whom she loved more than life. She wasn't ready to die, didn't want to. She just couldn't go on.

Eleanor, ahead of them, stopped and turned, the rain plastering her hair across her pale face.

'What're you going to do now, Thomas Carter?' Her voice was full of a wild triumphalism. 'If you shoot Bridget here there's no way you're going to get me too. And if I escape I'll blab everything, you know I will, and to anyone who'll listen. I'll go to the cops and I'll go to the press and to the law. So what are you going to do, Thomas Carter? What're you going to do? What're you going to do . . . do . . . do . . . do . . .?'

The chant, as she went on, and on, was caught in the wind and carried, whirling and falling, about them.

'It'll be your word against mine,' Thomas shouted, trying to drown her out. 'And the gun is yours, you're the one who brought Ted Morgan to Seattle, you're the one who moved into the hotel to keep an eye on Bridget.'

His voice sounded wrong: twisted and panicky and not his own. Thomas too was losing control.

'It won't be just my word against yours,' Eleanor called across to him. 'There's Lindsay's word too.'

'Lindsay won't speak against her father.' Thomas sounded more confident. 'There are loyalties you could never—'

'Loyalties? Father?' As laughs went Eleanor's was real, full-bellied. She scraped a ribbon of wet hair from her eyes. 'I wouldn't bank on Lindsay's loyalty, Thomas, if I were you.' She laughed again.

'Why don't you tell me about it,' Thomas invited.

He lifted the gun, pointing it in such a way that Bridget was its target, making it impossible for her not to look again into the black hole of the muzzle. Black and small and round, it cut through her growing hysteria, concentrating her mind terrifyingly on the prospect of death.

'I've got a much better idea. Why don't we go find Lindsay and hear what she has to say?' Eleanor was unconvincingly cool.

'Why don't we?' said Thomas.

He lowered the gun a little and Bridget felt the tension give inside her, like the snapping of an elastic band which had been holding her together. She turned slowly towards Eleanor, moving her head with caution. She had almost got the other woman in focus when Thomas, with a primitive, grunting sound, lunged, grabbed her round the neck and pulled her hard against him. Choking, the world darkening to a black-red landscape behind her eyelids, she tore at his arm and screamed. Once.

'You make a noise like that again and I'll kill you.' Thomas's breath was rancid with rage.

Bridget believed him. She kept her eyes shut and prayed wild imprecations that Eleanor would believe him too, wouldn't do anything which would make him carry out his threat.

She didn't plan what happened next. Maybe it was the fact of her eyes being closed to the sights around. Maybe it was a simple and primitive survival instinct. She was never able to say, even a long time afterwards, how it happened that she managed to grind the heel of her boot onto Thomas's shoe so viciously that he loosened his hold of her and dropped the gun, making it possible for her to whirl, bring her hands up to his face and begin a demented tearing at the flesh there, at his eyes and nose and mouth.

She couldn't stop. Not even when she felt hot blood running through her fingers nor even when she felt a jelly-like substance from his eye under her nails and heard his anguished, animal bellow above the sound of the wind. She was free of his hold on her, free of the paralysing fear that she was going to die any minute. And she was going to stay free, fight on, claw until he was abject, defeated, no longer had the power of her life and death in his hands.

'That's enough, Bridget, lay off him now.'

Eleanor's hand was on her shoulder, pulling her away from Thomas, halting the frenzy of the attack. She heard mewing sounds and knew they were coming from her own throat, felt a hot stream on her face and knew it was her own tears. When she stopped, shuddering, she felt Eleanor's arm go around her and she blinked, hard, shaking her head, seeing again the thunderous sky and cold, cold sea.

Hell couldn't have been any bleaker but it was a hell in which she was alive. She gave a sob that was sheer, agonized relief.

'Everything's going to be all right now,' Eleanor said. 'I'll look after you.' She pointed the gun at Thomas and together and silently they looked at him. He was hunched over, a bloodied hand covering one side of his face. As they stood he straightened and stared at them, unblinking, out of the uncovered eye.

'You've destroyed my eye,' he said.

'I'm sorry,' said Bridget.

She looked around. They were a good halfway along the pier, the timbers underfoot uneven and slippery in parts. This far out the water was truly convulsive, tormented in its lashings. Thomas took his hand away from his eye and the rain on his face ran with the pouring blood and diluted it until Bridget could see where her nails had torn and gouged along the side of his eye: it was a red, pulpy thing hung with slivers of flesh. With his good eye he looked past them to the city at their backs.

'Take a good look at me,' he said. His face was set and rigid and Bridget offered a half-hearted prayer that his pain wasn't too great. 'I built the business,' he said thoughtfully, as if speaking to himself, 'and I held it together and she would have destroyed it all, broken things up if she'd married Ted Morgan, given shares to you, Bridget.' He let out a long breath. 'To allow that to happen would have meant I'd lived my life for nothing. All of those years . . . all that I'd done . . . for nothing.'

The damaged eye glittered. With the blood pouring it was hard for Bridget to see exactly how much harm she'd done but at least it was functioning, shining as malevolently as the good eye.

'We killed that man together, Eleanor, you and me.' Thomas didn't even raise his voice. 'I did it because he couldn't be allowed to bring down what I'd built, but you were the one got him to come back to Seattle and that's what got him killed. You were as responsible as I was and you're going to have to live with it too.'

'Move.' Eleanor gestured with the gun towards the city.

'What if I don't? Are you going to kill me? What'll you do when I'm dead? Who'll run the business? Who else knows it? Shoot me, Eleanor, and you shoot yourself in the head. Let's end this thing.' He held out his hand and moved towards them and said, coaxingly, as if to a child, 'Give me the gun, there's a good girl.'

Bridget, instinctively, took a step backwards. This is all wrong, she thought, he's treating Eleanor like a fool and she's going to lose it.

Or maybe that's what he wants her to do.

Eleanor also stepped back. 'Don't come any closer, you mad bastard.' She waved the gun in a way that made Bridget whimper and close her eyes. 'I swear to you I'll use this. I'll decide what's going to happen here.'

Bridget opened her eyes and instantly regretted it. Eleanor was aiming the gun at Thomas's head, holding it very steady with her finger on the trigger.

'Don't!' she cried. 'Jesus Christ, Eleanor, please don't—'

'Keep out of this, Bridget,' Eleanor's tone was frighteningly normal, conversational even. 'If you can't cut it just turn away.' She kept the pistol pointed at Thomas's head as she went on. 'The prospects look more appealing from this side of the gun so why don't we deal, Thomas, like you said? I've been thinking and it seems to me it would be very stupid to bring the cops on to our case again. Looks like they can't prove anything about Ted, not unless I help them out. So why risk blowing the whole thing apart by giving them another body? Much better if the three of us could come to an amicable agreement.' She hesitated and then said, in a clear, slow voice. 'All I've ever wanted was a family to belong to. So, what about it, Thomas?'

'I think you're mad.'

Thomas turned and began walking slowly down the middle of the pier towards the open waters.

'Fuck you,' Eleanor's shriek, as she started after him, was full of an agonized loss. 'Don't make me shoot you in the back!'

Thomas laughed without turning round. 'You're not going to shoot me anywhere, Eleanor. But do you want to know something? I almost wish you would. I'm stuck with you, you and the widow. There would be nothing if it wasn't for me and now . . .' He came to the end of the pier and stood there, looking out to sea with a hand covering the damaged eye. He looked lonely and broken and Eleanor came to a fatal, undecided halt.

'Why can't we deal?' she called.

'Because it's too late.' Thomas leaned forward, over the water.

'No!' Eleanor began to run, her coat flapping about her in the wind. She reached Thomas and put a hand on his shoulder. 'No,' she said again.

Thomas turned and Bridget, ten feet away, saw what followed as if trapped in a dream from which she couldn't look away. In the time it took her to break from the spell of transfixed horror the worst had happened. Thomas's hands had caught Eleanor by the throat and lifted her into the air, a long, flapping rag doll to his frenzied executioner. The gun went off as he shook her, the sound dulled by the clamour all about, the bullet exploding harmlessly in the air. Bridget, shocked into life, screamed,

'No, for God's sake, no . . .'

Then, with the utmost simplicity, the seemingly inevitable happened, Eleanor's arm, as her head jerked forward, curved in the air above Thomas's head and the gun, in a randomly graceful gesture, became directly aimed at his face. Thomas couldn't have known anything as it went off and blew the side of his head away.

Bridget, running towards them, could see in front of her

234

only the spurting, splattering, volcano of red which, seconds before, had been his face.

When she reached her, Eleanor was standing looking at the collapsed thing at her feet with her face blank and her shoulders slumped. She didn't notice when Bridget stood beside her, made no response when Bridget put an arm about her. Thomas's body jerked a few times, then, apart from a thick, slow ooze of dark blood, there was no further movement.

'We should put him into the sea . . . or something . . .' said Eleanor.

The blood splattered across her coat was already beginning to stream and wash away in the rain.

Bridget looked from the dead man to the woman who'd shot him and shook her head. There would be nightmares later, dreams filled with black figures dancing in grey rain which slowly turned red. For now there were things to be done.

'We can't put him into the sea, Eleanor,' she said, gently. 'We'll have to call the police.'

Eleanor shrugged but was rigid and impossible to move when Bridget tried.

'This isn't doing you any good,' Bridget said. 'It's better if we go at once, get help . . .'

'There's no help for him now,' said Eleanor, 'nothing to be done for him anymore. Except to bury him. The sea would do that . . .'

She put her head back, closed her eyes and let the rain wash over her tight, white face.

'We need help, you and me,' Bridget pointed out. 'All of this mess has to be put right so that life can go on. We need to deal with it with some sort of decency – '

'Decency! Oh, God, Bridget, you're like something from another planet. Decency is dead; as dead as Thomas is dead . . .' Eleanor covered her eyes with a hand. 'Decency, in this family, died years ago, if it ever existed, if there was ever anything more than a malignant, cancerous growth where decency should have been.' She took her hand away from her eyes and looked around. 'I'm one of them and I'm diseased too and I've killed a man. I'll never be free of that . . . I'll never be . . . decent.'

She stepped from the circle of Bridget's arm and smiled at her, an infinitely sad smile that was full of the loss of hope and a chilling self-knowledge.

Then she lifted the gun to her temple and pulled the trigger.

Bridget sat with her for a long time, cradling her poor, blasted head in her lap, Thomas's body a dark and lonely outline beside them.

'Things are going to be OK,' she said more than once, to herself, to Eleanor's corpse. She didn't believe it, no matter how often she said it.

The rain had stopped and a pale moon had broken through the shifting clouds before a patrolling police car stopped at the end of the pier and two policemen got out and began walking towards them.

The cold was like nothing she'd ever known.

Chapter Twenty

'Living with Thomas did this to me.' Magdalena finished one drink and poured another. 'Had to blur the reality somehow.'

'He's dead,' Bridget said, 'you don't have to live with him any longer.'

'Might as well drink to his memory.' Magdalena shrugged, uncrossed her legs and stood. 'Not a lot else to do around here at the moment.' She paced restlessly before crossing the sitting room to a mirror where she stood teasing her newly platinumed hair. Apart from a rope of amber beads, she was dressed all in black. 'When do you leave?' She plucked critically at her roots.

'Friday,' Bridget said. Magdalena knew when she was leaving. She's asked Bridget once already that morning, twice the day before.

'Couple more days then,' Magdalena said, 'and you'll be gone.'

'That's right,' Bridget agreed.

In less than three days she would be home. Seattle would begin to become a memory. Some of it she could start trying to forget. She'd have gone home immediately after the night on the pier except that she'd had to stay to help with the police enquiries. In between times there had been the burials of Veronica, Ted, Thomas and Eleanor.

She wasn't at all sure Eleanor would have wanted to lie in a grave next to the Baldacci plot in a Seattle cemetery.

But that's where she was, in death as in life close to, but apart from, the family she'd hated and wanted to be a part of. Bridget prayed she would rise to haunt the living Baldaccis who had rejected her, but doubted there was that much justice in their world.

Bridget had told the police everything she knew as well as a lot that she thought they *should* know. They'd been kindly enough, in the way of police forces almost everywhere.

Ted Morgan's murder they attributed to Thomas, and Eleanor's death was proven a suicide. The evidence all pointed to Eleanor having shot Thomas.

What had happened to Grace Munro looked, like the identity of the area's Green River killer, as if it would remain unknown and unsolved. The police inclined to the view that either Frank or Veronica, or perhaps both of them together, had had something to do with it. Everything else, the years of incest, deceit and cruelty, were family matters and, in instances where the law had been broken, unprovable.

Lindsay, by plotting and bringing Bridget, Eleanor and Thomas together where Ted Morgan had last been seen alive had not broken the law. She'd wanted to create a situation, she said, in which the truth of things might emerge. The police, reluctantly, accepted this. Their witnesses were dead.

Eleanor's death haunted Bridget. Not just the last terrible act but the hour which went before it and the torment of all the maybes, the things she might have done to prevent it. She should have seen it coming, known where that last conversation was going. She could have stopped Eleanor using the pistol on herself. It would have taken so little; a different choice of words, a promise of solidarity, a gesture . . .

She *should* have stopped her. That she had not would stay with her for ever, her legacy from the Baldaccis.

Magdalena had moved back into her family home after Thomas's death. Less memories, she said, though Bridget found this hard to understand. Bridget had moved in too. Memories were the same for her wherever she went in Seattle and the Madison Park house was, in the end, given all she had to do with Lindsay and Magdalena, more convenient.

'The men are here to take down the tree,' Lindsay said coming through the door. She was wearing a suit of dark blue, long and lean on her slim frame. Her hair was smooth, skin glowing. Her move into the role of Chief Executive had been seamless.

'Ask them to be quiet, please, and quick.' Magdalena didn't look round. 'This house is so *busy*. I plan to change things.'

'You do that,' said Lindsay, 'and do you think you could lay off the booze while you're at it?'

'Why should I?'

'You tell her.' Lindsay turned to Bridget.

'Why should I?' Bridget countered. 'I doubt anything I say will affect your mother's decision to drink herself to death, one way or the other.' She walked to the French windows and stood there, watching the men who'd arrived to dismantle the Christmas tree. 'I can't, in any event, think of a single reason why Magdalena should stop drinking.'

'We have to talk.' Lindsay, coming up behind her, was curt.

'Do we?' Bridget sighed. 'I can't think of a single reason for doing that either.'

Magdalena laughed. 'How well you've settled in, Bridget. You sound just like one of the family. What a pity you have to tear yourself away from us.'

There were three men at work on the tree. One had set about dismantling the base structure, another was playing spiderman from a hoist and removing the lights. The third man was busy spreading a vast net over the frosty grass.

Suddenly, Bridget was aware of Lindsay moving from behind her and running down the room. She turned.

'Have another drink, why don't you,' the younger woman said frenziedly, and began pouring drinks from bottles on a table. She poured three in a row, great sloshes of vodka and Martini. She worked quickly, intently, messily. 'Have a few drinks, mother, and then a few more. Why the hell not?'

'How thoughtful. Don't mind if I do.' Magdalena drained the glass in her hand and moved languidly toward the table.

'You would too. You'd down the lot, wouldn't you. Bridget's right – you've decided to drink yourself to death.' Lindsay, white and shaking, used the back of her hand to send the glasses splashing and splintering across the room. 'Is that what you've decided? Is it? Tell me?'

'Looks like I'll have to get my own drink,' said Magdalena. Very slowly, with only a very slight stagger, she left the room.

Bridget, at the window, thought how Hugo would have hated the situation, the damage, the disintegration. These two women, alone with the disaffected Jack and the ineffectual Russell, were all that were left to keep the Baldacci dynasty going and the money machines churning. Hugo wouldn't have been able to tolerate Lindsay in charge either. Just as well he was gone.

'I need some air and I need to keep an eye on what those clowns are doing to the tree.' Lindsay, her hand shaking, lit a cigarette and walked back to Bridget. 'We'll talk on the patio.'

'There's not a lot I want to say,' said Bridget, 'or listen to.'

But fresh air sounded like a good idea and when Lindsay opened the French windows she followed her through. The air was sharp. She put her head back and took deep breaths and looked at the limpid, wintery blue of the sky above.

The man on the hoist was having difficulties with the reindeer on the top of the tree.

'Doesn't want to come down from there,' he called cheerfully, 'guess he likes being on top of the world.'

Lindsay, squinting up at him, said sourly, 'Strip the goddamn tree and get out of here. That's what you've been paid to do. I want you out of this place in thirty minutes.' She walked ahead of Bridget to the steps down to the grass. 'Last time there'll be a tree like that in this yard. Grandmother only had it put there to please that runt Hugo anyway, only kept it there for Ted Morgan's sake.' She flicked her cigarette end on to the grass, where it sizzled. 'Men were her weakness. Her only weakness.' She turned her cool, pale look on Bridget and half smiled. 'The old order changeth, yielding place to new.'

'What is it you want to say to me?' Bridget asked.

'There's something you need to know,' Lindsay said.

'There was a lot I needed to know, and for a long time. Now I know more than I ever want to.' Bridget folded her arms across her chest and leaned against the wall of the house. She'd been walking every day since the night on the pier. She walked by the lake, along the roads, even here in the garden. It kept her in touch with the realities of the mercurial weather, of the way days continued, reassuringly, to follow one another. She had a feeling now that Lindsay was about to start dealing in Baldacci realities.

'You need to know a few things about the old order.' Lindsay frowned at the man with the net and with an obvious effort stopped herself from telling him what to do. 'It will help you understand the new order, your place in it.'

'I have no place.'

'The old order was rotten,' Lindsay went on as if Bridget hadn't spoken. 'Take Hugo, your countryman, for instance. It would be better if you had no illusions about him. He double-crossed everyone in the end.' She gave a small laugh.

'Hugo Sweeney is a survivor, that's the most you can say about him. He helped Grandmother to die because he was jealous of her feelings for Ted Morgan and because Thomas paid him to. He came cheap, he was going anyway once Thomas told him of the wedding plans. He couldn't take that, after all the years. Then,' her tone held an element of awe, 'he did the dirt on Thomas by bringing in the priest to tip you off about Grandmother's wedding plans. He always knew how to play all sides against the middle. You do know,' she arched an eyebrow and lit another cigarette, 'that it wasn't an accident of Fate you were the one with Grandmother the night she died?'

'The thought had occurred to me,' Bridget said.

Nothing that had happened since she'd arrived in Seattle had been an accident, of Fate or otherwise.

'Thomas wanted you with her,' Lindsay said in precise tones, 'because he planned to make it look as if you'd influenced a suicidal and demented old woman into changing her will. A lot of Thomas's little schemes went awry. He really wasn't much good at anything once he stepped outside the boardroom. I'd no idea how dangerously useless he was until the night Grandmother died. The talk I had with Eleanor that night made a lot of things clear. That was when I discovered, for instance, that my daddy knew where Ted Morgan had been staying. Ted was a worry, both because he might have married Grandmother and because, once Grandmother gave him the news, he would almost certainly have told Eleanor about Victor being Grace Munro's son . . .'

'Please stop.' Bridget, leaving the wall, walked slowly to where Lindsay was standing. She looked the other woman in the face. 'There's something I want to understand and it's this. Why didn't you tell the police you suspected your father had killed Ted? You wanted control, you've made that clear, and loyalty isn't an obvious factor in this family. So – why not?'

'Ah, yes.' Lindsay gave a low laugh. 'That is the question that gets to the core of things.'

She turned her face away to look again at the men at work on the tree.

'Well, the fact of this little matter is that Thomas Carter wasn't my father. Not in the biological sense. When Magdalena was married off to reliable, well-connected Thomas for the business' sake, she took to the consolations offered by adultery and drink. Thomas never knew I was the progeny of one of Magdalena's infidelities.' She paused. 'I didn't know myself until she told me in a confessional mood brought on by Victor's death. I didn't tell the police my suspicions about Thomas because I thought, in the circumstances, it would be better not to involve them any more. I planned to trap Thomas into telling you and Eleanor what he'd done. Afterwards, when I'd told him the truth about my paternity, you, me and Eleanor would have had Thomas where we wanted him. Blackmail is an effective weapon of control. I would have taken charge, as I have now, and you and Eleanor would have—'

'I would have gone to the police,' Bridget said. 'How could you have believed I'd do otherwise?'

'I intended looking after Eleanor and she knew that. It would have been your word against hers and mine.' She sighed. 'Thomas had been in my face for a long time, voting against my plans, screaming caution, restraint.' She paused. 'He wasn't my kind of person; I thought so even before I knew he wasn't my father.'

'Eleanor . . .' Bridget said the name softly.

'I didn't want Eleanor hurt.' Lindsay shook her head. 'I truly didn't. She was a whacko but, Christ, how could she have been anything else in the circumstances? I didn't want you to get hurt either. I'm sorry about what happened.' She sighed and ran a hand through her hair, then she smoothed it again. 'It was all a terrible, terrible mess. Not the way I wanted things to happen at all.'

'Something was bound to happen once you started playing God,' Bridget said harshly. 'Thomas was falling apart and he'd become dangerous. You were setting him up to become a serial murderer.' She closed her eyes, briefly, and had a flash of Thomas, hunched and soaking and manic, before she opened them again.

'Wrong,' Lindsay snapped. 'He'd have been neutered. We'd have done it to him together.'

'If none of this had happened would you and Magdalena have gone on allowing him to believe he was your natural father?'

'Oh, yes.' Lindsay gave Bridget a sideways glance as she lit another cigarette. 'He'd have marginalized me if he'd known before and Jack, as his only issue, would have found power and favour coming his way. Jack!'

The idea silenced her. She sucked on the cigarette, her beautiful face only slightly flawed by a scowl.

Bridget said nothing for a while. Everything, it seemed to her, had already been said.

The tree was coming apart quickly now, the last of the lights coming off.

'I want you to know that I feel an affinity with Victor.' Lindsay, smiling a small smile, became confidential. 'His mother wasn't who he thought she was, my father wasn't my father. Odd, isn't it?' She thought for a minute. 'Strange too how it was Victor, the one who opted out and who had nothing to do with anything, who should have been the one to . . .' She shrugged, pulling on the cigarette and narrowing her eyes at the men and the tree.

'The one to bring about an accounting for the past?' Bridget finished for her.

'That's not the way I see it,' Lindsay said. 'Looks to me like your husband's death was timely. Magdalena's drinking was getting worse, Grandmother was getting older and beginning to lose it. Victor's death brought to a head a crisis waiting to happen.' She gave a light laugh. 'What we've got now is a fined-down instrument in which only the fit and able in this family have a say.'

'You. Magdalena. Jack. Russell. The fit and the able?'

'Oh, God, Bridget, you can be so mind-numbingly coy. I hope to God you're not going to be a problem in the future.' She tapped Bridget lightly on the shoulder. 'We'll have to get your attitude sorted.'

Bridget moved away quickly, closer to where the Christmas tree was at last beginning its descent on to the spread-out net. She brushed at the spot Lindsay's fingers had touched.

'My attitude is quite sorted, but your presumption, Lindsay, is obscene. *Don't*, please, come any nearer.' Bridget held up her hands as Lindsay took a step closer, 'and don't, please, presume to include me in your thoughts or plans for the future. I meant it when I said I didn't want Veronica's shares. When I leave on Friday . . .' she looked up along the high windows of the house, 'I'll be leaving all of this and all of you . . .'

'You're certainly entitled to make that decision for yourself.' Lindsay stayed where she was and went on smiling. 'But you've no right at all to deny Victor Baldacci's children their birthright. Veronica's last, and alternative, arrangements were very clear. Your daughter and son are to have a part and a share in things, independently of you. I've already written them.'

She turned, with a relieved sigh, as the Christmas tree sank finally and gently to the ground and spread its heavy plastic pines across the net.

'It's down. Done at last. Grandmother would have been

pleased to see it happen so smoothly.' The confidential tone came back into her voice. 'I do hope you learn to relax a little, Bridget. Your Anna and Fintan are blood of our blood, when all's said and done. They deserve to be a part of things.' She smiled. 'I want them on board. This family needs them.'

They watched as the men, with expert ease, spun and wrapped the great tree tightly into the net.